PRAISE FOR ⁄

Night Owl

"[T]he pace never flags. A brisk, competent thriller."

—*Kirkus Reviews*

"Andrew Mayne knows how to write intelligent, well-researched thrillers, and *Night Owl* is no exception."

—Bookreporter

Mastermind

"A passionate and thorough storyteller . . . Thriller fans will be well rewarded."

—*Publishers Weekly*

The Final Equinox

"Science fiction fans will want to check this one out."

—*Publishers Weekly*

"A lively genre-hopping thriller written with panache."

—*Kirkus Reviews*

"This mix of science, thrills, and intrigue calls to mind the work of James Rollins and Michael Crichton. *The Final Equinox* has it all and shows why Mayne is one of the brightest talents working in the thriller field today."

—Bookreporter

The Girl Beneath the Sea

"Distinctive characters and a genuinely thrilling finale . . . Readers will look forward to Sloan's further adventures."

—*Publishers Weekly*

"Mayne writes with a clipped narrative style that gives the story rapid-fire propulsion, and he populates the narrative with a rogues' gallery of engaging characters . . . [A] winning new series with a complicated female protagonist that combines police procedural with adventure story and mixes the styles of Lee Child and Clive Cussler."

—*Library Journal*

"Sloan McPherson is a great, gutsy, and resourceful character."

—Authorlink

"Sloan McPherson is one heck of a woman . . . *The Girl Beneath the Sea* is an action-packed mystery that takes you all over Florida in search of answers."

—Long and Short Reviews

"The female lead is a resourceful, powerful woman and we're already looking forward to hearing more about her in the future Underwater Investigation Unit novels."

—Yahoo!

"*The Girl Beneath the Sea* continuously dives deeper and deeper until you no longer know whom Sloan can trust. This is a terrific entry in a new and unique series."

—Criminal Element

Black Coral

"A relentless nail-biter whether below or above the waterline. Even the setbacks are suspenseful."

—*Kirkus Reviews* (starred review)

"Mayne's portrayal of the Everglades ecosystem and its inhabitants serves as a fascinating backdrop for the detective work. Readers will hope the spunky Sloan returns soon."

—*Publishers Weekly*

"Andrew Mayne has more than a few tricks up his sleeve—he's an accomplished magician, deep sea diver, and consultant, not to mention skilled in computer coding, developing educational tools, and of course, writing award-nominated bestselling fiction. They are impressive skills on their own, but when they combine? Abracadabra! It's magic . . . Such is the case in Mayne's latest series featuring Sloan McPherson, a Florida police diver with the Underwater Investigation Unit."

—*The Big Thrill*

"Andrew Mayne has dazzled readers across the globe with his thrillers featuring lead characters with fascinating backgrounds in crime forensics. The plots are complex, with meticulous attention to scientific and investigative detail—a tribute to the level of research and study Mayne puts into every novel. A world-renowned illusionist with thousands of passionate fans (who call themselves 'Mayniacs'), Mayne applies his skill with sleight of hand and visual distraction to his storytelling, thereby creating shocking twists and stunning denouements."

—Authorlink

"A solid follow-up with thrilling action, especially the undersea scenes and the threat of Big Bill. Here's to more underwater adventures with the UIU."

—Red Carpet Crash

"As with the series debut, this book moved along well and never lost its momentum. With a great plot and strong narrative, Mayne pulls the reader in from the opening pages and never lets up. He develops the plot well with his strong dialogue and uses shorter chapters to keep the flow throughout. While I know little about diving, Mayne bridged that gap effectively for me and kept things easy to comprehend for the layperson. I am eager to see what is to come, as the third novel in the series was just announced. It's sure to be just as captivating as this one!"

—*Mystery & Suspense Magazine*

"Mayne creates a thrilling plot with likable yet flawed characters . . . Fans of detective series will enjoy seeing where the next episodes take us."

—Bookreporter

"Former illusionist and now bestselling author Andrew Mayne used to have a cable series entitled *Don't Trust Andrew Mayne*. If you take that same recommendation and apply it to his writing you will have some idea of the games you are in for with his latest novel, titled *Black Coral*. Just when you think you might have things figured out, Andrew Mayne pulls the rug out from under you and leaves you reeling in fits of delight."

—Criminal Element

"The pages are packed with colorful characters . . . Its shenanigans, dark humor, and low view of human foibles should appeal to fans of Carl Hiaasen and John D. MacDonald."

—*Star News*

Sea Storm

"The fast-paced plot is filled to the brim with fascinating characters, and the locale is exceptional—both above and below the waterline. One doesn't have to be a nautical adventure fan to enjoy this nail-biter."

—*Publishers Weekly* (starred review)

"Strong pacing, lean prose, and maritime knowledge converge in this crackerjack thriller."

—*Kirkus Reviews*

"Fans of the Underwater Investigation Unit [series] will enjoy this installment, and those who love thrillers will like this too."

—*Library Journal*

Sea Castle

"The plot comes together like the proverbial puzzle, each juicy piece adding a bit to a disturbing big picture. A savvy police procedural that executes a familiar formula with panache."

—*Kirkus Reviews*

"Mayne combines a brilliant, innovative female lead with a plausibly twisty plot. Kinsey Millhone fans will love McPherson."

—*Publishers Weekly* (starred review)

"Mayne creates a world that blends the crime writing of Michael Connelly with high-tech oceanography in his Underwater Investigation Unit series . . . The series never ceases to be fascinating, making characters sink or swim as lives are on the line and the story veers in unexpected directions. Required reading for any suspense fan."

—*Library Journal*

"This is an above-average thriller that never ceases to surprise readers . . . [T]he experience that Andrew Mayne has created for us [is] one to truly savor."

—Bookreporter

Dark Dive

"A solid mystery with an underwater backdrop."

—*Kirkus Reviews*

"I have read all the entries in this series and will continue to read them as new ones come forth. Why? Because they are highly entertaining and have characters I relate to and admire."

—George Easter, *Deadly Pleasures Mystery Magazine*

IMPOSTOR SYNDROME

OTHER TITLES BY ANDREW MAYNE

The Specialists

Mr. Whisper

Trasker Series

Death Stake

Night Owl

Underwater Investigation Unit Series

Dark Dive

Sea Castle

Sea Storm

Black Coral

The Girl Beneath the Sea

Theo Cray and Jessica Blackwood Series

The Final Equinox

Mastermind

Theo Cray Series

Dark Pattern

Murder Theory

Looking Glass

The Naturalist

Jessica Blackwood Series

Black Fall

Name of the Devil

Angel Killer

The Chronological Man Series

The Monster in the Mist

The Martian Emperor

Station Breaker

Public Enemy Zero

Hollywood Pharaohs

Knight School

The Grendel's Shadow

Nonfiction

The Cure for Writer's Block

How to Write a Novella in 24 Hours

IMPOSTOR SYNDROME

A THRILLER

ANDREW MAYNE

THOMAS & MERCER

Text copyright © 2025 by Andrew Mayne
All rights reserved.

Published by Thomas & Mercer, Seattle
www.apub.com

Amazon, the Amazon logo, and Thomas & Mercer are trademarks of Amazon.com, Inc., or its affiliates.

EU product safety contact:
Amazon Media EU S. à r.l.
38, avenue John F. Kennedy, L-1855 Luxembourg
amazonpublishing-gpsr@amazon.com

ISBN-13: 9781662522505 (paperback)
ISBN-13: 9781662522499 (digital)

Cover design by Jarrod Taylor
Cover image: © David Kiene / Getty

Printed in the United States of America

IMPOSTOR SYNDROME

NOBODY'S CHILD

It seems strange to think about, but the sound of the truck was the worst part. That's when the anticipation started.

You could be a million miles away, reading a contraband book, pretending you were somebody else. But the noise of the muffler would claw you back to reality.

The fake smiles were bad too, because they meant a smile wasn't a smile. It always came before something terrible—a hideous mask meant to deceive you, and a mask you were expected to wear yourself.

After the smile came the look, as eyes stared through you and the others.

You could tell by the footsteps which one would be chosen.

The hand that grabbed yours probably wasn't as cold as it seemed, but there was no warmth either. These were the same rough, greasy hands that plucked pieces of meat from a chicken thigh and shoved it into the smile. The same rough hands that could come out of nowhere and strike you with such force you'd fall to the ground. But never hurt your face, never in a visible place, because then *they* would know.

And more than anything else, they must never learn what happened here. You could try leaving, but you wouldn't get far. Every time you turned to look back, you would see him watching you—high in his castle. Some people feigned obedience to find a way to escape. The sad trick was, the more you pretended to be obedient, the more obedient you became. But others had done it and word had returned: The secret was to keep running and never look back.

LOT

Refuge Officer Francesca Sauer stopped to scan the horizon on the South Point Trail in the northwest region of the Sheldon National Wildlife Refuge. She was there to track a pronghorn antelope herd that had wandered into a part of the refuge where food was scarce and predators were plentiful and hungry.

The coyotes had created a bottleneck for the antelope, forcing them into a narrow passage between the cliffs and lava flows. It wasn't a premeditated plan by the coyotes—they weren't tacticians like wolves—but an opportune situation they'd happened upon.

The ragged landscape of the refuge provided many fortunate situations for creatures that walked on four feet and two. Franky had seen all manner of predation in her six years working there.

Three months into the job, while patrolling on foot—a routine insisted upon by her boss, Curtis—Franky had found a dark pool of blood that had dried into a brown cake on the ground near the tracks of a truck. When she called it in to her boss as a suspected poaching, she didn't think much of it. Weeks later, when the lab results came back as not animal DNA but human, she realized it wasn't the snakes or mountain lions she needed to worry about.

Franky had encountered other strange and cruel sights, but that was the only one that chilled her. The others were merely acts of nature, whether it was watching a golden eagle carry a fawn in its talons hundreds of meters into the air or stumbling onto the sight of a mountain lion that had died of old age being preyed upon by vultures.

Seeing a majestic and fierce creature defeated by age and time was a little distressing. But Franky felt fortunate to witness it.

She'd ended up in the wilds of the refuge because she thought of herself as an explorer. When she was a child and watched reruns of *Star Trek* with her brothers, she would often tune out whatever the story was and fantasize about the alien landscapes and wonder what it would be like to just keep walking.

The steppes of the refuge reminded her of that. There were remnants of volcanoes, as well as cliffs, bluffs, and endless sagebrush in any direction she looked. No sign of civilization, no sign of humanity. This was an alien world and largely unexplored. While her younger colleagues tended to prefer sitting in their air-conditioned SUVs or, worse, running drone patrol from an office, she loved being out on foot.

There was something special about encountering the landscape one step at a time. It might not be as efficient, but you also tended to notice things that could be overlooked: poaching traps, litter, nests of threatened and endangered species, and the rare experience of being someplace truly wild.

In the distance to the northeast, something out of place caught her eye. It was bright white and almost gleaming in the early-afternoon sun. Franky patrolled through this area on foot once every two weeks and had an approximate idea of the rock formations and foliage. This was something . . . alien.

The word "alien" made her laugh because of all the crazy normal things she'd seen out here. Franky had never encountered anything that she would personally regard as paranormal or extraterrestrial. Not that a refuge officer should expect to, but she'd heard stories from senior officers and travelers who came through.

Her favorite story was told to her by a librarian of Paiute ancestry about the battles between her people and redheaded giants that had lived in the region.

Someone had speculated that perhaps it was an encounter with a lost Neanderthal tribe. Franky suspected the source of the myth was more mundane but loved the fact that a region that seemed sparse and devoid of people could have its own deep time and mysteries.

She continued walking in the direction of her present mystery: the unusual white object. By her estimation, it stood almost a mile away.

Were it not white, she would not have noticed it. Franky had not only been through this region on foot scores of times, but she had also made it a point to look at the most recent aerial surveys and drone footage before setting out on her hike this morning. She couldn't recall seeing anything like this object.

There was an endless number of boring possibilities: from a weather balloon that had crash-landed on a tree—something she had encountered twice—to a piece of meteorological sensing equipment placed by some other agency.

It wasn't moving, so it didn't look like a person, and it seemed too narrow to be a tent from where she was, but it was far enough away for her to acknowledge that she wasn't at the best vantage point.

As Franky drew closer, she started to notice more details. The object appeared to be two meters in height and a meter wide at its base. It was still bright white, and she could not discern any other features. It was set apart from the brush in a clearing. There were no trees or anything close to its height within a hundred meters. It reminded her of an ancient monument, like a sundial, the kind of thing she would see on the History Channel before she fell asleep at night. A word formed unbidden at the back of her mind: *ceremony.* The object didn't feel accidental; it seemed intentional. She had expected the mystery to resolve itself the closer she got but instead found it was deepening.

Franky stopped and removed her phone from her pocket and took a photo. It was an impulse she tried to encourage in herself and the younger refuge officers. Besides making reports more complete, photos were a great way to recall your own specific memories.

She was less than a hundred meters away from the object and still had no idea what it was. Its outer shape reminded her of a large crystal. The sun reflected off it, casting opalescent rays. Some small part of her felt like a deflated balloon as a realization set in. This probably wasn't some geological or natural mystery, but a prank. She began to suspect what she was really looking at was somebody's art project.

Five years ago, a prankster had started placing mirrored monoliths in random locations throughout the Southwest. The tall, triangular structures were made of reflective sheet metal bent around rebar and placed near hiking paths so they could be seen from a distance.

While creating a bit of internet hype, close inspection revealed that they had merely terrestrial origins. When Franky read about that, it made her sigh. Someday, she'd be reading about some hipster artist in New York selling photographs of their work for millions of dollars.

As she stepped into the clearing a few meters away from the white structure, the impulsive part of her brain told her she should just knock it down and deny whatever attention the perpetrator of this hoax was hoping for. But instead, she froze. She suddenly had an unsettling feeling. Something was wrong. It was a feeling she'd experienced periodically out in the wild. It happened when she was near danger or death.

The first time, on a walk with Curtis through a canyon, he had softly whispered to her that they were being stalked by a big cat. But not to worry—it's what large cats did. They made a habit of following anything unusual that went through their territory.

Now Franky had that sense that something out in the sagebrush, possibly a mountain lion, was observing the situation too. But she detected something else . . . a sensation she'd felt before coming across the carcass of a dead animal. She knew it was the scent of decay—too subtle for her conscious mind, but significant enough for the primal parts of her brain to recognize.

She was trying to understand in this moment: Was it a predator nearby? Death? Or both?

She unfroze and started to walk closer to the white obelisk. While the texture of it was rough and ragged, the shape and size of it suggested something about its possible contents . . .

Franky took several photos of the obelisk from different angles with her phone, then made a video walking around the perimeter, then scanning the area surrounding it.

Her dark suspicion didn't go away. Impulsively, she wanted to strike the surface of it, to destroy the object not out of spite but out of her fear for what it might be. Franky took off her backpack, set it on the ground, and pulled out the book-size satellite dish and turned it on. The Wi-Fi icon on her phone came to life. Radios were unreliable in certain parts of the refuge.

Thankfully, Curtis had found money in the budget to buy portable satellite internet devices, with his predictable admonishment that if he caught anybody TikToking or YouTubing or Friendstering, he would take them away and make them resort to smoke signals.

Franky found his grumpy-faced avatar in her Favorites menu and started a video call. A moment later, his even grumpier visage, overly backlit by the bright light streaming into the window of his office, appeared on her screen.

"What's up, Franky?"

Franky turned the camera around and pointed it at the white obelisk. "This. I found it near South Point Trail. It wasn't here two weeks ago."

Curtis leaned into his laptop screen, bringing his forehead so close to the camera it blocked the image of his face.

"What the hell?"

"Exactly."

"Is this some artsy-fartsy crap?"

"Maybe . . . From up close, it looks like salt," she said hesitantly.

"Is there anything else around? Tire tracks? A campsite?"

"Not that I can see. I'll do a closer inspection in a moment. What do you want me to do about this?"

"Well, I'll check my inbox. Could be some dumb thing the geological survey's done or, God knows, a military thing. You never know."

"Boss, I don't want you thinking I'm crazy, but I kind of got a bad feeling," she said.

Curtis looked concerned. He had worked with Franky long enough to know that she wasn't prone to flights of fancy or imaginative thinking.

"What kind of bad feeling?"

"I feel like I should take my shovel and see what this is made of," she admitted.

"I thought you said it was salt," Curtis replied.

"Well, the outside appears to be, but I can't shake the feeling that there might be something more to it."

Curtis took a moment to respond, probably thinking of the consequences, then replied, "Go ahead."

Franky set the phone down next to the satellite dish, with the camera propped toward the obelisk. From her backpack, she removed her folding shovel, used to bury dead animals that were within smelling distance of trailheads and relocate any snakes that got too close and curious. She walked around the obelisk to find a spot, roughly shoulder height to her. She pulled the shovel back into batting position, then swung it like a claymore into the glistening surface. Specks of salt flew away and pelted her in the face. Large chunks loosened and fell to the ground. She changed her position so she wasn't directly in the impact zone and swung again. A shard fell from the obelisk like a calving iceberg, revealing dark fabric underneath. Franky set the shovel down, pulled on her work gloves, and pried away at the salt around the fabric until an area the size of a deck of cards was visible. She then gently poked the fabric. Her finger reflexively curled in, and Franky felt her breath getting short as she stood back. She knelt to the camera and looked at Curtis.

She caught her breath and said, "Boss, I think you need to call the FBI and come out here."

LABYRINTH

Jessica Blackwood checked the text message on her phone, realized it was from the same FBI agent who had texted her last night, and closed it without replying. She had given him a tentative maybe but no promises, and that was the extent of it. For the former FBI agent—who had put more on the line than most and had been burned for it—the bureau's request didn't exactly stir a sense of duty.

She convinced herself she'd flown to Las Vegas to meet with her father and not because of any inclination to take the agent up on his request. Although she knew perfectly well that she'd been avoiding her father for months.

Jessica's relationship with her father wasn't exactly strained. "Cordial" was probably the better word for it. She had left home alone on her eighteenth birthday, not so much out of anger but a determination to avoid the gravity well of her grandfather's and her father's public lives.

Peter Blackstar, her grandfather, was a famous stage magician. Jessica had spent her childhood in front of TV cameras and in theaters, same as her father before her. While she didn't think of herself as having had a bad or particularly traumatic childhood, the older she'd gotten, the more she'd realized that her life had been set into motion before she had a chance to even think about who she was or what she wanted to be.

She loved her father, and they had reconciled years ago. Even her grandfather expressed his pride in what Jessica had done with her life. But that rebellious streak never went away.

Her father had been telling her about his "new" Las Vegas project for years. At first, he had asked her to be part of it, which she politely declined, only later realizing she had been acting selfishly. He wasn't trying to trade off her name or reputation; he was simply creating an opportunity for the two of them to work together. After the pandemic, and the economic impact that had on Las Vegas, his project had begun to wither away and then finally died.

He had texted her a few weeks ago, offering to show her what he had built. When Jessica replied I thought the project was dead, she immediately regretted it because she had misunderstood what he'd been trying to tell her all along. He just wanted his daughter to see what could have been.

When she received the FBI agent's text message the night before, Jessica, not a believer in the supernatural by any stretch, nonetheless took this as a sign from the universe.

Although she had grown up in Los Angeles in a run-down mansion in the Hollywood Hills, Vegas had always been a second home for the Blackstar stage show, which had performed there for several years in a row.

Jessica never considered herself particularly nostalgic; neither did Las Vegas. The city seemed to reinvent itself on a decade-by-decade timescale, tearing down the past and rebuilding the future. But it couldn't shake the echoes of what had been.

As Jessica waited in the parking garage, the sounds of traffic along the Strip and the hot, dry air blowing down the breezeway brought her back to her childhood.

When most people think of the performing arts, they think of what happens onstage, but Jessica's most vivid memories were of sitting on loading docks or watching cases be moved into and out of the backs of theaters from semitrailers.

One of the last engagements her family had performed here took place in an air-conditioned tent not three blocks from where she stood.

While she could remember the order of acts in the show, including the production of a very elderly lion that had been beaten down by show business and looked at her wistfully every time she passed by, her fondest memory was sitting on the edge of the loading dock at the back of the theater, talking to the other entertainers in the show: the dancers, the jugglers, the mime acts, and the two brothers with the thick Czech accents who did a balancing act.

They had escaped from behind the Iron Curtain to make it to the United States, where they shared a studio apartment off the Strip, survived on cheap buffets and infrequent shows that barely paid the rent, and thought they were in paradise.

It was backstage, among the laughter and camaraderie, that Jessica had realized it was hard to tell millionaires from paupers when it came to show business. A person's happiness seemed more dependent upon the people around them than the size of the marquee or the kind of car that took them home at night. And even though she was much younger than everyone else, she felt at home. She'd realized that they were all just kids like her, trying to find their way in the world.

Jessica heard squealing tires and the squeak of the fan belt of her father's roughed-up Suburban as it entered the parking garage.

When she was younger, she used to pay a lot more attention to sounds. Was this something all kids did, and it went away? she wondered. Or just her?

Jessica could see the suntanned face of her father through his dirty windshield and the flash of his white teeth as he smiled upon seeing her.

She realized that when she had texted, he was back in Los Angeles. He must have left soon after she called and driven nonstop. Suddenly, she felt horrible for postponing and delaying coming to see whatever it was he wanted to show her.

He parked next to her rental, stepped out, and threw his arms around her, reminding her that he might not have always had the right words, but he expressed himself eloquently with his warm embrace.

"Theo couldn't make it?" asked her dad.

"No, he's off in the jungle helping a friend vaccinate some villagers."

Jessica said this casually, not letting on how much it stressed her out. The first time she met Theo Cray, the infamous biologist-turned-serial-killer-hunter, was in a Southeast Asian prison, where he had been held after another effort to provide medical help to remote villagers in the middle of a civil war conflict.

Things had gone bad, very badly.

When Theo said he was going to help this time, she knew there was no point in having a discussion. Clearly, his sense of moral responsibility and his determination to put the past behind him had motivated him to do this.

Just in case, Jessica kept a tab open in her browser with up-to-date flight times to the nearest airport.

"So, the FBI wants your help again?" asked her dad.

"I think somebody just wants a second opinion so they can tell their superior 'I told you so,'" she said with a laugh.

"Do you regret leaving?"

"No."

She retained physical and mental scars from her experiences. Still, like Theo, as much as she hated dark places, she always found herself drawn to them.

"Well, I'm glad you could make it out. This is all going to be gone in a few weeks, and I just wanted you to see it," he said as he went back to the open door of his truck and retrieved two small flashlights. "We're going to need these."

Jessica looked down at the flashlight he handed her. "Something tells me the power's not on."

"No, they shut that off, but it'll look just as cool. Trust me," he said confidently.

"I can't wait." A genuine smile formed on Jessica's face.

The flashlight and her dad reminded her of childhood games of hide-and-seek in empty resorts and steam tunnels under hotels. Her childhood was certainly chaotic but probably, on net, much more enjoyable than most. As she grew older, she realized how much of this was her father constantly trying to engage her sense of wonder and help her find joy in even the most trying of times.

One memorable hide-and-seek had taken place when they'd arrived for a six-week engagement in an English resort town, only to find out that the booker had gone bankrupt and the hotel shut down. While her grandfather hastily put together a fill-in tour, there wasn't much money for entertainment or dining out. Her dad had made the best of it with ghost stories and hide-and-seek and fed Jessica by bartering magic tricks for fish and chips at the local pub.

Jessica's memory of it was that it'd been a fun start to summer. She learned later that her dad and grandfather's experience was quite the opposite.

Now, as they headed toward a double-door entrance, her dad explained his latest trick: "The main entrance was going to be an elevator in the middle of the casino. We never got that part finished. That was going to be pretty cool, though. At first, it was going to feel like it flew several miles into the air, then fell into the center of the earth before arriving at the labyrinth. We're going to enter through the emergency exit. It'll be down a couple flights of stairs."

Jessica's father took a key ring from his pocket, unlocked the door, and held it open for her. The interior of the stairwell was lit. Steps went both up and down into the lower section.

"This way," he said as he took the steps in stride, eager to show her what lay below.

Although Jessica's father had followed in his father and grandfather's footsteps and performed, he was known more as a thinker, someone who created magic effects. For most of his life, the only canvas he really had to work on was his father's show and the occasional magic apparatus that he sold to help make ends meet. But when a friend had come along asking for help designing an entire magical experience in Las Vegas, her father's creative spirit soared. It was an opportunity to design not just one trick or one show but an experience lasting several hours across several floors underneath a casino.

Her grandfather had been skeptical because he didn't think the economics made any sense. He knew Jason was getting screwed over in the deal. But Jessica's dad didn't care. It wasn't about how much money he was getting paid to create; it was about the paint and canvas he got to work with. He would have gladly done it for free. Jessica suspected he'd probably lost quite a bit of money in the deal and had, in fact, been doing the work at a loss.

In their sporadic conversations, he'd mentioned parts of what he was working on but never the whole picture or any detail.

A select few permanent magic-show installations were well known. The most famous was the Magic Castle in Los Angeles, an old mansion turned into a private magic club with nightly shows. There had been a magic-themed attraction at Caesars Palace, built at roughly the same time her dad had started working on the labyrinth. David Copperfield had once planned a chain of magic-themed restaurants in the spirit of Planet Hollywood, including a location announced in Disney World. The New York version got as far as having some of the installations put in before the project vanished, like so many other themed restaurants.

They reached the bottom of the stairs. Her father unlocked another door and opened it to a dark corridor.

Jessica aimed her flashlight at the bare wall studs and electrical conduit that ran along the unfinished concrete floor. "Well, this certainly is something, Dad," she said, immediately regretting the sarcastic comment.

He walked over to an electrical panel, opened it, and flipped a switch. "It gets better."

Blue light began to glow from the gap underneath a door at the opposite end of the corridor.

There was a look in her father's eye. She hadn't seen it often, but when she did, she knew what it meant. It was his *I've done something really clever* look.

She knew three things about this look. One, he was always right. Two, Jessica always ended up experiencing a sense of wonder her cynical eyes didn't think she was capable of. And three, her grandfather, frustrated at being fooled by his son, would curse and complain after he found out how it was done, calling it cheap tricks and theatrics.

"The problem with all of the other magic experiences is they try to take what happens onstage or something out of a magic book and make it bigger or expand it into some kind of theme-park attraction. But that's wrong. You've got to think opposite," he explained.

"Opposite . . . What do you mean?"

"You need to borrow from the really great magicians, the ones that play directly with our imaginations: the Walt Disneys, the H. G. Wellses, the George Lucases, the Eschers. You have to take what was in their heads and find a way to make it real," he said and dramatically opened the door.

As her eyes adjusted, he gently guided her by the elbow to a platform inside the door. Jessica looked all around, speechless. Her father watched her, experiencing her delight vicariously.

She was both amazed and confused. "Dad," she started to say but couldn't find the words.

Before her appeared a room infinitely large, staircases in every direction at every possible angle. To describe it as M. C. Escher–like would be to minimize what she was looking at.

She stared across the cavernous interior and saw herself upside down, looking in a different direction. She was on the ceiling, she was below, and she and her father were in a corner looking back.

To say the illusion used mirrors would be like saying an infant was a collection of atoms. The experience was almost transcendent.

"I'm not even going to ask."

"Well, I'll tell you anyway," her dad said with a grin. "The answer is simple. I used every trick in the book, including a few new ones."

Jessica suddenly felt sad, and she realized no one else was going to be able to experience this. "I wish this had a chance to open."

"It's okay. I've got the blueprints and videos and photos. We might be able to sell it off to some theme park in Dubai. But I got to build it, and that's what really mattered. Well, that and . . ." His voice began to crack. "You got to see it."

"Dad, I'm proud of you. I've always been proud of you, but I just want you to know that."

"Thanks, kiddo, but the other reason I wanted to see you wasn't just to show you this. I realize there's something that's been broken that I need to try to fix," he told her.

"Hey, I'm good with Grandpa. I get him. I understand him. I love him. He's crotchety, grumpy, foulmouthed, and there's probably a lot more of him in me than I care to realize. But I still love him, and I think he knows that, and I hope you know that," she assured him.

"This isn't about me or Grandpa. I want to talk to you about your mother."

"Ah, I see." A pit grew in Jessica's stomach. She had a more regular relationship with her fourth-grade pen pal from Brazil than she did with her own mother.

Jessica's mother had exited her life when Jessica was a small child. Her mom had been a dancer in the show and developed a romantic relationship with her father.

Her mother was nineteen when Jessica was born, and a young nineteen at that. Although the reasons why her mother decided not to put her up for adoption were never made apparent to her, Jessica suspected that it was probably pleading from her father and perhaps some influence from her grandfather. She got the sense that an arrangement had been made. And while her mother had been around early on, she quietly faded away, leaving Jessica to be raised by the two men.

There was the occasional card on her birthday and the less occasional phone call, which was more reminiscent of a conversation between distant relatives than a mother and daughter. Still, Jessica had never harbored any ill will toward her mother. She understood the pull of the family's legacy and the overbearingness of her grandfather. Jessica wasn't much younger than her mom had been when she decided to leave the family business.

"I owe her a call," Jessica said.

"You don't owe her anything. What I would like you to do is at least get to know her a little," he said.

"She left you. She left me. What else do I need to know?"

"It's more complicated than that."

"Grandpa screwed her. Maybe he's my dad?" she snapped.

Her dad's face went pale. "Is that what you think?"

"Listen, we both know how he was . . . *is*. I wouldn't say that I'd never considered that it was a possibility. Don't get me wrong—wherever the DNA came from, you're my dad, and I love you, Dad. Never think anything else," she insisted.

He took a moment to regain his composure. "Let me make it very clear to you: You're mine. You're only twenty-five percent your grandfather, although twenty-five percent of Grandpa is basically a thousand percent of any other person."

"I'll accept that," she said with a smile.

He nodded and paused for a moment. "I lost two friends this year. One I expected, one was sudden. I know I've only got a certain amount of time left; don't worry, I'm healthy. Your grandfather defies expectations, but we all go eventually. And that doesn't mean we have to be at peace with everybody around us, but sometimes it's helpful to understand. Grandma left too, and I think I know why, but there's still a lot that I would have liked to have known about her. You don't have to make that mistake with your mom. I made my own peace with her. I talk to her, not a lot, but I keep in touch. And I know you two are friendly, but I don't think you ever got the chance to know her. She's a very interesting person, and there's a lot of her in you."

"So you've been talking to her," Jessica asked.

"She lives in North Las Vegas. We've had lunch. She's done okay. But not knowing you is probably her biggest regret. You're both pretty stubborn. When you're done talking to the FBI folks, maybe you give her a call, get together," he suggested.

Jessica thought about her tentative agreement to potentially meet with the FBI agent. "I don't know if I really want to talk to the bureau," she admitted.

"I'd tell you don't do it, which is really how I feel. You've done more than you've been asked, more than anybody should. And they don't have any right to ask you. But I also know *you*. Even when the smart thing is to walk away, you'll never do that when somebody needs help." He shrugged.

"Well, I was *going* to say no until you just guilted me into it." She sighed.

"Or you're saying yes as an excuse to avoid talking to your mom," he noted.

"When I get a chance, I'll talk to her. I don't know really what she could possibly say to change how I feel, because I don't really feel anything. But I'll do it. In the meantime, this is amazing and all, but is there anything else here? Is this it?"

Jessica's father let out a laugh that echoed through his infinite labyrinth. "*Is this it?*' she asks. Kiddo, this is only the entrance. Prepare to have your mind blown."

FLOODLAND

Sloan McPherson watched as the rain pelted the warm hood of her SUV and turned into a fine mist, making the already poor visibility even worse. Her headlights managed to create only a dim glow a few inches in front of her bumper. Tropical Storm Rupert was making its way across South Florida and already had dumped more rain than most hurricanes.

"What's it like on Biscayne Road?" she called out to her phone in its cradle.

"Still blocked off, but we've cleared all the cars," replied Rachel Zuniga, the dispatcher handling the emergency calls on a conference line.

The storm had so overwhelmed the emergency radio systems that they had resorted to holding conference calls between groups of South Florida law enforcement to coordinate public safety.

Since morning, Sloan had rescued six people who had stalled their cars trying to traverse the flooded streets. While it was reckless for them to be out during Rupert, she understood that some people had jobs to do and/or family members to check in on. And she herself was driving around in the middle of the storm. Although her SUV had a snorkel and could endure this weather without issues.

Sloan was a member of the Underwater Investigation Unit, a special task force that focused on crimes that took place in and around Florida's waterways. As an adjacent agency to the Florida Department of Law Enforcement, they often assisted in large-scale emergencies. Part of it was civic responsibility. The other reason was to collect interagency favors they might need to cash in later.

"McPherson, are you still near Twenty-Second Avenue?" Hughes asked.

"Heading northbound on it now towards University. We've got another stalled car?" Sloan inquired.

"Negative. There was an armed robbery at a drugstore two miles north. Miami-Dade lost sight of the suspect when they were able to make it through a flooded street that the cruisers couldn't," her UIU partner explained.

"What was the suspect driving?"

"A stolen blue F-1 pickup truck with jumbo tires and a jacked-up suspension."

"Basically, a swamp buggy," Sloan noted. "I'll take a look."

"Don't get too close, just look for the truck and call Miami-Dade. I know I don't need to tell you that, but I have to tell you that."

"Understood," Sloan acknowledged.

Sloan McPherson and Scott Hughes had been partners at the UIU for almost five years. They understood each other well and willingly took flak for one another, in some cases bullets. His warning came out of fraternal concern rather than Hughes trying to put Sloan in her place. She understood as much and took it that way. But she also knew that Hughes interpreted an "understood" from her not as agreement, but more like, *I heard you.*

Sloan preferred to be underwater rather than being pelted by it. "Underwater" meant scuba diving, which she was known for, but it also included sitting in her oversize bathtub at home with her husband drinking a beer and watching football.

The word "husband" still felt funny to her. She and Run, her partner of fifteen years and the father of her daughter, had quietly gotten married four months prior.

Having come from a family with a less than stellar reputation in South Florida (including an uncle who was serving time for drug trafficking and a father who was known as a hard-luck treasure hunter), Sloan had long feared that marrying Run would make her out to be a social climber.

Deep down, she knew it was more her fear of Run's mother implying that. His family was extremely well off and his mother a bit of a socialite. As independent as Sloan thought herself to be, she understood that certain aspects of her behavior were purely reactionary.

Her family, while eccentric and at times quasi-criminal, was extremely loving. They'd never made her feel ashamed for getting pregnant in high school. Whether Run would be part of her life hadn't been as important to them as Sloan's happiness. She had a whole extended family to look out for her: Run was free to be part of it or not.

Now, one child and a decade and a half later, her resistance to marriage had finally eroded—this after an offhand comment by Run's mother, of all people.

The two of them had spent the afternoon on one of their polite make-nice shopping trips ending as usual with lunch at a schmancy restaurant, where they carried on in a cordial manner, if not slightly more business-formal than the typical mother-in-law/daughter-in-law vibe.

After a second glass of white wine, Run's mother said, "I still don't understand your resistance to marriage."

It took all of Sloan's scuba training and breath work to not spit her water across the table.

Her mother-in-law was a smart, or perhaps shrewd, woman. It wasn't a casual comment, nor was it something she had been contemplating for years. It must have come from the sudden realization that Sloan would continue to be in her son's life, now and forever.

To the woman's credit, she loved their daughter, Jackie, as dearly as any of her nieces or nephews. More so, given that Jackie was her only grandchild.

Mrs. Jacobs had even taken to coming to Jackie's swim meets, though her ass had probably never sat in anything that didn't have more than three inches of padded cushioning and the price tag of a small car. But there she sat, and sometimes even stood, screaming and cheering Jackie on with as much love and affection as one could feel.

Watching the cantankerous woman embrace Jackie as her own made Sloan realize that the woman was being sincere about marriage. If not for Sloan's sake, for Jackie's.

Sloan kept moving her eyes from the road to the flooded parking lots and ditches along the way, looking for anyone stranded . . . and the fugitive pickup truck.

This part of Dade County consisted of industrial buildings and sporadic RV parks. When a storm like Rupert came through, residents of mobile home parks were the first to be moved by emergency officials.

People were either very happy to be taken to an evacuation center or extremely reluctant to leave their home. Sloan had noticed no middle ground in such situations.

A plywood sign with the name Dolphin Cove was barely visible above the water in front of the trailer park. Beyond the white fence made of horizontal slats of concrete, the place was a lake littered with mobile homes, some of which had gone adrift and collided with one another at the far end of the park.

Some of the homes stood out defiantly, like tiny islets in the middle of a furious ocean.

"How's it going out there?" Hughes asked.

"I feel like I'm in the middle of Dunkirk. Any update on the fugitive?"

"No sign of him yet, although we have a potential name, Ronald Flavius," Hughes said. "He was let out of jail four months ago—basically a serial armed robber who's spent more of his adult life behind bars than outside."

"You got a description?" Sloan asked.

"White, forty-eight years old. Hair down to his shoulders, a black mustache, and a thin build," Hughes reported.

Sloan had slowed down to get a better look at the mobile home park. She was about to continue when she saw someone sitting on the roof of a trailer in the south corner.

"Hold up, I think I have somebody here," Sloan said.

The figure, seeing Sloan's vehicle, stood up and started waving his red T-shirt, flapping violently in the wind. A thunderclap boomed, creating a loud echo that reverberated through the rain. The Black male in his late sixties or seventies dropped flat on the roof and spread himself out.

"We've got a problem here," Sloan said.

"Mr. Flavius?" Hughes inquired.

"I don't think so. But not everyone got clear of this park," she replied.

"Need me to send over search and rescue?"

"How far away are they?"

Hughes paused. "Thirty to an hour, to be honest," he said.

"I've got a guy on the roof in the middle of a thunderstorm. I don't think we have that much time. I'm going to use the kayak."

"I wish we hadn't given our Zodiacs and Whalers over to Marine Patrol," her partner lamented.

They'd let other departments use their smaller watercraft because they had more staff use of them in twenty-four-hour shifts.

"Hey, I've got my rescue kayak, no problem," she said.

"You've got seventy-mile-an-hour winds too."

"I've dealt with worse."

Sloan wasn't exaggerating. Having spent most of her life on the sea, she'd been in terrifying conditions, including rogue waves and gale-force winds that had managed to strip not only the sails but the mast off the family sailboat.

Sloan put her earbuds in and slipped the phone into her pocket before climbing out of her truck.

As a precaution, she grabbed a rope from the back of the SUV and tied one end around the submerged trailer hitch and the other to a carabiner on her gun belt.

She quickly flipped the latches holding the kayak to the roof of her vehicle and pulled it toward herself, stepped back, and let it fall to the water, which was up to her knees.

The kayak was a flat, orange plastic, arrow-shaped craft designed for stability, not speed.

She grabbed the rope that ran around the side and pulled the kayak behind her as she moved into view of the man on the roof of the mobile home. The wind had died down a bit, but the water had a steady current as it flowed downhill.

Where she stood, the water was two feet deep. Unfortunately, the park sat in a low spot. The water stood at least eight feet deep near the trapped man.

Some of the people she'd rescued earlier in the day had been trapped in water barely past their ankles, which, while not enough to stop an able-bodied human, was more than adequate to bring a car with a low air intake to a dead stop.

The man on the roof began to get up when he saw her, but Sloan waved and shouted, "Stay down."

The last thing she wanted was for him to slip off and break his neck on a railing or submerged station wagon. Besides the horrific rain, the lightning, the wind, and the flooding, the other great danger was what you couldn't see. With floods came debris, which meant everything from broken timbers and nails to glass shards and sheet metal.

She knew a rescue diver who had broken his tailbone jumping into dark water and landing on a shopping cart. That was one hell of a way to end up on disability.

Sloan guided the kayak until the water came up to her waist, then slid herself up and into the craft's simple seat. She unstrapped the paddle attached to the side and began to guide the craft at an angle into the current toward the entrance of the trailer park.

The water in the newly formed lake occupying the trailer park was choppy but without much current in the center. Her immediate concern was the tiny river that had started over the irrigation ditch next to the now submerged road.

She used all her strength to paddle as quickly and forcefully as she could and not get carried too far away and miss the entrance to the park.

Just as her kayak's nose began to reach the slower-moving section of water, there was a loud thud. Sloan turned around to see that she'd skidded over a row of mailboxes that had been uprooted and relocated. She used her paddle to push away from the debris and moved the craft into calmer water.

The rain was still pouring down in sheets and made a staccato rhythm as it hit the hollow kayak like thousands of metal pellets striking a plastic drum.

Sloan allowed herself to catch her breath, then felt her body violently jerked backward, almost out of the seat of the kayak. She had to lower her torso in order to regain her balance; now she felt something constricting at her waist. She turned around again and realized that the mailboxes had snagged her safety cord. She set the paddle across her lap, grabbed the cord, and gave it a swift yank, flipping it up and over the mailboxes, then continued her journey toward the stranded man.

While the cord kept her from going adrift, it also presented a hazard. She debated cutting it free but decided that would always be an option if it became snagged on something else. It wouldn't be difficult to unknot it from the carabiner or cut it with one of the multiple knives she carried.

Ahead of her, the man on the roof was leaning over the edge as if trying to slide himself off. Sloan shouted to him again, "Stay put, stay put!" She would figure out how to help him down once she got closer, but she did not want this job to turn into body retrieval.

The area around her lit up like a strobe light. A moment later came a tremendous crash of thunder.

The man on the roof gave her a look like, *What am I supposed to do? I don't know, maybe evacuate when they tell you?*

Sloan was halfway across the lake when she noticed something out of place. In the northeastern corner, near the cluster of mobile homes that had drifted together, was a jacked-up blue pickup truck with water up to the door handles.

"Heads up, guys," she said on the dispatcher's agency conference line. "I think I may have spotted our fugitive. There's a truck matching your description in the trailer park."

Hughes, also on the conference line, was the first to respond: "Is anyone in it?"

The rain made telling at that distance impossible.

"Hard to say from here, but it looks like the window's down, and I can't see anyone."

"McPherson, I'm going to suggest you wait for backup before proceeding," Zuniga advised.

"It's a little too late for that. I'm here on a rescue, and the person I'm trying to save is exposed to the elements," she told the group.

"Just be careful," Zuniga cautioned.

Sloan steered her kayak toward the side of the victim's house the currents were pushing up against. Her plan was to bank it there in the hopes that it would stay in place.

As she brought the tip of the kayak alongside the mobile home, the man poked his head over the top of the roof. "Took you long enough, lady," he said with an affable grin on his face.

"You should have ordered an Uber," she shot back.

The man began to edge his body over the side of the roof.

"Hold up a second," Sloan said. "I need to check to make sure you're not going to fall on anything sharp."

She shoved her paddle into the water and probed the area to the side of her kayak. Finding no immediate danger, she shoved the paddle under the nylon straps, then pulled a life jacket from the deck and held it up to the man. "I need you to slide this on," Sloan instructed.

"I can swim," the man said.

"So can I, but let's not be stupid."

The man lay on the roof and reached down for the jacket, then began to slide it on and fix the straps.

"Did you see the occupant of that truck?" Sloan asked, pointing toward the vehicle across the lake.

"Yeah, that guy came tearing up in through here a few minutes ago before you got here. Then it stalled out. He climbed out the window and then disappeared behind the Reynoldses' home. Or what used to be."

Sloan scanned the area around the truck. Chances were, the fugitive was either behind or inside one of the homes right now.

Rethinking his escape strategy.

"The witness says the fugitive might still be in the trailer park, possibly in one of the flooded homes," Sloan said over the open line.

"Backup is still ten minutes out. They're having trouble getting their cruisers through," Hughes reported.

"Of course." She sighed.

The man on the roof slid his body over the edge, bracing himself with his elbows.

"Okay, you can—" Sloan was about to say "drop," but the man was already a step ahead of her and let go, splashing down at the front of the kayak. He grabbed the line as he bobbed in the water.

"How do I get into this thing without knocking you out of it?" he asked.

"Slowly. Just slide your body over, and I'll balance it out," she instructed.

As the man pulled his upper torso over the edge, Sloan grabbed him by the belt loops of his pants, hauling him in to lie flat in the kayak.

He turned over and sat up in the small well directly in front of Sloan's feet. "Do you need me to paddle or something?"

"Nope," Sloan replied. "I need you to hold on because we're going to get the hell out of here as fast as we can."

"No problem with me. The sooner we get out of this lightning, the better."

"That and the fact that the man who bailed out of the truck, and who may be hiding in your friends' house, is an armed fugitive. Just FYI," she added and began paddling the kayak in an arc that would try to take them as far as possible from the end of the lake where the fugitive was likely hiding.

She was halfway back when she heard the sound of a man yelling from that direction.

"I think I see the guy," said the man in her kayak. "Look over there by the side of the home."

She saw he was pointing to a gap between two of the units that had drifted near each other.

A wet and desperate-looking version of the fugitive who had been described to her clung to a door, waving furiously at Sloan and shouting for help.

"We've spotted the fugitive, and he seems to be in a dire situation. He's waving for help," Sloan reported.

"One person at a time," Hughes advised.

"I know, but I think this guy's struggling," she said.

"I can try to make room," said her passenger.

"What's your name?" she asked.

"Adam."

"Listen, Adam, this is barely built for one person. I'm going to take you over to my truck, and then I'll go back for him."

"I can swim; it doesn't look like that guy can," he said.

"All he has to do right now is hold on to the door."

The sound of the fugitive's pitiful "help" cried out across the lake again.

I got an innocent victim in my kayak, a raging storm, and a potentially armed fugitive calling out for help. She realized it was like that goddamn logic problem about the farmer with the cabbage, the goat, and the wolf.

"The man's likely armed. I don't want to put you in harm's way," she explained.

Adam turned to her. "Does it look like he's holding a gun?"

"Sloan, just get your guy to safety—focus on one person at a time," Hughes urged.

The current had picked up. By Sloan's estimate, it would be another six or seven minutes before she reached the SUV and about the same amount of time to get back to the fugitive.

She looked at Adam, then to the man clinging to the door, waving his free hand at her.

As if to remind her of the direness of the situation, the heavens let loose another bright flash, followed by a crash of thunder louder than the last one.

This wasn't the cabbage, wolf, and goat, she realized. This was the trolley problem, where there was no winning solution.

She couldn't bring Adam and the fugitive close to each other. Although there was no visible gun, the man had a record of violence. There's no telling what he would do in a desperate situation.

The logical thing to do would be to take Adam to the SUV, make sure he was safe, then go back for the fugitive. But it was becoming apparent to her as the waters picked up speed and the rain grew harder that Adam was correct: The fugitive probably didn't have much longer.

If he drowned, no matter his past or the crimes he'd committed, that wouldn't sit well with Sloan.

It was an impossible situation that required an improbable solution.

She unclipped the safety line from her belt and fastened it to Adam's life jacket, putting the rope into his hands. "I need you to keep pulling. It will take you straight to the truck, and I need you to do it as fast as you can," she instructed.

"What about you?"

Sloan slipped off her boots and removed her rain jacket. "I'm only going to slow you down."

She grabbed another life vest and, against all reason and training, dived over the side of the kayak and began to swim.

She realized she had left her AirPods in when Hughes's voice crackled over the line. "What the hell are you doing?"

"Just a quick detour," she said, tilting her head to the side for a moment to speak.

She rolled over on her back to make sure Adam was doing as she had instructed. He was holding the line but was drifting toward her, his face etched with concern. He seemed like a good guy and was clearly wrestling with his own ethical dilemma.

She shouted, "Go to the truck and call for help on the radio."

It was a ruse—the people he would be calling were already on the line with her. But she needed to give him a purpose—one that didn't involve trying to help her when he would only get in the way.

Adam nodded, then began pulling at the line with the intensity of a fraternity tug-of-war, and the kayak lurched across the lake. Sloan felt guilty for abandoning him, but he had the safety line, a life vest, and the kayak, which was more than she had now.

The currents pushed her, but Sloan instinctually knew how to swim in such a way that she could continue to make progress, tacking like a sailboat against the current while shunning the wind.

"You okay?" asked Hughes.

"Me? I'm great. I'm about ten meters away right now. This guy looks very scared."

She realized her iPhone was in the kayak with Adam. Yet, remarkably, the range of the AirPods was greater than she had expected.

"How the hell are these things still working?" Sloan said aloud.

The fugitive was holding on to a screen door that had begun to rip away from the trailer. It looked like he'd tried to break in through a locked door but only managed to crack the window.

"Are you armed?" Sloan shouted to the man as she drew closer.

"What?"

"Is your name Ronald Flavius?" Sloan was dog-paddling in place, keeping a careful distance from him.

"No," the man replied. "My name's John."

He was clearly lying. "Is this your home?"

"No, it's my friend's. Can you help me?"

Sloan realized now was not the time to confront the man about the lie. It was better for them both to indulge in the make-believe in order for him to behave like a normal person hoping to be rescued and not a fugitive who realized he'd been cornered.

Sloan tossed him the life vest. "Slide this over your head," she explained, "then put an arm through the loop."

He caught the life vest with his free hand and began to do as Sloan had instructed. She took this moment to swim toward him.

When she was an arm's distance away from him, Sloan said, "Turn around so I can tighten up the jacket. Cross your arms over your chest."

Pale and in shock, he did as instructed and let go and splashed into the water. She grabbed the back of the life vest and began swimming back into the center of the lake.

"Kick with me," she said to him. "That'll help us go faster."

Sloan wasn't sure where she had found the strength, but they were making good time as she pushed into the current and headed for the exit to the RV park. Behind her, she heard a loud crash and stole a glance over her shoulder, witnessing a mobile home getting crushed by the impact of another that had come undone from its foundation. Water gushed inside, and broken timber and aluminum siding jutted out at vicious angles. With a cracking sound, the trailer Ronald had been clinging to crumpled like an aluminum can.

"Jesus Christ," he exclaimed.

Sloan reached her free hand out to sidestroke, and it bumped into rope.

She looked ahead and saw that Adam had managed to pull himself to the road near the SUV and was standing in ankle-high water looking back with the kayak bobbing near the bumper. A length of the safety line had looped back out toward the lake. She grabbed hold of it and pulled Ronald toward the line and quickly tied his vest to it.

Adam realized what she was doing and began hauling them in as best he could. She wanted to shout to get in the vehicle but didn't have the energy.

Suddenly, a bright flash—whiter and more intense than the previous lightning strikes—blinded her.

When she could see, Adam had collapsed in the shallow water.

Sloan let Ronald free and swam as fast as she could to the fallen man.

STOIC

Twenty-five minutes in the FBI office and already the fuckery has begun, Jessica thought.

The conference room looked like a thousand others that all blurred into the same liminal space of fluorescent lights and cheap wooden veneers. This meeting was made different by the people attending and Jessica's imaginary compass that showed which direction the conversation was going. At present, that was definitively south.

Special Agent Donna Monroe, a well-intentioned FBI agent in her mid-thirties who had done solid investigative work on the cartels out of Albuquerque, was the one who had asked Jessica to come to Las Vegas.

Her colleague, Ben Treynor, was several years her junior and had formerly been a police officer in Michigan. He was matter-of-fact and polite but basically kept to himself and let Monroe do the talking. Neither of them was the problem.

It was their supervisor, Special Agent Isaac Callis, who had pushed a document in front of Jessica and was asking her to sign it.

On the surface, it read like a straightforward nondisclosure agreement. Except instead of levying civil penalties for divulging corporate secrets, this agreement held her criminally liable for the release of sensitive information relating to bureau cases. There were several problems with this. First, it would make absolute zero sense for her to sign it, given that it offered her zero protection, and more importantly, it gave the FBI the discretion to determine what they considered "sensitive."

If Callis had it in for her, he could claim later on that merely divulging the fact that they'd had the conversation was a violation.

While ultimately a judge would probably find that an overreach, it would come long after she'd had all her personal electronic devices seized and searched and her friends interrogated and threatened with procedural traps.

This wasn't typical FBI behavior, but not something completely alien to them, especially when a grudge was involved.

Jessica had a good relationship with most FBI agents and had worked with the current director of the FBI and considered him a friend.

She pushed the document away. "I think I'm good."

"This is just a procedural form," Callis stated.

"And it's my procedure to decline this," Jessica replied.

Callis leaned back and shook his head. "Your reputation for being difficult precedes you," he said.

"As should my reputation for not giving a damn. I guess I'm done here."

"Your legal responsibility doesn't change whether or not you sign this," he insisted.

"I've sat where you're sitting more times than I care to remember and said the same bullshit. We both know that's not true. Me signing this is the difference between you having a form you can take before a judge and make whatever claim you want to, or you actually having to do some work, or rethink whatever it is that you're up to."

"Ms. Blackwood, I'm not up to anything. I just need to be thorough."

"Well, I don't need to be here. I came as a favor to Agent Monroe. I have no reason to think you have some sort of vendetta. I also have been burned enough times to know when to avoid a potential problem."

Callis glanced over at Monroe and Treynor, as if to blame them for the situation. Jessica felt for them a little. She had been in similar spots with higher-ups, but at the end of the day, they were adults accountable for their own actions. She wasn't going to let him guilt her into a mistake.

"How much do you need her help?" Callis asked.

"I don't think it would hurt," Monroe replied. She looked to her colleague Treynor, who nodded.

Callis turned back to Jessica. "It would make my life a lot easier if you signed this," he said.

"And it would make my life a lot more complicated if I did."

She could tell he was a stubborn man, not used to giving in. At the moment, it wasn't as much a matter of her signing it as Callis pitting his will against hers. But he had massively underestimated Jessica, whose willpower was nearly infinite.

The scowl vanished from his face as he took on a different approach. "Part of the reason we need you to sign this is because of the potential implications of this case. It might involve"—he paused to say the last words dramatically—"the Warlock."

Jessica made her own dramatic gesture of checking her watch and feigning indifference. "Well, good luck to you, then. Monroe, would you mind leading me out?"

Callis was surprised by her reaction. "Aren't you curious to know more?"

The Warlock—real name, as far as was known, Michael Heywood—was a serial killer Jessica had caught early in her career. He had created a series of impossible-looking and media-savvy murders to attract attention to his half-baked, chaotic worldview.

"Heywood is sitting in a maximum-security facility right now, being monitored 24/7. I'm not worried about him," Jessica said.

Two years prior, that wasn't the case when Jessica found out that Heywood, under a cooperation agreement with a national intelligence agency, had been helping them while covertly using internet access and computer resources for his own criminal acts. The people responsible for his detention now took it much more seriously, and the individuals who had created the prior arrangement were embarrassed and disciplined.

"Anytime a cryptic message is left at a murder scene, or they think some computer programmer was involved, somebody calls me. I hear his name half a dozen times a year," Jessica said.

"Well, this is more than that. I would say it's what you would definitely call weird," he told her.

Jessica was bored with the stalemate. Instead of verbally responding, she stood, grabbed her handbag, nodded to Callis, and walked toward the door.

She wasn't acting; she really didn't care.

Callis was smart enough to realize it wasn't a bluff. "Fine. Fine," he said, and picked up the paper and tore it in half. "Just know, burn me, I burn you." Then he got up. "You guys can fill her in if she deigns to stay. I've got other things to do."

Jessica stepped aside to let him pass. He gave her a glance, then shook his head as he walked away.

"I've never seen him give in like that," Monroe said quietly, clearly afraid he would hear her from the hallway. Treynor said nothing, but his expression agreed.

"Can I give you two a little bit of personal advice?" Jessica said. "Don't get bullied. Don't put yourself in that situation. If you're like, 'Oh, but my job,' screw it. It doesn't matter. Take it from me. You'll be a lot happier with yourself."

But are you happy with yourself? the voice at the back of Jessica's mind asked her.

"What have you got?" she asked as she sat back down.

Monroe pulled a large-screen tablet from her briefcase and pushed it in front of Jessica, revealing a photo album. "These photos were taken two days ago at Sheldon Wildlife Refuge. It's in the northwest corner of the state."

Jessica flicked through the series of images, beginning with a distant shot of a white obelisk and then closer images showing it from different angles.

"Let me guess. Salt? And you found a body inside of it?" Jessica asked.

"How did you know it was salt?" Treynor asked.

"Because it's biblical, and I can see it with my own eyes." She smiled at the irony of her own statement. "Who found it?"

"A wildlife officer named Francesca Sauer," Monroe replied.

"Any other witnesses?"

"Just her. She patrols the region once every two weeks on foot," Monroe explained. "The latest drone images, which had been taken four days prior, didn't show anything, so we estimate that it had been placed there no more than a day before. They found signs of animals using it as a salt lick."

"And the victim?" Jessica inquired.

"He was killed about a day earlier by our estimate, but it's a little bit tricky," Monroe said.

"Let me guess—his body's filled with salt; he choked on it?" Jessica asked. "That's also messing up the forensic analysis."

Treynor exchanged glances with Monroe, looking slightly suspicious. "Exactly. Nobody else briefed you on this?"

"No, but more importantly, who's the victim?"

"We're in the process of narrowing it down," Monroe said. "There was no ID on him, but he was in his early twenties. Caucasian."

Jessica flipped through the photo album to images of the body laid out on a sheet of plastic. Close-ups of the mouth and nostrils showed that they were packed solid with salt. He was wearing a black T-shirt and pajama bottoms and was barefoot.

"So you know the name, but you don't want to tell me right now, which suggests this is a known personality. I'm not exactly up to date on social media, but if I had to guess, well, I would say an Instagrammer, but given the paleness of the skin, more likely a YouTuber or live streamer."

"Why would you jump to that conclusion?" Monroe asked.

"Everything about this is symbolic. This person had to represent something. The fact that you don't want to say the name tells me that it's a known person. But given that we haven't heard about a prominent actor missing in the news, it suggests that this is somebody who is probably famous but outside of traditional media circles."

Jessica took out her phone, tapped on it a few times, read something, then clicked it closed and put it away.

Both Treynor and Monroe could tell that she knew something.

"You already got the name?" asked Treynor.

Jessica wasn't in the mood to toy with him. "Dustin Fonseca. A live streamer and YouTuber. He hasn't been active for four days. He has an erratic streaming schedule, so nobody is alarmed yet."

"It took us half a day to figure that out. His face wasn't in the FBI database," Treynor told her.

"And his face isn't in any of the photos," Monroe remarked, tapping on her phone and trying to figure out what Jessica could have searched for. Frustrated, she set it on the table.

"I live with a guy who only thinks in zeroes and ones."

"Theo Cray," Treynor said.

"That would be him," said Jessica. Her relationship with Theo Cray was the topic of several true-crime podcasts.

"Well, I think at this point you know as much as we do. Maybe more. We're trying to figure out how," Monroe said.

"What about tire tracks?" asked Jessica.

"There is one set of recent ATV tracks that end a few hundred feet away. It looks like it was pulling a small wagon," Monroe told her.

"So one person could have done this?" Jessica replied.

"Certainly one person could have placed the body. We're not ruling out an accomplice. Our focus is how he did the salt embalming," Treynor said.

"I don't think *how* is as important," Jessica told him. "We need to worry about *why* and who's next."

"What makes you think there's going to be another victim?" Monroe asked.

"Have you caught the guy that did this? Do you know why he did it?" Jessica asked. "The answer to both of those questions is no. So we have to assume this is just the start."

She knew there was something else they hadn't told her, whether this was per Callis's instruction or a strategic holdout. She sighed inwardly. Such silly games only hampered investigations.

"Let's focus on the how for a moment," said Monroe. "How would you encase somebody in salt like this?"

"I would take a saline solution and suffocate somebody with it, then shove salt in. I don't think it's terribly complicated. People die in industrial accidents like this all the time," Jessica said. "This isn't the mystery."

"Forensics says otherwise," Monroe stated. "They say there wasn't enough time for the salt to dry out between when Fonseca went missing and when the obelisk was found. They say it's almost as if his body was transported into the salt. Well, not their exact words, and they're not claiming that. But right now, there's no good explanation."

Jessica pointed to the wedding band around Monroe's ring finger. "Can I borrow that for a moment?"

Monroe, knowing her reputation, slid it off and handed it to her without question.

Jessica stood and grabbed a sealed water bottle sitting to her left. She held it at eye level in one hand and brought the ring resting on her palm up and into the bottom of the bottle, smacking it hard. When she lowered her hand, the ring was gone.

Monroe and Treynor leaned in and saw the wedding band floating at the bottom of the water bottle. Jessica leaned over and set it down on the table.

"What the hell?" Treynor exclaimed.

Monroe picked up the water bottle and scrutinized it, then stared at Jessica. "How?"

Jessica said, "How isn't important right now; it will be later on. The question is why."

Monroe said, "Well, if we're talking about motive, then obviously whoever did this probably didn't like Fonseca very much."

Treynor added, "We're going through logs of his live streams looking for angry fans in chat."

Jessica said, "I don't know if that's going to help you or not—probably worth doing—but I'm not really talking about motive. Well, not in the sense of why they wanted to kill Fonseca. The question is why *this*, why the dramatic gesture?"

"Does it need to be any more complex than that? It was a flourish. Why place my wedding ring inside a water bottle?" said Monroe as she picked it up again to look more closely.

Jessica said, "To call your attention away from something else." She pulled the left side of her jacket open, reached into a pocket with her right hand, and pulled out a phone. She held it in front of Monroe, clicked the side button, and the wallpaper appeared, showing Monroe, her husband, and her child standing in front of Cinderella's castle at Disneyland.

"That's your phone," Treynor blurted.

Monroe snatched the phone from Jessica's hand. "Da fuck?"

Jessica said, "I wouldn't call this obelisk, as you called it, a distraction. It is certainly an announcement. But the real play is something we're not seeing. My guess is there will be others, but that's not the point, or not the final act, as much as I hate using theatrical terms for all of this."

The pair still seemed distracted by her magic tricks.

"What about the message?" she asked loudly.

They looked at her in shock.

"We didn't say anything about a message," said Monroe.

"I know, but clearly there's something to go along with this. At first, I would guess some sort of cipher placed at the scene, but the goal of this isn't for them to give you clues to catch them. The goal of this is for them to distract you or to make a point, and if they want to distract you or make a point, they're not going to risk, you know, some super-complex Zodiac Killer mumbo jumbo. They're just going to point and say 'over here.' So if they haven't done that, I'm surprised, and maybe I have to rethink this."

Monroe shook her head. "Nothing. We don't have one."

Jessica asked, "Really? There wasn't anything left? A note? Something carved into the stone? Something on or in the body?"

"We removed the salt from his esophagus and searched inside his cavities for something, but . . . nothing. We looked on the ground around the obelisk and couldn't find anything."

"Interesting," Jessica said, leaning back. She took out her phone, dialed a number, and a moment later, spoke. "Hey, Marco, it's Jessica. I'm over at the Las Vegas FBI office with Agent Monroe and Agent Treynor. Can you do a quick search? I want you to check the tip-line email inbox for the words 'lot' and 'salt.'" She looked over at the agents. "What was the name of the wildlife park again?"

Monroe started to answer, but Jessica remembered. "Also, Sheldon Wildlife Refuge. Biblical. No? Okay." She thought this over for a moment, then clicked on the info icon on the photo. "Let me give you a latitude and longitude." She proceeded to call off the location numbers where the photo had been taken. "Oh, you got something?" She nodded to Monroe. "Can you send it over to the Las Vegas FBI office right now? Thanks." Jessica clicked off.

Monroe picked up her phone, which Jessica had set on the table, and opened her email. "Goddamn," she muttered.

Treynor was staring at his phone too.

"Goddamn," Monroe said again, then turned the screen toward Jessica. "What the hell does this mean?"

The image was that of a young woman's face, eyes open, almost serene, surrounded by a pale green glow.

It appeared to have been taken underwater.

"This looks to have been emailed an hour ago," Monroe said. "The subject line is just a bunch of numbers. That might be why they missed it. Are they coordinates?"

Jessica nodded. "Marco says they were a close match to where Dustin's body was found."

"But this isn't Dustin," Monroe replied.

"Oh, damn. I think my wife follows this woman on TikTok," Treynor told them.

"Jesus." Monroe pinched and zoomed the image and then looked at the email header. "I don't see anything else here. How the hell are we going to find this one?"

Jessica said, "I know somebody, if she's not too busy right now."

Sloan McPherson was sitting on the couch watching the water slowly recede from the lawn of the waterfront home she shared with her husband and daughter when she got a text message from Jessica Blackwood. Her boat, a cabin cruiser she used as an office, was suspended out beyond the dock by fiberglass davits and had thankfully avoided smashing into her living room during Tropical Storm Rupert.

Fortunately, her rescue mission had succeeded. She'd managed to administer CPR to Adam after the lightning strike. It hadn't been a direct hit, but it was plenty to stop his heart. It was a miracle that the line she'd been holding hadn't electrocuted her as well.

Ronald nearly drowned as he struggled in the current, but the life vest Sloan had given him kept him alive. That didn't stop him from threatening to sue Sloan and every emergency responder who showed up afterward.

Her colleagues congratulated her on the rescue, but she knew how close she had just come to losing both men. Despite the plaudits, she regretted having put them in jeopardy. She and Ronald had gotten lucky. Adam hadn't.

"How you doing?" Run asked Sloan for the fifth time since she got home.

"Jessica's in Las Vegas. She wants me to consult on something. I could do it from here," she said, her voice drifting off.

"Vegas? That sounds a lot drier than here."

"Fort Lauderdale and Miami airports are closed, though," she said.

"And Palm Beach?" he asked, knowing she'd already looked it up.

"Opening in an hour."

Run laughed. "I never thought I'd see the day a McPherson got sick of the water."

"I'm realizing I have my limits. And I think it would be nice to hang out with Jessica a little," she admitted.

"Okay. But just don't turn into a cynic like her. There's still good out there in the world."

"She knows that," Sloan assured him. "And I do too."

THE OUTSIDERS

Sloan was sitting next to Jessica in the FBI Las Vegas field office auditorium, her backpack and duffel bag next to her feet. Jessica had picked her up from the airport twenty minutes earlier and updated her on the way to the meeting.

Dustin Fonseca's family had identified his body a few hours earlier, and social media was already blowing up with the fact that his death was being handled as a murder investigation.

Nia Stratos, the newest victim—at least, they assumed she was a victim because nobody had been able to reach her since the FBI tip line received the image of her underwater—had even more followers than Dustin Fonseca. Her last social media post was a TikTok movie review she'd uploaded less than twenty-four hours prior.

Her seeming death had not yet been reported to the public.

The FBI was trying to contact her social media management company to find out if her last video had been a timed post or uploaded live by Stratos.

In addition to Callis, Monroe, and Treynor, half a dozen other FBI agents had gathered in the auditorium, as well as a representative from the US Fish and Wildlife Service, two Las Vegas Metropolitan Police Department detectives, and an officer representing the Nevada Department of Public Safety named Vera Pinellas.

A map of the southwestern United States was projected onto the overhead screen. Bodies of water large enough to hide a body were circled in red.

"I always expected the desert to be a lot drier than that," Sloan remarked as she observed the hundreds of red circles.

Callis closed the laptop that was sitting on his armrest, stood up, and addressed everyone in the room. "Can we go back to the image?" he requested. Nia Stratos's drowned face appeared on the screen. "Right now, we want to figure out what the pattern is. Is there a clue to be found? Is there something we're overlooking? If there's a pattern, we have less than twenty-four hours before the next abduction."

An agent named Tanya Running Deer held up her hand.

"Yes?" asked Callis.

"Did we find any other emails that were sent? Perhaps another clue?" Running Deer asked.

"Headquarters is looking into that right now." Callis turned to the image and gazed up at Nia's face. "What is he trying to tell us?" he wondered aloud.

"I just got an email from one of the bureau's consulting experts on mythology," said Treynor. "He said the salt might not be as significant as we think. It could be earth, and we're looking at water. We should expect wind and fire." He shrugged.

"The Valley of Fire," Vera Pinellas noted aloud.

"Put the map back up," Callis commanded.

The Valley of Fire State Park was northeast of Las Vegas and butted up against Lake Mead.

Callis stood under the map, staring up at it with his arms crossed, as if trying to look through the screen into the water to see where Nia Stratos's body was located.

Jessica raised her hand.

Callis made an unpleasant face, then reluctantly called on her. "Blackwood?"

"Did we find anything else in the inbound emails or other tip lines?" she inquired.

"Um, I said not yet, but we're looking. It was the first thing we thought of."

"No, I mean *prior* to Dustin Fonseca's body being found," she clarified. "The location of the obelisk was sent *after* he was found—along with the image of Nia Stratos. What I'm asking is, did we get a photograph or some tip about Dustin in the days before this?"

"We'll look into that," Callis replied, then nodded at Monroe and Treynor.

It was obvious no one had thought about that.

"I'm not sure how urgent that is right now, though," Callis added.

Jessica didn't bother raising her hand. "I think it makes all the difference. If he's sending us emails after the victims are killed and just confirming what we already know, I don't think there's a pattern here for us to find, at least not one that he's consciously presenting to us. All he's doing is fucking with you, getting you to chase down crazy leads."

Callis's frustration mounted. "I know you have a lot of experience in this area, and I respect that," he said, unconvincingly. "I've got one body, a photograph, and that's it. There isn't much else for us to go on." He addressed the room: "Let's focus on Lake Mead for now. Ask the sheriff's department for any citations written in the last forty-eight hours. Let's see if we can get security footage."

Jessica didn't think his strategy was too off base, but it was far too narrow. If Lake Mead didn't lead anywhere, then they would have lost precious time.

"Should we issue a warning?" she asked.

Callis looked up from his laptop at her. "A warning to who?"

"A warning to the public. Right now, we have two random social media influencers that are dead with no indication this is going to stop anytime soon. We should tell people to be careful, watch out for strangers, use their common sense," she concluded.

"I don't know what good that would do. That seems overly broad. Every day, dozens of people are kidnapped and murdered in our country. I don't think that warning is going to have much effect."

"Well, I don't know a whole lot about social media, but news spreads fast, and it seems to me that if we want people to be safe, telling them to be careful wouldn't be the worst idea."

Callis shook his head. "I think that could cause a panic," he said, then turned to speak privately with Agent Monroe.

"He thinks he can solve this in the next twenty-four hours," Jessica said under her breath.

Sloan was keeping quiet, but her jaw was clenched.

"What are you thinking?"

Sloan turned her laptop toward Jessica. The image—the underwater image of Nia—was visible, along with some markup she had done with traced contours, lines, and highlighted reflections.

"Clearly, I'm a one-trick pony, and I get why you asked me here. But the water," Sloan said.

"What about it?" Jessica asked.

"We know the photograph was taken with an Android phone because of the image specs, which means the phone was in an underwater housing. Also, this suggests that somebody took the photo underwater *with* Nia," Sloan explained. "By my estimate, this photograph was taken around two or three o'clock yesterday—if you look at the light rays and the brightness of the water."

"Broad daylight," Jessica noted.

"Exactly. Now, Lake Mead is a very big lake, and you can do a whole lot of whatever you want without anybody seeing you. But there's no guarantee of that, because it is by far the most active lake for hundreds of miles around. That would *not* be where I would risk getting caught posing and photographing a body. Notice where Dustin Fonseca's body was found, in an area deserted for weeks at a time. Whoever put him there wanted to make damn sure they didn't get caught in the act. It stands to reason they'd apply the same logic to Nia Stratos."

"You need to tell this to Callis."

"Between you and me, I think you're better at standing up to bullies," Sloan admitted.

"He's about to bounce me out of here, in case you haven't noticed."

"Fine." Sloan raised her hand. When Callis failed to notice her, she called out, "Excuse me."

He looked up. "Yes?"

"That photo was taken probably in the late afternoon. I don't think any sane person would have been out on Lake Mead at that time to pose and photo a dead body. We probably want to be looking somewhere else."

Callis pulled up the image again on the overhead projector and turned to look at it. For a moment, he appeared to be ready to raise an objection, then folded his arms and stared again. "What did forensics say about the apparent time of death compared to when the photo was taken?" he asked Monroe.

"Given the coloration of the skin and condition of the hair, maybe a few hours," Monroe replied.

"They could have planted the body at night and come back during the day," said Callis.

"No," Sloan told him. "Look closer."

The entire room leaned in, scrutinizing the photograph for some detail they had missed.

When she realized they weren't seeing it, Sloan got up, moved past Jessica, walked down the aisle and up to the screen, and pointed.

"There," she said, indicating an air bubble under a tuft of hair tucked behind Nia's ear. "That would dissipate within three to five minutes max."

Callis considered this. If true, that meant Sloan was right. This body was planted during the day, not under the cover of darkness.

Sloan could feel the tension in the room as she returned to her seat.

"Nobody loves the killjoy," Jessica whispered.

"So we don't search Lake Mead?" asked Officer Pinellas.

"Of course we do, but we'll have to broaden our scope," Callis said with a touch of bitterness.

"What else do you notice?" Jessica asked Sloan.

She was scrolling through internet images of people scuba diving in inland lakes around Nevada.

"I'm not sure. But I agree with you. I don't think we're looking for an intentional clue, just an accidental one."

"Heads up," said Tanya Running Deer as she hoisted her phone into the air. "Looks like this already leaked."

Callis rushed over to look at her screen. He glanced at it, then stared straight at Jessica.

"Ms. Blackwood, thank you for your help. We have it from here. Agent Treynor will show you to the exit. McPherson, you can stay," he added in an ice-cold voice.

While Sloan didn't have the confidence of Jessica to calmly take down someone in authority, she did possess an impulsive nature. And zero tolerance for bullshit.

"What the hell is up with you?" she asked the man.

"It's okay, let it go," Jessica said quietly.

"Nope," Sloan said as she stood up and walked over to Running Deer. "Let me see."

She took the phone from the agent's hands and looked at the screen, then handed it back.

Running Deer had screenshotted a social media post from a Las Vegas gossip columnist saying that Jessica Blackwood had been brought into the Fonseca investigation because it was a suspected serial killer case.

"You're an idiot if you think Jessica said anything," Sloan told Callis.

Callis was surprisingly measured in his response. "We have to be careful here. Anybody with a badge stays. Anybody without a badge has to go. No disrespect to Ms. Blackwood."

It was a weak attempt at trying to save face.

"I'm here because Jessica asked me. Where she goes, I go," Sloan said defiantly.

"Thank you for your help. I will pass my thanks on to your supervisor," Callis said coolly.

Asshole move, Sloan thought. Plus, it was all the justification she needed to bail. If his ego was too big to tolerate Jessica, then this was the wrong place for her to be.

"Got it," Sloan replied, then turned around and walked back to where Jessica was preparing to leave. "Any good restaurants in this town?"

"I used to love the Circus Circus buffet when I was a kid."

"Sounds scrumptious."

Jessica shook her head. "Lord, no, not there. I think we can do a little better."

WATER SHOW

Sloan watched from the restaurant window as the Bellagio fountain erupted high into the air and thought to herself, no matter how hard she tried, she couldn't get away from water. Water wasn't the problem, to be fair. At this point she was certain that if she'd grown up in the Sahara, she'd be fighting a compulsion to enter dangerous situations involving sand dunes and cacti.

"Are you enjoying the wine?" Jessica asked.

Sloan took a sip. "Yes, it's great," she replied absentmindedly.

"That's your water glass."

Sloan looked at the liquid. "Oh, sorry, just a little bit out of it."

"Jet lag, stress, the bullshit we just encountered, or all of the above?"

"I think the second one."

"Anything you want to talk about? Now, be warned, I am probably the last person to give advice on dealing with stress. I'm what you'd call a Russian doll of anxiety," Jessica confessed.

Sloan was watching the camera flashes from the tourists who were standing along the sidewalk by Las Vegas Boulevard, watching the fountain show. "You seem pretty well composed to me."

"The FBI psychologist said I was a bullshitter extraordinaire bordering on psychopathy," Jessica admitted.

"Hmm. Well, I do feel like the version of me I present to the world is different from who I am," Sloan replied.

"Yeah, well, we all feel that. It just means you're honest."

Sloan turned away from the water show and let out a small laugh. "I came here because I got sick of the water. Now, that's not quite true. I found myself in a damned if you do, damned if you don't situation."

"I'm pretty familiar with those. Anything you want to talk about?"

"During the storm, I had to rescue somebody off of a roof in the middle of the flood, as well as an escaped fugitive. Classic textbook ethical dilemma here. Tried to save both; both men lived, but I put one of them in harm's way, and he had a heart attack from a lightning strike that hit nearby. It's not the kind of thing where I need to be told, 'Oh, you made the best choice you could,' and whatever. I get that. And that's not the problem for me. I'm not sitting here thinking, 'I should have done things differently,' although you could argue that. I guess it's that I don't feel well equipped to make those decisions anymore—not that I ever was. I just never thought about it."

Jessica nodded ruefully. "You realize nobody's equipped to make these decisions, right? If you don't stress out about it, you're a sociopath. If you stress about it too much and you can't make a decision, then you're ineffective. You realize your job isn't making the perfect decision, yeah? And it's not even necessarily a matter of making the right decision in the moment. It's just getting up again and making that decision again and again. I think people fixate on how physically resilient you are, Sloan, but your real strength is mental—how you keep going."

"Yeah, I get it. That makes sense. I just don't know how many more of these kinds of decisions I have in me. How did you manage?"

"I didn't have any patience left. I quit. That's how I dealt with it," Jessica admitted.

"But you're still out here helping people."

"When I want to, when I feel like picking up the phone." Jessica crossed her arms and looked down at the table. "But I don't always answer. That's the difference. With that badge, you have to, and that means you know you have to put everything you have on the line every time you get that call."

"I hadn't considered it that way."

"We walked away today. We found ourselves in an impossible situation and weren't able to do what we do to the best of our ability. That's enough of that. Maybe that's something you need to think about. Anyhow, I'm terrible at this; let's order."

The two of them sat there for a few minutes, pretending to look at their menus in silence.

Sloan set her menu down and shook her head. "We're not walking away, are we?"

Jessica looked up from hers. "Uh, I was kind of gonna ask if you were. But . . ." She trailed off.

"You can't stop thinking of Dustin Fonseca and Nia Stratos?"

"Yeah. Those poor kids. And whoever's next," Jessica said, checking her watch. "Probably soon."

"The last time I got pulled into one of your traveling sideshows, there wasn't an active FBI investigation, just a few different cases that you and Theo thought were connected. How do you proceed in a situation like this?"

"We do our own footwork. We keep the FBI investigation updated. Any development we find, we send to Monroe and Treynor. It's up to them to decide what they do, how much they pass on to Callis. The key is we keep them in the loop, but we don't tell them what we're doing next, only what we did."

"And that usually works?"

Jessica shook her head. "Almost never. Because if we make progress, it means we're finding things out that they're not, and somebody's gonna get embarrassed. Which means either they pull you in or they threaten you to make you step aside."

"I see you know this routine quite well."

"Yes, you might have noticed the lack of warmth Callis directed at me. I found the best thing you can do is just keep out of their way. Let them do their thing, as misdirected as it may be, while you do your thing."

"He was afraid of being embarrassed by you," Sloan said.

"A guy like him is probably well intentioned, but he's never dealt with a suspect capable of pulling off what took place. He knows that. And while leaning on expertise from the bureau is what you're supposed to do, my involvement brings about that kind of scrutiny that somebody like him doesn't want."

"Yeah, the PR scared him. Okay. So we stay out of their way, send any tips to Monroe, and do what we can with the understanding we can walk away whenever the hell we want," Sloan said.

"Exactly. But it really is time to order dinner. I'm starving."

"Me too. So, where do we start?" Sloan asked.

"The gnocchi sounds good," Jessica said.

"No, I mean with the case," Sloan explained. "But yeah, that sounds good too."

"I was hoping you could tell me. This is your area of expertise."

"I've dealt with a few sociopaths and serial killers, but nobody with this much of a theatrical sense."

"Don't focus on that right now. We need to think about the physical evidence and who's being targeted next. In particular, looking where we know the FBI investigation is not. They're going to be covering quite a lot of ground and hopefully will have a breakthrough. But what does Sloan McPherson know that they don't?"

"I don't know about that other than the observations I'd made about the water. Here's something I can't get out of my head. This is a pretty elaborate murder scene that we found, and the photograph of Nia is incredibly staged. A lot of work to pull off. I watched my kid in a play, and they had a month to practice, and everything went wrong. How does somebody nail it the first time?"

"It's a great observation. In the case of the Warlock, he had been planning things for years. There were some slipups, but he still managed to pull it off, and mostly by himself. He had some assistance, but nobody knew the full picture of what was going on. Here, it could be similar. That's why they wanted to bring me in—because they're worried that maybe Heywood slipped his leash again, but I'm reasonably sure it's not him; if anything, it's somebody who took notes on the Warlock. The other thing to consider is that they do make mistakes. We just don't know what they are yet. In hindsight, they become obvious. Every major investigation, you find out they slip through your fingers because you came very close or missed a detail. I don't need to tell you that. The key is we just have to look for where he slipped up or the thing he doesn't want us to see."

Sloan took an iPad from her backpack and opened it to the image of Nia underwater and studied it. "Well, this image is intentional, and he wanted us to see it, but there's a lot more information here than he, or maybe even the forensics group at the FBI, realizes."

Jessica played with her fork absentmindedly, twirling it around her thumb as she thought something over. After a long silence, she nodded at the iPad. "I think he already screwed up."

Sloan squinted at the image on the screen. "Where?"

"I'm sure there's more there that you could see, but I mean the fact that we got the photo at all. We're assuming that this is a clue about the next murder, which clearly it is, but what it really is, I think, was a clue about the first murder."

"I'm not sure I understand."

"The subject line was the location of Dustin Fonseca's body, right? The message . . . was an image of Nia," Jessica clarified.

"Dustin's body hadn't been announced yet, so I assume that was the killer's way of proving who he was in the email," Sloan said.

"Right, that's what we all assumed: He used the location of his first victim as a calling card to tell us who the next victim is. But you asked me how somebody could pull this off without screwing it up. I think he did screw up. I think that wildlife refuge officer found Dustin's body before the killer meant us to."

"The email came in earlier today, right?"

"Correct, but Dustin's body was found two days ago."

"What does that mean for the investigation?" Sloan asked.

"I don't know. It might have forced him to change his plans or act differently, because he felt like he had more time. If we weren't aware of the case until today, then he would have had more time to work unnoticed. He was certainly able to abduct Nia without us realizing, but this might have affected his plans. I'm not sure how." Jessica nodded at the iPad. "I think you're right—that photo might tell us more than we realize."

Sloan looked at the picture, then Jessica. "How much do you trust the FBI's forensics on this image?"

"Given enough time, they're great. Their first twenty-four hours, forty-eight, even the first week, not so much. They're usually brought in after the crime has been committed, and they have time as a luxury. Why?"

"That's been my experience too. I try to stay in my lane, but I've spent a lot of time underwater and I've taken a lot of photographs, both in my work as an investigator and as a PhD student in archaeology. I know way more than I care to about how water photographs. They're like fingerprints. A good photo can tell you a lot about the sediment, the location, the temperature, the salinity, and a lot of other stuff. I would love to run this through some computer program, which I'm sure probably the navy or somebody has, but going on my gut here, I think they missed something."

"Oh? Explain," Jessica prompted.

Sloan set the iPad on the table and rotated the photograph for Jessica to see. "The color, brackish green. We can tell probably the time of day by the reflections, which we commented on before. But you can also tell something if you know the camera. And I've taken a lot of photos in the ocean. I've taken a lot of photos in canals. I've taken a lot of photos everywhere. This is salt water," she announced.

"Like the Great Salt Lake . . ." Jessica noted.

"Yeah, but not necessarily. There are dozens of saltwater lakes in the West, but we can narrow it down by salinity. This appears to have one of the higher levels of salinity, from looking at it. Nowhere near as salty as seawater, but a kind of brackish water that I'm familiar with."

Jessica started scrolling on her phone, looking up data about lakes in the region.

"What about here?" Jessica said, turning her phone around to Sloan and showing her the Wikipedia page for Pyramid Lake.

The lake got its name from a large, roughly pyramid-shaped rock that jutted out of the water. It was an ancient body of water, one of the two leftover lakes from the massive inland sea that covered the region millions of years ago.

"I have some subsurface topological data I can look at," Sloan said as she opened a portal on her iPad. "Oh boy, this lake's big—seventy miles around. Deep too."

"Yes, but if you look at the roads, there's only a few places that you'd probably have easy access to, which could narrow it down, assuming they went for convenience."

"But if they put a boat in the water, they could go anywhere," said Sloan.

"Definitely. You have to remember, though, that they want to spend as little time as possible transporting a dead body around. Assuming she was dead when they moved her."

Sloan shook her head. "No, she didn't drown here." She scanned a map showing satellite data of the floor of the lake. "Interesting," she said, turning the satellite map around so Jessica could see it. "You're right: This lake is deep, but I'm not sure that matters. The key is putting the body somewhere that's easily accessible to you and first responders but not detectible while you're doing the deed . . . Oh, look here: This is Anaho Island. It's protected. You're not allowed within a thousand feet of it, but between here and the shore, the deepest it gets is twenty feet. You could hold your breath, go down, touch the bottom, and go up again several times. It would be a great place to dump a body that you wanted to reveal at a later point but not be too worried about somebody finding it until you told them where it was."

"That seems searchable," Jessica noted.

"Totally. How long do you think it would take for Callis and his team to get organized enough to take a look?"

Jessica shook her head. "The question is whether they'd do it. But . . . if we were to get a guide and a boat—and assuming you brought one of your small little underwater drone thingamajigs—what are our chances of finding it?"

"It depends upon the condition of the water—maybe a few hours. Are you sure we don't want to just tell the FBI?"

"Don't worry, I'm not going to ask you to go in the water, I promise. We'll tell them, but I don't think they're going to be jumping on this lead anytime soon. And no offense, it's a bit of a wild lead. I doubt they'd make it an immediate priority."

"No offense taken. I agree. We tell them, we look anyway. And if we don't find anything, we tell them never mind. Then again, there are a lot of other bodies of water, and I could be wrong about the salinity."

"I trust your instincts. And doing something is better than just sitting here," Jessica said, looking around at the restaurant. "Well, this is a pretty nice place."

The water fountain outside the window erupted again as the next show started. Sloan gave the attention-catching attraction a moment's glance, then turned back to her iPad.

"It's a seven-hour drive," she observed.

"We'll get dinner to go." Jessica smiled. "I don't take you for the kind to just sit still."

"Nope. But now that I shared my hunch, I'm curious to hear yours."

ANCIENT HISTORY

"You've had your own history with ritual killers," Jessica pointed out as she drove her rented SUV north on the dark desert highway.

The pair had planned to take shifts driving while the other one slept but found themselves engaged in conversation instead.

"That's one way to put it. I've dealt with a couple of different kinds of whack jobs. The Swamp Killer certainly fit the ritualistic type. He'd make little shrines out in the Everglades. And these weren't meant for other people to find; they're just some weirdo fetish. The Warlock, on the other hand, I can't even fathom what was going through his head."

"He wanted to be a cult leader. The problem was, he was very lacking in the charisma department. The closer people got to him, the less interesting he was. That's why he resorted to theatrical murders."

"I've read up on him, and everybody has a different opinion," Sloan said.

"Yeah, I think people want to read more into it than there was. He's a very clever guy, can be very manipulative, but he's just a psychopath. Also, killing people was a means to an end."

"And whoever killed Dustin Fonseca and Nia Stratos . . . that feels different?"

"I leave it to the experts to get into the head games, because even they're pretty bad at it. I try to focus on physical evidence, what killers say, what they're not saying, and how they do it."

"And what is this guy saying right now, assuming it's a guy?"

"Well, we've both made that mistake before, but I don't know. Dustin Fonseca, Nia Stratos, they're, I guess, what the kids today would call famous. I'm sure the FBI team back in Vegas is going over everything they've ever said or done and any fan that ever interacted with them with a fine-tooth comb, which is what they should be doing. Our killer could be the world's angriest chat troll. But he's not stupid, he's not a spree killer, this isn't *really* ritualistic. The salt thing's weird, the underwater thing's weird, but they're also designed to draw attention."

"That kind of sounds like the Warlock. He literally made it look like a girl fell from the sky into the middle of Times Square and dragged a World War II airplane onto a beach," Sloan noted.

"I know, I know," Jessica said as she stared out ahead into the highway. "But with Heywood, the victims were selected because they had biological twins they didn't know about. It was a weird thing. He wanted to make these things look like impossible crimes because he was trying to make people think that he could perform magic. Literally, that's why he called himself the Warlock. He wanted the world to think that he was some supernatural entity. The victims were just people with really bad luck. Dustin and Nia, on the other hand, were targeted. I think that's the difference here, and I think it's important. Why were they targets? How they're killed and where is important, but *who* they are is critical. And that will probably tell us more about their murderer."

Sloan nodded as she thought this over. "So the victims are chosen for a reason. The way they're killed is a message."

After a long silence, Jessica spoke up. "The Warlock had this manifesto—you've probably heard of it—the 'Eternicon,' and it didn't make a lot of sense. It was like he read *Dianetics* and the Unabomber's manifesto and decided he had to have one. It was hollow. He's a hollow man. There wasn't a lot there. Not to get too analytical, he was a very intelligent person who was extremely unfulfilled and fixated upon the most ridiculous kind of compensation mechanism you could imagine."

"Why does this killer want us to find the victims?" Sloan asked.

"I've been thinking about that too. Problem is, I keep thinking about previous cases. Heywood was doing it for attention. Marta was revenge."

"The crazy cartel lady who wanted to kill the pope . . . she was a piece of work," Sloan remarked.

"Yeah, say what you want, but she had her reasons. Wrong ones, but reasons."

Sloan looked out her window at the glowing horizon, silhouetted by the dark mountains. "Probably a lot of buried bodies out there."

"The Vegas Mafia had a certain way of dealing with problems," Jessica agreed.

"I was actually thinking a little bit further back in time than that. There's been continuous human occupation out here for at least ten thousand years, maybe fifteen thousand years. You know, it may not look like much right now, but this was a lot greener in the past. Well, wetter. We would have been underwater a few million years ago. But even ten thousand years ago, this would have looked different. Would have been different animals out here. Giant sloths, dire wolves. Terrifying birds."

"I keep forgetting that you were studying archaeology before you got pulled into all of this."

"Me too. My husband likes to joke that the only thing that changed was just the recency of the bodies I find." Sloan gave her a wry smile.

"Ten thousand years . . ." Jessica mused as she looked beyond her headlights into the dark desert wilderness.

"Could be fifteen thousand. There are petroglyphs in Nevada that may be that old," Sloan said, stopping for a moment and tapping on the window with her knuckle, lost in thought.

"I don't know why he chose Sheldon Refuge, but if we find something in Pyramid Lake, it ain't gonna be an accident," she said at last. "At least, I don't think it is. It could be a coincidence, but it might be a pattern . . . But it'd also be an obvious pattern."

"Say it, for crying out loud," Jessica urged.

"Okay, this is going to sound a bit crazy," Sloan began, "but we chose this location because I looked at the water, and it looked like salt water. It's the shallowest part of a salty lake. Convenient place to drop a body. But what I didn't even think about is how significant this location is. It's only a few miles from Lake Winnemucca."

"Is that another salt lake?" Jessica asked.

"Just salt now. It used to be called Lake Mud. I remember there was a skirmish there at the end of the Civil War between soldiers and Paiute Indians. I don't remember the details . . ."

"Well, that's an interesting piece of history. But what makes the proximity meaningful?"

"The point I'm going to get to is what's really fascinating, at least to the archaeologist in me, but probably useless to the cop side of me. But Lake Winnemucca has the oldest petroglyphs in the United States. They don't know if they're ten thousand or fifteen thousand years old, but even if they're just ten thousand years old, they're still the oldest ones."

"Interesting," Jessica responded. "What do the petroglyphs depict?"

"I'm a horrible archaeologist. I don't recall offhand, but I think it was just, like, abstract patterns and diamond shapes, that kind of thing. Maybe something that looked like trees or plants. I don't recall any animals. It could have been astronomical information or somebody just high out of their mind on fermented honey or whatever they used. But it is archaeologically significant. Probably nothing to do with this, though."

"Sounds pretty significant to me," Jessica remarked.

"Maybe, but if we were in Europe, we could be visiting a crime scene that was on top of a medieval battle, on top of a Roman battle, on top of some Neanderthal tribal raid, for all we would know."

"True, but think about it: Is there anything similar about the Sheldon Refuge?"

"I'll look it up, but now that I think about it, the killer could just be a hiker type seeking out-of-the-way places to leave bodies. We'd be better off looking at AllTrails data," she said with a sigh, referencing a popular hiking app.

"We could send that idea to Callis and his team. It's exactly the kind of data analysis the FBI is good at crunching," Jessica suggested.

"I just pulled that out of nowhere. I don't know how useful it is," Sloan admitted.

"You never know. In an alternate universe, I was asleep right now and you were driving, and we never had that conversation and didn't realize that. So probably good for something."

"Yeah, but in another alternate universe, I'm driving, you're sitting here, and you're thinking, and we already solved it," Sloan remarked.

"Fair point. Do you ever revisit your cases and look at the points where you missed, and you could have solved it sooner?"

"I don't, but I should. I've certainly had other people point that out to me. Gwen, our ex-detective researcher, she's great at pointing out all the things I missed."

"If I had a dime for every true-crime podcaster that went over my cases and pointed out my mistakes, I'd have a lot of dimes," Jessica agreed.

"Want me to drive while you count those?"

"I'm good for now. Why don't you grab a nap."

"It's okay. I'll keep you company," Sloan replied.

"Actually, I was hoping you'd grab one so I wouldn't feel guilty when I ask you to drive and I fall asleep," Jessica explained.

"Ah, got it."

"Before you doze off, if you want to work on finding out how we're going to get hold of a boat by the time we get there, that would be great."

"I'm sure I can get someone to lend me one."

"Even out here in the desert?"

"Boat people are everywhere," Sloan assured her.

PYRAMID LAKE

Just past 6:00 a.m., the sun was beginning to create a glow along the eastern horizon as Mr. Briar, a retired surveyor with a trim gray beard and a camo hat, turned the winch, lowering his twelve-foot aluminum boat into the water at the edge of the jetty.

When Briar had gotten out of his truck to meet the two women, Jessica noticed that it took him only a second to size up Sloan as a woman who knew what the hell she was doing.

As much as Sloan described herself as an awkward klutz, she radiated a certain physical confidence. In another life, she might have become a competent soccer player or judo champ.

The boat rolled off the edge of the ramp and into the water with a splash. "I take it you know how to work the outboard motor and all that," said Mr. Briar. "There're life vests in the well up front, paddles if you need them. If you get in any trouble, just call me on my cell. You should get some reception out here. Stay away from the island across there. That's a protected area. Other than that, try not to get in any trouble."

"As long as there aren't any explosive cylinders on board, I think we're going to be fine," Sloan remarked, making an inside joke about the last time she and Jessica had taken a waterborne trip together.

"Not last I checked," Mr. Briar replied, clearly not sure if she was joking.

"Have you seen anything weird around here lately, maybe within the last week?" Sloan asked.

Jessica observed Briar's reaction as his eyes narrowed and he tried to think of what Sloan meant by "weird." While she would have taken a more indirect or subtle approach, she appreciated Sloan's bluntness and had observed in the past how effective it could be, probably due in no small part to the fact that Sloan was who she presented herself to be: well-intentioned, good-hearted, sincere, open, and honest. If she had an agenda, it was well hidden.

"We get some people coming out here doing stupid stuff on their Jet Skis, if that's what you mean."

"Anybody out here that didn't look like they were here to fish or do normal outdoor recreation?"

"Other than you two, no."

Sloan realized how odd her line of questioning probably sounded to him and decided to be a little bit more open. "I'm a law enforcement officer from Florida. My friend here used to be an FBI agent. Sorry if our questions sound odd."

"Then you probably know about the fella from Nixon," said Mr. Briar, nodding in the direction of the town five miles to the south, "who killed his girlfriend a couple years ago. Then, of course, the Pyramid Lake War back in the 1800s," he continued, gesturing to the east over the mountain range between the lake and the dry bed where soldiers had encountered the Paiutes.

Jessica nodded in agreement. "So, a different question, and again, this is going to sound odd, but are there any people around here you'd consider eccentric, say? Maybe the kind who keep to themselves? Maybe somebody you don't quite trust?"

"Lots of people. You don't exactly end up out here if you fit in anywhere else," said Mr. Briar.

"Anyone in particular?" Sloan asked.

Mr. Briar turned around and held open his hands, gesturing toward the small town. "Knock on any door. Each one of us is a bit odder than the next one, but crazy likes company."

Sloan looked at Jessica to see if she had any more questions.

She shrugged. "Well, thank you very much. We should be back in a few hours. We have your cell phone number. We'll give you a call, if that works."

Sloan held on to the bow of the boat, getting knee-deep into the water as Jessica climbed in. She pushed the boat away from the ramp and hopped aboard. Mr. Briar gave them a wave, then walked back to the cab of his truck and drove off.

Sloan pulled the cord on the ancient outboard motor, and it roared to life. She turned the handle and swung them in a sharp loop toward Anaho Island. Pyramid Island, the smaller, triangular-shaped isle that gave the lake its name, lay a mile or so to the north of Anaho.

After they were a good distance away from shore, Sloan called out to Jessica over the sound of the motor, "You want to handle this while I get our gear ready?"

Jessica took over steering the boat as Sloan started to assemble a small underwater drone she pulled from her duffel bag. It consisted of a thick Frisbee-shaped submersible craft and several hundred feet of thin, yellow, rubber-covered cable connected to a device that resembled a hockey puck.

"The one you used last time was a lot bigger. Is this an updated version?" Jessica asked.

"I could fit this in a carry-on. It can only go wireless for a short distance, so I just use the fiber-optic cable. If we see something interesting, we'll have to figure out another means to pull it out of the water."

"Another means . . ." Jessica replied, eyeing the swim fins and mask at the bottom of Sloan's duffel bag. She hadn't brought Sloan out to Nevada with the expectation that she would need to go scuba diving. The fact that Nia Stratos was apparently found underwater made it a lot easier to justify Sloan's inclusion. But Jessica mostly had wanted to have another person to talk things over with. And despite their different personalities—Jessica's intense introversion and Sloan's high-flying extroversion—or maybe because of the contrast, she enjoyed being around Sloan.

As the robot powered up, Sloan opened an app on her iPad to connect to the Wi-Fi in the hockey puck. The view from the drone's camera was visible on the iPad, as well as a depth map showing the interior of the boat as a bunch of pixels. Satisfied that everything was in working order, she powered it down and turned to Jessica. "Let's go south a bit in case anybody's watching us. Probably somebody is. Just so it's not obvious we're making a beeline to Anaho Island," Sloan suggested.

"Aye-aye, captain," said Jessica. "Did you ever get your captain's license?"

"When I was twenty-two. In my family, it was more important than a driver's license or a college diploma."

"Why am I not surprised?"

Sloan turned her attention back to the lake. It was a calm day with little wind and not much chop to the water. From where they were, they couldn't see any other craft. The lake couldn't have been more different from the ones Sloan was accustomed to in South Florida. Lake Okeechobee was vast enough that the flat shore was hard to see from its center. The absence of anything taller than a palm tree could convince you that you were in the middle of a small ocean, whereas Pyramid Lake sat between small but steep mountain ranges to the east and west. The absence of vegetation and the dull brown terrain made Sloan think of what it would be like on Mars.

Jessica guided the boat across the water at the angle Sloan had suggested. She kept it at the right speed to move across the slight chop without too much vibration.

"I guess you've done this before," Sloan remarked.

"A little bit," Jessica called back over the sound of the motor. "I get the attraction, to be honest with you. I've never been much of an angler, but this part's kind of fun. The ability to just point the bow in any direction you want and go wherever you please."

"That, in a nutshell, is my family's motto. Land is where we store stuff we can't fit on our boat."

"How often do you end up on the water?" Jessica asked.

"When it comes to work, I probably spend more days at my desk, but every night when I go home, my office is in my boat off the dock in our backyard."

"Salt water in your veins," Jessica noted.

"More like brackish brown Florida canal water at this point, but yeah."

Sloan turned toward the bow of the boat and scanned the horizon, then checked her watch. Jessica had no idea how far they had traveled, other than a rough estimate from looking at the lake on Google Maps, but she had a feeling Sloan had a much more precise understanding.

"About seven minutes," Sloan said, confirming Jessica's suspicion. "While we're on the topic of salt, how the hell did Dustin Fonseca end up inside of a giant salt cube?"

"When I was a little girl, my father explained to me there are two kinds of mysteries in magic: the good kind and the bad kind. The good kind are ones where you are left with no explanation other than the supernatural. The bad kind are where you're left with a number of implausible or improbable explanations, none of them impossible."

"How do you mean?"

"If I had you pick a card, put it in the deck, and I shuffled it, and then I found your card, you might assume that I got lucky one out of fifty-two times. If you're a little more analytical, you might think that all I had to do was keep track of where five or ten cards were after the deck was shuffled, then figure out where yours was. Maybe my odds are one in ten. But if I let you shuffle the cards, and I do the trick again in such a way that seems truly impossible, then it becomes a good trick.

"Of course, if you're convinced the deck is shuffled and then I reveal your card in such a way that you're also convinced that I am one hundred percent absolutely positive that it's your card and not just me getting lucky one out of fifty-two times, my confidence influences the overall effect. It becomes a miracle, even though mathematically it's not," she explained.

"So Monroe and Treynor and the others at the FBI are making a bit more out of it than what it is?"

"I think so. None of them thinks it's paranormal or supernatural, which is good, but I can think of a half dozen ways that you could pull that off, and I'm sure there's probably an even better way—maybe the one that this person or these people used. That's why I was telling them getting too caught up in the method is a distraction. There might be a clue in the method that could tell us who it is, but at this point, finding the bodies, finding more physical evidence, is the most important part of the case."

"So you're saying it's not that impressive?"

"I'm saying there's no Hula-Hoop," Jessica said.

"Hula-Hoop?" Sloan asked.

"It's a phrase we used in my house growing up. Let's say you're sitting in the audience, and the magician has his assistant lie on a couch, and he waves his hands over her body, and she begins to float up into the air, up above his head. Are you amazed?" Jessica asked.

"I guess that depends."

"What does that depend upon?"

"Well, I guess if he's using strings."

"Exactly. It looks impressive, but you've heard that magicians might use things like wires, so you're awed, but maybe not completely amazed," Jessica explained. "The magician needs to prove to you the explanation in your head is wrong. And that's where the Hula-Hoop comes in. If he then takes out a Hula-Hoop and passes it over her body, removing the possibility that she could be connected to wires, now you're truly astounded, because it went from an improbable-yet-possible to a miracle. What we saw wasn't a miracle."

"Whereas the Warlock's murders were," Sloan concluded.

"At first glance, absolutely. They were impossibilities. They had me stumped, and that's what has me concerned here."

"You're more worried that our killer's not as clever?" Sloan asked, confused.

"I didn't say he wasn't as clever. I said whoever's doing this has a different motivation, from what I can understand. With the Warlock, the murder was the point. For this killer, I can't fathom a motive."

Sloan watched a large white pelican skim across the water, then come to a landing on Anaho Island.

"You never said how he did it, though," she pointed out.

"If you put a gun to my head and said I had to do the same thing, I would have started with a block of salt cut in half with a space for the person. Shoving the salt inside of them—not too difficult. We'll do a toxicology report eventually and find out that he was sedated or drugged, and they just crammed that into him as fast as they could. There are different kinds of salt, laboratory grade with fewer impurities. They might have pumped him full of salt, took out a bunch of moisture, sucked it out again with a vacuum, then primed it full into him, filling up his lungs. Then packed a bunch of salt around him, wedged him into the salt container, used a little bit of moisture to get it to seal, possibly in an oven. Again, laboratory results will tell us something and, boom, you've got a guy encased in salt. Even though it looked like it took a lot longer to do it, it probably didn't take that long at all."

"I guess that makes sense," Sloan said.

"It's probably not how they did it. My point is, right now, trying to figure it out without a lot of physical evidence or details is pointless. If it's not that method, it's something else. Because the reality, which I tried to get everybody to understand in the Warlock case, is that he's not special. Not supernatural. There's an explanation that we simply haven't arrived at yet. But what's frustrating here is, if we'd found Dustin Fonseca nailed to a cross in the middle of the desert, we wouldn't be fixated on how he was nailed to the cross. We'd be asking ourselves, *Why* the fuck is this guy nailed to a cross? And directing the investigation that way."

"And that's why you're so eager to find Nia Stratos, isn't it? You don't think we're just going to find a body."

Jessica used her free hand to make a shrugging gesture. "We probably could spend our time sitting in a hotel room on our laptops, watching all their videos and going through every interaction we could find, but that's probably not going to tell me as much right now as what the killer left out here. That might be important later, but my hunch tells me we can narrow down the killer's motive a lot from whatever clues might be underwater . . . partially because we got a bit of a head start on this."

Jessica slowed the boat as they entered the area between Anaho Island and the mainland. Sloan checked the depth map and pointed to a spot three hundred meters east of where they were.

"It's only about twenty feet deep here," she said.

Jessica looked from the island to the land and realized it was a much larger area than it appeared to be on the map. "A lot of water to cover."

"That's why we brought this guy," Sloan replied, holding up the yellow ROV before tossing it into the water.

JULES

Sloan watched as the ROV sank beneath the surface and faded from view before barely reaching a meter. There was a jerk on the yellow fiber-optic cable as its motors came to life, and the drone started moving away from the boat as it acclimated itself to the lake.

Her iPad showed a view of dark, murky water that was nearly opaque, with occasional particulate flecks drifting by. The more interesting image was from the underwater 3D positioning sensors that used a combination of ultrasound and specially tuned lasers to map the floor and objects within ten meters of the little robot.

"Jules, how are you doing?" Sloan asked.

"Great, boss. Just getting myself adjusted to the surroundings. Looks like we're in Pyramid Lake," said Jules, a cheerful voice emanating from the iPad speaker.

"This one talks too," Jessica remarked.

"Well, they're so smart now, me controlling it with a joystick doesn't really make much sense. It's a lot easier just to tell it what you want it to do and let it do its thing," Sloan said. "Didn't you tell me Theo has conversations with his robot dog?"

"It's gotten worse. He's talking to our Roomba now."

Sloan had her eyes on the depth map. "That sounds a bit intense."

"He actually has a rational explanation for doing it, which is the infuriating thing about Theo," Jessica said. "He suggested you could use a Roomba with a camera and some other sensors aimed at the ground for crime-scene investigation. As it swept along the floor, it could track and map everything it picks up. While probably not a substitute for a full forensic team, it could be a great tool for investigations that don't have the human resources or budget."

"See, that makes sense," Sloan said.

"Maybe, but I don't really like having something telling me how many times I've dropped my toenail clippings or spilled my tea in an automated email report," Jessica said.

"Fair point," Sloan conceded.

"Have you considered telling Theo you would like more privacy?" Jules suggested.

"Butt out, Jules. You're not part of this conversation."

Sloan pressed the mute button for a moment. "We used a general-purpose chatbot for this. We'll have to refine it some."

Sloan reached her arm into the water and faced her palm in the direction of the sun. "Jules, take a photo and get a light reading on my hand."

"Done," the robot replied.

Sloan's palm appeared on the tablet. She held it up for Jessica to see.

"If we adjust for the angle and depth, the sun would have to be higher than it is now for the photo," said Sloan.

"So it was taken in the late afternoon like you guessed?" asked Jessica.

"I think so. Jules, continue your mission," Sloan commanded.

Jessica and Sloan watched as the robot started to move in a sweeping pattern, painting in dots on the screen as it mapped the lake bed. When it was almost at the limit of its tether, Sloan had Jessica start the motor and move the craft forward so the robot could continue its sweep.

"There's a lot of sediment between Anaho and the shore—boulders and smaller deposits. Once upon a time, this lake stretched for hundreds of miles down past Lake Tahoe and up north into Oregon. With the tributary that ran almost completely across the state, people probably lived all around here, and this lake was a source of life. Not that you would think so looking at it. Although they've reintroduced the cutthroat trout here because, apparently, that was good fishing—almost too good for a while, to the point of extinction here."

"Interesting. I've still been thinking about what you said with the petroglyphs and the deep history of this area," Jessica said.

"I wouldn't read too much into that," Sloan told her.

"Hey, boss, I just want to let you know my long-range sensor is picking something up," said Jules.

"What's that?" Sloan asked.

"Some kind of object twenty-seven meters northwest. It's a consistent background noise, so I don't think it's a glitch. I can't find any patterns in the database that match. Do you want me to skip scanning the rest of the floor and go take a look?"

"Affirmative," Sloan replied.

She pressed the mute button for a moment. "I know it's just a machine, but . . ."

"Yeah," Jessica said.

The robot shot off to the side, pulling the fiber-optic cable with it. Sloan turned the boat toward its path and followed along behind. The forward sensors started to show a cloud of dots in front of the ROV as it probed the dark water ahead of it.

A large, oval cloud formed in front of Jules that stood out from the noise.

"That's interesting," Jessica said.

Suddenly, the cloud vanished.

"I think that was a school of fish. Jules, can you still pick up the signal?" Sloan asked.

"Affirmative, four meters ahead," Jules confirmed.

"Stop where you are and collect data," Sloan told it. Although the underwater robot was normally adept, she didn't want it to disturb a potential crime scene.

"Would you like me to rotate around the perimeter?" Jules asked.

Sloan thought about it for a moment. "No, I don't want the tether getting in the way. Just hold this position in a lateral line and collect as much data as you can."

They watched as the screen began to fill with more data. Small white dots appeared, at first in random places, and then started to form above the lake floor into a jagged object like a spike.

"Is this another salt obelisk?" Jessica asked. "Was the photo of Nia a ruse?"

"Too early to tell. It's creating a diffusion map, so there's not a lot of data. It'll take a while for it to fill in. I could run Jules in closer if you want, but I'm hesitant to because I don't want to disturb anything. The water's relatively still here, and there's a good chance there might be some physical evidence in or around the area." Sloan had spent thousands of hours watching images like this one at crime scenes and on archaeological expeditions.

"Is it okay to turn off the motor?" Jessica asked as the engine hummed behind her.

"Go ahead. There's not too much wind; we're not going to drift a lot. I'll keep my eye on the tether."

Jessica killed the engine, then scooted forward at the edge of the seat so she could lean in and get a better look at the display. The jagged edges had turned into polygons and were growing in detail. There was a large object midway between the bottom and the surface of the lake that appeared to be less than two meters in height. A pattern of faint dots led from it to the lake bed.

Suddenly, the polygons multiplied, then transformed into a much more defined shape.

"My God," said Jessica. "It looks like . . ." Her voice trailed off.

"A medieval statue," Sloan said. The face was recognizably Nia's. Her body resembled a figure in prayer, with her hands clasped before her. It was too hard to tell through the computer rendering if they were bound or clasped, but there was an almost religious aspect to it. Her ankles were close together with something bound around them, connected to a cable running to the seafloor.

"I'm going to move the robot in closer so we can use the camera." Jessica nodded.

"Jules, I want you to move in, but do it slowly. We don't want to disturb anything. Try to keep at least a meter between you and the object. You understand?"

"Affirmative, moving in slowly," Jules confirmed.

As the robot carefully moved toward what they believed to be Nia's body, the pixelated image began to fill in and a silhouette emerged from the darkness.

"Lights on, Jules," Sloan whispered.

The silhouette burst into a bright glow as it became brighter than the background. The robot's camera adjusted, revealing their first view of Nia Stratos's face.

"Oh, man," Sloan said under her breath. "This just got real."

"It never goes away, no matter how many times," Jessica agreed, shaking her head.

Nia Stratos's pose was the same as that in the photograph, the only difference being the angle from which they were viewing it. Mouth slightly open, eyes open, looking up to the sky as if to the heavens. Jessica couldn't tell if that was intentional or not. She had seen that expression before in people who died under certain conditions. For all she knew, it might have been the same expression medieval painters used to show a person in the presence of the divine.

As the drone descended deeper, the camera revealed that Nia was wearing a loose white dress that almost resembled a toga. Her hands became visible, and the light from Jules reflected off something shiny.

"Jules, move ten centimeters to the left, but keep your focus on the object," Sloan instructed.

The robot did as it was told, shifting slightly so they could get a better view of what was causing the light to be reflected.

"Is that a metal chain?" asked Jessica.

"I think so. It looks like how they bound her wrists. Probably chrome or something," Sloan said.

"It looks like the Siberian chain escape," Jessica remarked.

"The what?"

"Nothing, just a magic trick from my childhood. Your hands are wrapped with a chain in a certain way, and you're able to get out," Jessica said as she leaned in closer to look at the monitor. "That's not how you would bind it for it. This looks like she was legitimately tied up with the chain, which means there's going to be a lock underneath it. Or should be."

As the robot descended below the level of Nia Stratos's hands, a small padlock became visible near her wrists. Her dress had billowed out in the water, almost as if frozen in mid-movement. Her knees were visible below the hem.

"Scrape marks," Jessica observed, pointing at abrasions near the knees. "It looks like she might have been dragged."

"Jesus Christ," Sloan growled.

"I know, I know."

The robot continued to descend. There were more abrasions on Nia's shins. A larger, thicker silvery chain was wrapped around her ankles. The bottom of the chain ran down to the lake bed.

The robot came to a stop and hovered in front of Nia's feet. There were more abrasions on her toes and crusted blood around the toenails.

"It looks like she went through hell before she died," Jessica said.

"From the expression on her face, I think she was drugged. Not that that really makes much of a difference, but if I had to die, I guess I would prefer a drowsy death than one where I was fully aware."

"Can we take a look at how she's anchored?" Jessica asked.

"Jules, maintain distance from the subject, but keep descending. Maintain half a meter from the floor," Sloan instructed.

Jessica turned her head sharply to the side and squinted into the distance. "Did you . . . ?" She stopped.

"What?" asked Sloan, looking up from the iPad.

"For a moment, I thought I saw, I don't know, a flash from out there," said Jessica as she pointed toward the hills to the east of them. "Hopefully just broken glass."

The robot continued its descent, following the silver chain downward. Algae had clung to it in places, but it otherwise appeared brand new, as if it had just come off the shelf of the boating supply store.

"Is this thing getting photos?" Jessica asked.

"Yeah, it's sending video and high-quality stills up to the cloud as well," Sloan confirmed.

"I guess we should call this in to our friends at the FBI and send them what we have so they can do a recovery."

"Yeah. We should." Sloan hesitated. "But . . ."

"I'm not asking you to go into the water," Jessica said.

"I know that. It's just that we're in the middle of nowhere in Nevada, and it'll be half a day before they get somebody out here who can do a competent body recovery. That's assuming the locals don't just grab a hook and pull the chain up out of the water, which they've been known to do."

"And the most competent person for doing a body recovery within a hundred miles is sitting right next to me," Jessica added.

"I don't have a hero complex. It doesn't have to be me. I'm just concerned that time is not on our side. At the very least, we need to preserve her to the best of our ability. Every minute counts. There could be a fingerprint under the eyelid, material under her nails, something important. She's been out here too long already. Once we call this in, they're going to call Fish and Wildlife, then the FBI. We're going to have several boats over here churning up the water, not to mention what the salt water is already doing. As an active law enforcement officer, I'm going to make the call to preserve the crime scene," Sloan decided.

"Agent Callis will be pissed," Jessica replied.

"But the forensics team will thank me," said Sloan as she started digging through her duffel bag for a box of clear plastic garbage liners.

The robot stopped its descent. The end of the silver metal chain was wrapped through the center of five cinder blocks. A large padlock fastened it.

"Well, that's just sloppy craftsmanship," Jessica commented.

"What's that?" Sloan asked as she leaned over to look at the screen.

"Not even an anchor, just a bunch of blocks."

"Well, if the FBI doesn't have a nickname for him, I suggest the Home Depot Killer."

"Corporate will love that. Still, I don't know why it bothers me. I don't think he's trying to tell us something with it, but it certainly says something." She picked up the iPad. "Can I get another look at her face?"

"Jules, find the subject's face and hover while maintaining distance," Sloan instructed.

The robot began to ascend, this time a little more quickly, but not so fast as to create a wake that would disturb the body.

Jessica studied Nia Stratos's corpse as it passed by the screen. She wasn't looking for anything specific, only trying to take it in and understand.

Jules came to a stop in its original position in front of Nia's face. Her eyes still looked to the heavens, her mouth agape, as if confused and frightened by something she had seen. Sloan leaned over to look at the screen with Jessica. Nia wasn't a victim; she was a person. There was a story there. One that had ended tragically.

A loud squelching sound blasted through the air, startling the women.

"For fuck's sake," said Sloan as she whipped her head around to see where the noise had come from.

A man in sunglasses, a baseball cap, and a law enforcement uniform stood at the center console of a twenty-foot boat with a green hull and the word "RANGER" across the side. He was holding a megaphone and glaring at them.

"Fish and Wildlife?" asked Jessica, expecting a state game warden.

"Worse, tribal police. Let me try to handle this," Sloan said.

She dropped what she was doing, stood up, and waved to the ranger. She pulled her badge from her back pocket and held it aloft. "Hello," she called out. "I'm Detective McPherson."

"I don't care," he shouted back at her, his voice amplified by the megaphone. "You are in the middle of a protected refuge. This is off-limits for all pleasure craft."

"I don't want to split hairs," Sloan yelled back, "but we're about fifteen hundred feet from shore. The limit's a thousand feet."

"I don't think that was the right approach," Jessica said quietly.

"Yeah, my mouth gets away from me sometimes," Sloan muttered.

"You're about one minute from being placed under arrest," the ranger shouted back.

He throttled his engine and started to bring the boat closer.

Sloan realized this could disturb the crime scene and held her hands up in the air. "Wait, wait," she shouted. "We're in the middle of a body recovery." She pointed toward the water. "I'm assisting on an FBI case. There is a body just ten feet below us. Don't come any closer, or you could wreck the crime scene."

"Are you insane?" the ranger shouted back and continued toward them.

"Stop, stop," she shouted. "My name is Sloan McPherson. I'm with the Florida Department of Law Enforcement assisting an FBI case. You can contact the Las Vegas office and ask about this. Please stop your engine. Do not come any closer," she implored.

He slowed his boat to an idle, turning the bow aside. "I'm going to need you to stop whatever you're doing and follow me back to shore."

"Time is extremely important here. We cannot wait. We have to preserve the crime scene."

"Lady, FBI investigation or not, this is tribal land," the ranger explained. "Everything needs to go through me. You're out here without permission, probably without a permit. So I'm going to need you to follow me to shore. We can settle this there."

"You don't understand," Sloan said.

"Follow me in now!" screamed the ranger, his patience gone.

"How important is it we preserve her body as soon as possible?" Jessica asked Sloan.

"Very. We need to get her hands and head bagged, at the very least, before they start sending their watercraft around here. Let me try again."

Sloan raised her badge again. "Can we talk about it here?" she asked the ranger.

The ranger made an angry face and reached for the throttle as if preparing to ram them, then froze. "What the hell?" he yelled.

Sloan turned around at the sound of a splash and saw Jessica's legs disappearing into the water. She had taken the plastic bags with her.

CRIME SCENE

Although Jessica hadn't spent as much time in the water as Sloan, she had plenty of professional experience with it. In her family's magic act, known for escape artistry, Jessica had learned to hold her breath for an uncomfortably long time before entering middle school.

Her grandfather had even inquired about getting her a certified Guinness World Record for the achievement but was rebuffed and told that attempting to do so would be tantamount to child endangerment.

Soon, Jessica had refined her breath-holding and underwater lock-picking skills. She was never particularly fond of water stunts, though, and the breaking point with her father and grandfather came as a teenager in Mexico City when she was trying to perform an underwater escape on live television. She had a close call with death, although she knew her father and grandfather didn't wish her ill and thought the act safe. It was then she understood that she had a much more realistic understanding about how the world worked than either of them did.

As she dived into Pyramid Lake, she made it a point to throw herself to the side and as far away from Nia's body as possible.

The water was colder than expected and chilled her as it seeped into her clothes, displacing what warm air had been there.

Jules was hovering in place two meters in front of her, its light casting a glow on Nia like an aura. Because Jules's camera showed only a limited field, the full halo effect hadn't been apparent on the iPad screen. In the dark-green light, the resemblance to a medieval statue was even more pronounced. It seemed intentional, but she knew better than to read too much into it.

Her lungs already pounding, Jessica knew she didn't have much time. While she'd been able to take a deep breath before jumping in, she was a bit out of practice at breath holding. (Her last try had been with Sloan when they ended up in Puget Sound.) She made a mental note that practicing holding her breath would be advisable if she planned to spend more time around McPherson.

She pulled one of the plastic bags from her pocket and opened it up, letting the water flow inside it like a jellyfish.

She guided it over Nia's left hand and up to her wrist. Jessica then took another one, opened it, and guided it down over Nia's head like a shroud.

Although she was certain Sloan would have more finesse and technique in preserving the body, any preparation was better than none.

She brought the edge of the next bag like a shroud over Nia's other hand, careful not to move her limbs.

Before moving to the legs, Jessica pulled a length of plastic twine from the roll and cinched it around Nia's torso.

As she fumbled in her pocket for her knife to cut the twine, her face drifted closer to Nia's, and she could see straight into the young woman's eyes.

They were bloodshot. Jessica didn't consider herself a forensics expert, but between training, investigations, and research, she had looked at hundreds of photographs of corpses that had died under various conditions, ranging from explosives to poisoning and asphyxiation.

Nia's eyes didn't resemble the bulging, bloodshot orbs of somebody who had been strangled or drowned. These were the eyes of somebody who had been crying.

The realization sent a gut punch through Jessica. But instead of feeling exhaustion, she felt a rush of adrenaline and anger giving her strength.

Satisfied with Nia's upper body, Jessica swam down to her feet. She cut off a long strand of twine, wrapped a plastic bag around the area where the chain had secured Nia's ankles, and tied it off. Her lungs had begun to protest despite the rush of energy, but she had more to do. She tore the seam on a bag, slid it over the top of Nia, past her shoulders, by her hands, and then around her waist, and wrapped the twine around that section. Murderers who raped their victims sometimes left their bodies in water to remove evidence of the crime. While Jessica didn't have any specific reason to suspect that Nia was violated, it was important to make sure that nothing was overlooked.

Jessica readied to surface, then remembered the weight holding Nia to the lake bed. Quickly, she used her remaining oxygen to swim to the bottom of the chain, where it was wrapped around the cinder blocks.

Even down in the depths of the lake, the shiny metal of the chain glinted from the light above. This didn't look like an ordinary chrome chain. It seemed shinier, like the polished metal she'd use in a magic act, in stark contrast to the brutalist cement anchor below.

Jessica swam around the cinder blocks, looking for any kind of clue, but saw none. She contemplated wrapping the blocks in the plastic bag but realized she was more than likely to disturb their positioning. While it didn't look significant to her, she had been wrong about that kind of detail before.

Her lungs were angrily protesting now. She was on the verge of passing out. Even though only two minutes had gone by, for someone out of practice, this was the edge of suicide.

As she ascended and saw her handiwork from afar, she felt ashamed. It looked like an incompetent Mafia hit man had tried to wrap the body so it could be shoved into the back of a Cadillac. She was mortified at the thought that Sloan was watching this from Jules's camera.

Despite Jessica's clumsy work, Nia's face was still visible through the plastic. From Jessica's vantage point, the girl looked like a drowned doll. It was such a cold, dark, and lonely grave.

Something had gnawed at the back of her mind since she first viewed the photo of Nia. This wasn't a theatrical murder or a ritualistic killing. This was no public fetish display. No . . . this was, for lack of a better word, *private*.

If it hadn't been for the photograph sent to the FBI, this murder would have served as a remote and permanent burial.

As the edge of her vision began to darken and she kicked for the surface, Jessica had another thought: What if the person who sent the photograph of Nia's body wasn't the same person who had murdered her?

HIDDEN AGENDA

When Jessica reached the surface, the ranger was no longer threatening to ram their boat, but he still scowled from his craft while pointing at Sloan and lecturing her. To her credit, Sloan wasn't being argumentative. She was nodding and keeping the situation from escalating. At the sound of Jessica surfacing, she set down the iPad and helped her out of the water.

"Next time, you're going in the water," Jessica said between gasps.

Sloan pointed at the iPad screen. "You did a pretty good job, all things considered."

"Did you show him?" Jessica asked.

"Yes," Sloan said more quietly. "That's the only reason I'm not in handcuffs right now. Although that's still a possibility."

Behind her, the ranger was talking into his phone.

"Do you think Mr. Briar tipped him off?" Jessica asked.

"Maybe, but not if he didn't want his boat impounded, although I have no idea how things work out here." Sloan shrugged.

"So what's going on now?" Jessica asked, drying herself off with a towel Sloan had handed her from her bag.

"Pretty much the same thing that would have happened had we just called it in. He's speaking to his boss, who is then going to probably talk to the Nevada State Police, who will then speak to the FBI or the Department of the Interior or however they work things out here."

"What did you tell him?" Jessica asked.

"The truth, or at least fifty percent of it—that I had been asked to assist with an FBI investigation and was trying to preserve the crime scene. Of course, if Callis wants to make a stink about it, we could find ourselves in trouble, although he strikes me as an asshole, not stupid."

"They'll want to make the chain of custody look as clean as possible," Jessica told her. In other words, for any of this evidence to be admissible in court, they had to prove within a reasonable doubt that the crime scene had not been tampered with. While the act Jessica had just committed could be arguably considered tampering, Callis would understand it was in his best interest to not protest and would likely gloss over who specifically performed the recovery.

The ranger lowered his phone, then yelled over to Sloan and Jessica. "My chief called it in to the FBI. I need you to follow me back into the marina." He then scowled at Jessica. "Assuming there's no more plans for recreational swimming."

"One second," said Sloan as she reached into her duffel bag and pulled out a deflated vinyl ball attached to a cord and a weight.

A little after 1:00 p.m., Jessica and Sloan were sitting at a picnic table under a windbreak near the Pyramid Lake Marina building, which housed both a gas station convenience store and the Paiute Tribe ranger station.

FBI Agents Monroe and Treynor were in a huddle with the chief of the local tribal police, Vera Pinellas from the state police, and a rep from Nevada's Department of Wildlife. The agents had flown on an FBI jet from Las Vegas and brought two more bureau colleagues who hadn't been at the briefing.

Jessica and Sloan had spent the intervening hours informing the local officials and a Reno FBI agent about what they knew and how they had taken it upon themselves to search for the body. The FBI office in Reno had been aware of the Dustin Fonseca case because it had been the first bureau office to respond.

After the initial interviews, Jessica and Sloan had taken turns catnapping, head down, at the shaded picnic table. In their work, both had developed a knack for falling asleep in any situation—which Sloan found both a useful and sad skill.

Now she was reviewing the footage from Jules on her iPad.

"See anything?" asked Jessica as she lifted her head and wiped the sleep out of her eyes.

"No, I'm just having trouble sitting still. This is the part that I don't have a whole lot of patience for," Sloan said.

"Yeah, desk work was never really my thing, although I miss it at times," Jessica said as she pulled at her hoodie. She was watching Sloan carefully as she scrutinized the footage.

Sloan caught her out of the corner of her eye. "Say it," she said.

"I'm sorry, just a bad habit I picked up from somebody," Jessica admitted.

"This wouldn't happen to be a world-famous computational biologist with a reputation for coldly rational analysis, would it?"

"He likes to let people come to their own conclusions. At first, I thought it was the most annoying thing in the goddamn world. Then I realized that while that was true, it also served a purpose."

"That purpose of being extra annoying," quipped Sloan.

"Yes, but sometimes the way another person comes to the same conclusion can reveal something," Jessica explained. "Theo would use the metaphor of the blind men trying to identify an elephant with each one touching one part of it. Well, their experiences were different. When you looked at all the information they were gathering collectively, you had a much better idea of what an elephant was, or something to that effect. The point is, I was waiting to see if you saw something I noticed . . . and then there's something else that only came to me as I was about to black out underwater."

"Killers with fancy motives aren't my expertise, to be honest with you. I'm curious to hear what your blackout eureka was."

"Well, this is just my gut instinct and kind of backs up something I'd said before. And it kind of leads to my . . . maybe a eureka moment, or perhaps a touch of brain damage. But if you look at where she was found and the circumstances of it, this wasn't a public killing, and neither was Fonseca, to an extent. This killer didn't want a lot of attention, like, I don't know, somebody who drops a body in the middle of a crowded city. These are out-of-the-way locations." Jessica pointed at distant Anaho Island. "Had we not got that email, she could have remained there forever. It's as protected a location as you can get."

"She was in only twenty feet of water. A mile to the south, it's three hundred feet deep," Sloan pointed out. "Why not drop her there? Feels to me like they wanted us to find the body."

"I thought about that, and I don't have a good answer," Jessica admitted.

"But something tells me you have a bad one. Let's hear it."

"The photograph is curious for a couple of reasons. First, why it was taken. Sometimes killers like to visit a scene again, but usually those crime scenes aren't underwater in the middle of a wildlife refuge."

"I get your point. It's inconvenient, but not impossible."

Jessica pulled her foot to the bench, rested her chin on her knee, and stared out at the water. "And then there's the other thing—my passing-out epiphany."

"I'm listening."

"Fonseca was found by a refuge officer who happened upon his body. It's a very bizarre murder scene and MO, and at first, we think it's a calling card or some attention-getting killing. Then, two days later, we get a clue from the killer, which is the location of Fonseca's body and a photograph of Nia Stratos, who nobody had realized was missing until then."

"But we're making a big assumption somewhere, aren't we," Sloan said.

"Maybe, and it doesn't make a lot of sense; it's just a guess. We assumed the email came from the killer, but without the email, if we never got it, the whole private-murder thing makes a little more sense. Forget the email existed. What does that tell you?"

Sloan thought this over. "Well, to your point, these are both out-of-the-way places. They aren't public. Visually speaking, the scenes—the murder scenes—are kind of attention-getting, but Fonseca was more notable because he was covered in salt like some rock thing from *Star Trek*. Whereas Nia, without the photograph, we never find her. Was she not supposed to be found? Then why send the email?" Sloan wondered aloud.

Jessica simply raised her eyebrows and said nothing.

"Oh," Sloan realized. "What if the killer didn't send the email? But then who the hell did? Why don't they just tell us what's going on?"

"I've got a couple scenarios, neither good," Jessica said. "First, having an accomplice would have made these elaborate killings a lot easier. Two people, maybe a difference of opinion. Somebody with a motive to kill them, somebody assisting them who has their own ideas. A whack job could get lucky enough to find a partner in crime. The likelihood they're going to have the same exact ambitions in life? Not so much."

"I don't know how long that partnership's going to last if one of them snitches to the FBI," Sloan noted.

"Like I said, dumb idea, but there could be another explanation. What if someone else happens to know what the killer's up to? Maybe a family member, somebody close to him who's aware and trying to let us know."

"Or he's got Tyler Durden disease and doesn't realize he's ratting himself out," Sloan added.

"I guess that's just as likely as anything else. The other problem with that theory is we really don't have a lot to go on."

"Yeah, I was kind of hoping for a Ziploc bag with a note inside with a bunch of pasted-up letters spelling out our next clue," Sloan joked.

"I'd like to believe that Nia is the last victim and the killer got it out of his system," Jessica mused, then shook her head.

Sloan checked her watch. "Is this guy killing on a regular basis? Is our next victim dead already?"

"I don't know. I don't think he's acting by any specific timeline other than what works for him."

"Yeah, for all we know, though, if there is another victim, they could be dead and there's another email sitting inside the FBI inbox. Not that Callis would let us know about it." Sloan glanced upward as a shadow passed over, and a pelican swooped across the water, dived in, then emerged a moment later, took to the air, and flew toward Anaho Island.

"A pelican colony in the desert," Sloan noted. "Birds must have been nesting on that island since before there were people on the continent."

"I admire the fact that your brain can be in two places at once," Jessica said.

"I'll pretend that was a compliment."

"It was. Did the death of Fonseca or Stratos strike you as angry?" Jessica asked.

"Like in a passionate way? Not as far as I'm aware. Certainly, Fonseca was killed in an excruciating way, and the wounds on Nia imply it was not a quick or painless death, at least at the start." She thought for a moment. "But no mutilation or abuse that I could see.

It felt more . . . I don't know . . . 'Torture' seems the wrong way to describe it."

"'Technical' is the word I'm thinking of," Jessica said.

"Uh-oh," Sloan said. "FBI's headed our way."

Jessica turned as Agents Monroe and Treynor separated themselves from Vera Pinellas and the tribal chief and came over to their picnic table.

"You two have a moment?" asked Agent Treynor.

"McPherson was just giving me the twelve-thousand-year history of the area," Jessica said.

"Keep this under your hat, but there's been a third potential victim," said Treynor.

"Goddamn it," Sloan cursed.

"The good news is, he got away, so we have a live one," Monroe finished.

"Well, that's a lucky break. Do we have a name?" Jessica asked.

"Michael Radley," replied Monroe, "but you didn't hear it from us. Callis wants this locked down."

"So why are you telling us?" Sloan asked.

"We know who our friends are," Monroe said, pointing a thumb toward where they'd found Nia Stratos's body. "We try to return the favor."

"That's appreciated," Sloan said.

Jessica typed quickly on her phone. "He's a live streamer, focuses on fantasy games, lives in Boulder, Colorado." She showed Sloan her phone and a video of Radley playing a game.

"How do we know it's the same case?" Sloan asked.

"We don't know yet," replied Monroe. "This came from headquarters. Apparently, Radley had some details that connected to this. It seems like we've got a pattern here. Callis is convinced there might be others."

Treynor looked up from his phone. "Apparently, there was some kind of pipe bomb planted behind his monitor. He had ducked down out of the way momentarily and came within a millisecond of losing his life."

"A pipe bomb? That doesn't sound anything like these other murders," Sloan said.

Treynor shrugged. "I'm just telling you what I got. And like I said, you didn't hear it from me."

"Were there nails in the pipe bomb?" Jessica asked.

"Nails? Let me see. There's a photo attachment." He zoomed in to an image. "Huh. Yeah, looks like it." He turned the photo around for Jessica to see.

A long, sharp, pointy nail that looked like a thin chisel was stuck into a metal YouTube million-subscriber button.

"Is that steel?" Sloan asked.

"No, gold or plated gold. You get it for having a million subscribers," said Treynor.

"She meant the nail," Monroe replied. "It looks old."

"It's iron," Jessica stated.

Everyone turned to her.

"At least it looks that way. Thanks for keeping us in the loop. We appreciate it," Jessica said. "McPherson, I don't know about you, but I could use a few hours of sleep before we head back to Las Vegas."

The two women made their goodbyes and walked back toward Jessica's rented SUV.

"Let it out," said Sloan.

"I probably should have told them, but I want to think about it a little bit more because it's gonna sound really goddamn crazy."

"We're both punch-drunk from lack of sleep, sun, and exertion, so might as well let me have it."

Jessica held out her hand. "Salt. Silver. Iron," she said, counting each one off on her fingers. "What do these things have in common?"

"I don't know," Sloan replied.

"Magic. Not my kind of stage magic, but old-school supernatural magic. These are things you use to bind the supernatural—specifically, how to bind or kill a witch: salt, silver chains, iron nails."

"Wait, what? Like a witch, like the Warlock?" Sloan asked.

Jessica shook her head. "No, no. Like how you traditionally kill a witch. As in, somebody thought Dustin Fonseca, Nia Stratos, and apparently this Radley kid were witches. Or at least wanted to bind them, or trap them, or kill them in the same way you kill a witch."

"Are you saying that they might have been in some kind of coven?" Sloan asked.

"Not at all. I've had people think I was a witch, simply because, whatever. The victims could have no idea what's going on, but whoever's killing them might have a different idea."

"So somebody just pointed at their computer screen and screamed *witch*," Sloan said.

"Crazier things have happened, but I think we understand a little bit more about who we're dealing with."

"So how many more victims are there going to be?" Sloan asked.

"How many influencers are there?"

"Like, in the world? There's one born every minute."

"Exactly. And now we know this guy won't be stopping 'til he's stopped."

INTRUDER

When Sloan and Jessica reached their rented SUV, Jessica glanced through the back passenger-side window and paused.

Neither had returned to the vehicle since they got back. The tribal police officer had escorted them straight to the station, where they'd awaited the FBI agents and the others.

"Have you been to the car since we left?" Jessica asked.

Sloan shook her head. "I've been with you the whole time, except when I used the bathroom. Why?"

Jessica was staring through the window. "I tend to keep my handle for my laptop case pointed toward the front seat so it makes it easier if I have to reach back and grab it. It's facing the other direction."

Sloan was about to grab the handle to the rear hatch so she could drop in her duffel bag but stopped, set her bag down, and walked over to Jessica.

"I don't think I moved it, but it's possible," she said.

"I'm probably just sleep-deprived," Jessica admitted.

"Maybe, but let's not be careless." Sloan knelt, unzipped her duffel bag, and pulled out a small pouch. "I can grab some fingerprints."

"We might be acting a little too paranoid," Jessica said.

"I'd rather be paranoid than regretful," Sloan replied as she sprayed the door handle with a small bottle, then placed a piece of clear plastic tape over it. She pulled the tape away and fixed it to a card. There were dozens of overlapping smudged fingerprints.

"Theo's got some software for this if we want to take it to the next step," said Jessica.

"It couldn't hurt. Let me get a few more off your bag and around the interior. It might have been some local, curious, wanted to see what was in our car. Bored kid. An opportunistic person driving by." Sloan turned around to look at the gas station and ranger's office. "I don't see any cameras aimed this way. If we're curious, I guess we could probably call later on and ask."

"I'm sure the FBI will grab copies of everything. Worst-case scenario, we can just reach out to them."

As she waited for Sloan to finish gathering the fingerprints, Jessica turned back toward the lake and stared off into the distance. The small flotilla of boats, consisting of the rangers' craft, Department of Wildlife, and an FBI evidence-recovery boat, were barely visible at the opposite end, but her attention was on the hills behind the shore. They were largely barren, consisting of light-brown sediment and rock.

"You look like you're walking between two worlds," Sloan said as she put away the fingerprint kit.

"I'm pretty sure one of those worlds is Sleepland."

"What about the others? What are you thinking?"

In her experience with Jessica, Sloan had begun to learn the true meaning behind the expression "still waters run deep." Sloan had grown up in an environment where you said what you thought, sometimes before you even thought, whereas Jessica Blackwood was deeply contemplative and pondered silently for considerable lengths of time. Sloan wasn't sure if this was due to some kind of concern on Jessica's behalf or the way a truly smart person was supposed to behave.

While there was always plenty of reading material around the McPherson households and boats, it tended toward popular fiction and anything ocean-themed. She'd had a friend in middle school who Sloan's mother had described as bookish. Their house was filled, floor to ceiling, with bookcases holding a vast library. She loved walking through the rooms and pulling out random paperbacks to see their covers. The musty smell and scent of cat pee hardly bothered her. Tressa, her friend, was quiet like Jessica, although once you said the right word, it triggered her and revealed a vast and complex inner world. The girl could sit quietly while thinking about characters in an Anne McCaffrey novel, or how somebody would hem a dress in the eighth century. This while Sloan tried to figure out how many Goldfish crackers she could shove into her mouth, or if she could live on Hi-C fruit punch alone.

"How sleep-deprived are you?" Jessica asked.

"If there's something else you want to do, I can shotgun a couple Red Bulls and be good for days. At least I'd like to think so. I'm fine. What is it?"

Jessica was still looking across the lake. "It's nothing, but while we're on the subject of indulging in paranoia, I just want to check something else out."

"If you want to dive back down there, I can get some air tanks."

"No, it's not that. This is going to be very dumb, but while we were on the water, remember I saw a flash of light from the hills? I want to take a look. Although I know it's probably just a piece of broken glass."

Sloan nodded to the car interior. "Given this, I don't think it'd be out of line for us to go take a look. Let's see if anything's missing or has been messed with first, then drive around the lake and have a look. I'll call the tribal cop, make sure we're okay. I don't want to get yelled at again."

❦

While the opposite side of the lake was three miles distant as the pelican flies, it took them twenty minutes to get there in their car. Jessica stopped the vehicle on the side of the road near a bluff that was almost directly across from Anaho Island. The recovery boats were clustered near where Sloan and she had been a few hours earlier. Nia Stratos's body had been pulled from the water and was on its way to the Reno medical examiner's office. The FBI forensic team was using an underwater camera less sophisticated than the one Sloan had used, to probe the area around where Nia had been anchored in hopes of finding discarded pieces of evidence.

"I'm not sure what they're looking for at this point," Sloan said.

"I know," Jessica replied. "I'm sure Callis is convinced his self-declared adversary has left him something."

Sloan opened her door and set a foot on the ground, scanning the ground around them. "Maybe he did."

"Well, I didn't spot a golden arrow pointing to the ground telling us to look here. I probably saw a beer can or foil from a cigarette pack."

She exited the car and stood next to Sloan at the edge of the road, overlooking the rocky incline. There was a large mound of metamorphic rock between the road and the shore. It was almost directly parallel with the eastern peninsula of Anaho Island and Nia's final resting place.

"Don't worry, I won't keep us out here too long," Jessica told Sloan.

"Stop apologizing," Sloan replied as she started walking and half skipping down the hill.

When they reached the base of the mound, Jessica said, as she surveyed the area, "I'm going to walk around. You want to go over the top? It's a lot of ground to cover, and I don't really know what we're looking for."

"You got it!" Sloan replied and started bounding up the hill like a mountain goat with inexhaustible energy.

Jessica shook her head in amusement and shouted after her, "Nobody should have that amount of pep. I'm ready to pass out and use the nearest rock as a pillow."

Sloan turned around and shouted back, "Trust me, sister, if I stop now, I won't even use a rock pillow. I'll be flat out on the ground, and the scorpions can come and eat me. And I won't care."

She turned around and continued to ascend. Inwardly, she knew she was performing for Jessica, trying to show how determined and strong she was. The reality was she was on her last legs and wanted nothing more than to sleep for a week. If she was good at anything, Sloan surmised, it was hiding what she felt physically. That might've been why she wasn't as good at concealing her emotions. So much focused on making her seem invulnerable . . . Part of that had to do with growing up with older brothers and never wanting to be left behind, as well as being born into a family that didn't know how to sit still.

Sloan kept her attention on the ground as she climbed the hill, both to make sure she didn't step on a rock or rattlesnake but also keeping her eyes open for any kind of clue. Chances were Jessica was right and it was just a piece of glass or some reflective material, but you never knew. It wasn't impossible that whoever put Nia's body into the lake had also come back to see what progress the investigators had made. There was also the matter of who sent the email. Sloan thought Jessica's intuition was spot-on. If true, then another player was involved. Given those possibilities, it didn't seem entirely impossible that somebody could have been up here watching as they searched for the body.

Sloan reached the top of the mound and perched herself on a boulder. Jessica was working her way around the north end of the hill, her attention on the nooks and crannies between the stones that formed the outcropping. The wind blew across the lake and made a whooshing sound as it picked up speed and swept up the hillside.

Sitting there, she considered the nature of crime scenes. Though often photographed, a crime scene wasn't a fixed picture. It wasn't a diagram. It didn't even occupy a fixed point in time. It was part of a continuum.

Only twenty-four hours ago, if Sloan had been sitting exactly where she was at that moment, she would have seen everything. If she'd had a pair of binoculars, she might even know the identity of the killer.

"It's not just a matter of knowing where to look, it's when to look," Sloan said under her breath.

Jessica had reached the point directly in front of the mound and across from the peninsula of Anaho. She had her hands on her hips and was staring at the formation with intense scrutiny. Likely unaware that Sloan was watching her, Jessica crossed her arms, closed her eyes, and appeared to be concentrating.

The last time Sloan had worked with Jessica, Theo had joined them. The pair were a bit intense, even by Sloan's standards. They used a subtle system of sign language that Jessica had learned from her family to perform mind-reading tricks and transmit information. You could be having a conversation with one of them while they were secretly passing messages back and forth.

Initially, Sloan had found this a little bit rude, but then she realized the communication had become almost unconscious to them. Like a couple sharing an expression or an inside joke. Beyond the passing of info, though, it was clear that sign language had become something of a comfort for the pair.

While they were both fiercely intelligent and quite capable of making compelling vocal arguments and expressing themselves, Sloan had the sense that this nonvocal form of communication was a more natural way for them to share what they were thinking.

Along with their secret sign language, Sloan had observed that Theo and Jessica had embraced all kinds of mind games, tricks, or mnemonics—that was the word—to make fuller use of their mental capabilities.

It was interesting as an observer allowed into their inner circle. Theo came from an extremely scientific and analytical world, where these kinds of mental tools were academic and, in some cases, purely theoretical, whereas Jessica, coming from a family of entertainers who used similar systems to survive, had a similarly pragmatic approach. On the surface, the two were from wildly different worlds, but deep down, they had everything in common.

Sloan and her husband, Run, complemented each other in different ways. Both were driven and outgoing. Both liked to sit back, watch a football game, and drink a beer.

Run was smart and could think about something for a long time, but Sloan would never describe either of them as "complicated." Who they were was pretty much right on the surface.

Jessica's eyes opened, and her head jerked up suddenly as she looked at a point midway up the rock formation to her right. This startled Sloan, because it looked like Jessica had snapped out of a trance.

Her friend began climbing the hill with forceful determination. Sloan almost began walking down to her but decided to wait. Jessica was moving with purpose.

She reached the section she had been staring at, then stopped, her eyes focused on the ground. Her head swiveled around, almost in a precise manner, as she visually gridded off the zone and searched each section. After a minute, she looked up at Sloan and waved. Sloan walked down the rocks to meet her.

"You had an intense look about you," Sloan said.

Jessica's face relaxed, and she smiled. "Yeah, sorry, I was trying to remember everything about what I saw. Given our mind's habit of making things up and filling in details that aren't there, it can be a bit challenging."

"So, what's the trick?" Sloan asked.

"I'm still trying to figure that out myself. The problem is, you can practice all kinds of methods of recall and use memory palaces, but you have to be using them at the moment, for the most part."

"For the most part," Sloan repeated.

"Well, one method is to not try to specifically remember the thing you're trying to recall. I know that sounds counterintuitive, but what I mean by that is, I was on the boat and I saw a flash of light out of the corner of my eyes. So instead of trying to imagine where it came from—emphasis on *imagine*, because that's what happens—I tried to recall everything else. What was the temperature? Was I cold? Was I warm? Was the wind blowing? Where was the sun? These other little things, these adjacent memories, can help you bring back the one you're looking for. Maybe I heard a jet or a pelican, and that could trigger something else."

"And?" Sloan prompted.

Jessica said, "I think I may have just seen a piece of broken glass or the sun hitting a particularly shiny rock."

"Or somebody could have been up here with binoculars or a riflescope watching us, then left."

"We don't have to invent convenient theories to make me feel like less of an idiot," Jessica said.

Sloan searched the ground around her feet. "Hold up a minute. Let's think this through. Let's assume you did see something. Maybe it wasn't a person. What could it have been?"

"I think I just covered that: a piece of broken glass, a shiny rock."

"I understand that, but let's say our killer is responsible for it. What would it be then? It's too bright and pointless for a camera flash. So what you could have seen was the sun reflecting off a piece of glass or metal."

"But only for a moment," Jessica added.

"We found her body at, what, 7:23 a.m., which would put the sun about right there," Sloan said, pointing to a specific part of the sky. "Well, at least right there from where I'm looking. You'd have to look over my shoulder to see."

Jessica walked up to Sloan and put her head next to Sloan's to see the part of the sky she was pointing at. The woman's nautical navigation skills were clearly on display.

"That feels about right. It was a bit overcast too," Jessica said.

"Yes, but there were some cloud breaks. Either way, though, if we were looking for something under a rock, it wouldn't have been the reflection from the sun, because it would have been in shadow."

They both looked around the boulders in their immediate vicinity.

"I don't see anything sitting out in the open," Jessica said.

"There's also between rocks," Sloan replied as she started jogging laterally across the hill. "We just have to look for a good place to put something, not search every possible place you *could* put something."

"Would that be from up here or from looking from down there?" Jessica said, pointing toward the base of the hill facing the shoreline.

"I think from up here, when they were scouting the location. If they had landed the boat during the day, that would have attracted too much attention. I think our killer probably came to where we are right now to survey the location."

"But he placed Nia's body at one of the shallower parts of the lake, so he had to know the depth."

"Which he could have got from the same tables that we looked at. I mean, I'm making a bunch of assumptions here, but I'm going to go by what I think is logical. I think—hold on." Sloan stopped and stared at a large boulder. It was almost cube-shaped and had been cleaved into two pieces with a gap of at least four inches between the sections. She stepped down the incline and brought herself directly in front of it and leaned in.

"Watch out for rattlesnakes," Jessica cautioned.

"I'm hopefully out of biting distance right now," Sloan said as she pulled a small flashlight out from a fanny pack and aimed it between the rocks. "Snakes, if you're in there, come out with your hands up!"

"I would think you'd have a better idea of snake anatomy, growing up in Florida," Jessica said.

"I have a plenty good idea. I've seen a few with legs too. They go by names like Marty and Chris."

Jessica moved to where Sloan was standing. "Let me stand here. You go on top of the rock and do your best to impersonate the sun."

Sloan leaped on top of the boulder and held the flashlight above her head, doing her best approximation of where it would have been, and aimed down into the crevasse.

A sliver of light danced across Jessica's body for a moment as the light moved slightly in Sloan's hand.

Jessica took her phone from her pocket and snapped several photos.

"What do we got?" asked Sloan.

Jessica walked over to Sloan and showed her the image on her phone screen. Nestled inside the crevice was a black box with a round protective lens over what looked like a camera.

"Given the location and direction," Sloan said, indicating how the crevice was aimed directly at where the recovery operation was taking place, "it would seem statistically unlikely this is some Department of Wildlife camera."

"Damn it," Jessica grumbled. "We could have brought a signal sniffer out here to find out how it's transmitting. It's probably cellular, but picking up some of the packets might have been useful."

"I guess we need to call our friends across the lake and let them know it's here. I'd love to take it apart and have a look, but fair is fair," Sloan said.

"Yeah, we should tell them. I don't even want to go near it. Goddamn it. Whoever put it there could be watching us right now," Jessica said.

"Damn." Sloan glanced down where the camera was hidden. "Well, in that case . . ." She leaped off the rock and landed in front of the crevice, sticking up a middle finger. "You can go fuck yourself. We're coming for you."

BELIEVERS

Jessica and Sloan watched, along with Monroe and Treynor, as a technician from the Reno FBI office pulled the device from the crevice between the rocks. While they were certain it was a camera, one couldn't be sure what was inside. Deranged and vengeful criminals had, on occasion, left booby traps for investigators.

The bomb tech, a bald man in his late fifties, wore a plastic face shield and heavy body armor. His movements were slow and precise, and he spent the first half hour using a fluoroscope and mirror to investigate the area around the device. He then used explosives-detecting chemicals to test the surface.

Checking the chemical kit he brought with him, he nodded and said, "I think we're clear." Just to be on the safe side, he used a mechanical grasper at the end of a four-foot pole to reach into the crevice and grab the device.

Jessica and the rest were watching from fifty feet away, at the base of the outcropping.

"I had to help clear out a homeless camp last year where they'd set up boards with nails driven through them, buckets of broken glass, and a bunch of other booby traps. Imagine if the kid from *Home Alone* became a meth addict with a real hatred for the police," Sloan told Jessica.

The bomb tech stepped back, turned around, and lifted his shield. "It looks like a cell phone with an extra battery pack and a long-distance lens attached. Do you want me to take it apart here or bring it back to the lab?"

"Bag it up. We'll try to get prints and see if cyber can find something else out about it," Monroe instructed.

"I'm fairly sure we're not going to get anything," Treynor said.

"You never know, even bomb makers make mistakes. I heard about a case where they got a partial print off the threads of a screw. Everything else had been wiped down, but they forgot that," Monroe told him.

"So what's the point of the camera? To watch us?" Treynor asked.

Jessica and Sloan had been thinking that question over since they found it. While they'd come to different possibilities, they were hoping Monroe or Treynor would have an explanation that made more sense.

"Either way, we should probably check the immediate area at Sheldon Refuge for a camera," Jessica suggested.

"There aren't a lot of places out there unless you wanted to stick something in the ground, but I think you're right," Monroe said.

Treynor stared at the rock where the camera had been hidden and looked back toward the water, where there was only one boat left near where Nia Stratos's body was found. "Is it like getting your jollies or something? Is that what he does? Just watches, cackles, and rubs himself down with cocoa butter?"

"Cocoa butter . . . that's a pretty specific kink," Sloan remarked.

Treynor shrugged. "Well, who knows what goes on in the minds of those weirdos—not like us normal people."

"Although you do have a point," Sloan conceded.

"I do?"

"Did you guys watch *Squid Game*?" Sloan asked.

Jessica shook her head, but Monroe replied, "My husband and I did. Why do you ask?"

"Do you think this is, like, some rich sicko billionaire pay-TV thing?" Treynor asked.

"No. No, not at all," Sloan replied. "I mean, that's kind of what bothered me about it. I grew up around rich people. I mean, my family certainly wasn't, but being around them, you observe them. And one of the things you know is they just can't shut up about whatever interesting things they do. I could buy a lot of the things in *Squid Game*, but the idea that rich people would watch something messed up like that and *not* be blasting it all across social media, telling everybody else about it? I found that the hardest part to believe."

"But you're saying the camera was here for a purpose not completely unrelated," Jessica clarified.

"Monroe, you used to work out of the Albuquerque office on the cartels, right?" Sloan asked.

"For nine years. Why do you ask?"

"Instead of Nia being an influencer, imagine she worked for a Sinaloa bank or some other occupation and we found her like this? What would you say?"

"I'd say it was the cartel. It was a revenge killing and a message," Monroe stated.

"And the messages aren't always for the public or the police, are they?" Sloan asked.

"They're to family members, friends, any enemies of the cartel. That's the whole purpose—it's to scare them, to warn them."

Sloan turned to Jessica. "You picked up on the fact right away—this wasn't a message to the police or even necessarily to the world. You picked up on the fact that these killings seemed *private*. But what if it's not just between the killer and victim but maybe within a small group, and the people who this message is meant for know what it means?"

"Okay, interesting theory, Florida woman, but the Radley kid says he has no idea why he was targeted other than the fact that he's famous. You'd think he'd want to tell us," Treynor pointed out.

"I didn't go to the FBI Academy, but police academy taught us about something called—what's the word—oh yeah, a *lie*," Sloan shot back.

Treynor held up his hands. "Easy, I'm sorry. I'm just speaking out loud," he said apologetically.

"No, we're good. I'm just sleep-deprived. Don't you guys talk shit a bunch out here in Nevada? Anyhow, my point is, were this a cartel killing, would potential victims be running to tell the police?"

"Not in my experience, but this isn't Mexico," Jessica stated.

"I understand that, but you don't go to the police for one or two reasons. You might think they're in on it, or you're afraid they're not going to be able to do anything to protect you." Sloan pointed at Nia's body site. "Whoever did this went to extreme measures. I don't know if, quote, 'police protection' would be enough for a witness or insider to blow the whistle. At least, I wouldn't think that it was. Would you?" she asked.

"Not if you were really, truly scared, like almost supernaturally so," Jessica said.

"The silver chains and the salt," Monroe pointed out. "These people believe magic is real."

"We all believe magic is real. It's why we say things like 'God bless you' or 'we'll keep you in our thoughts and prayers' or 'pray for Ukraine.' The skeptical part of us is always doubting, but the other part of us wonders."

"Sure, but witchcraft?" Treynor questioned.

"Do you know how many copies of the book *The Secret* were sold? Have you seen how obsessed with astrology influencers are? When Oprah Winfrey is pushing magical thinking as a product, what makes you think that the average person is any more rational?" Jessica asked.

"I think faith is important. It's helped me a lot," Monroe said.

"I'm not attacking anybody's faith here. I'm just trying to say that we have to understand that it comes in different forms and intensities. We might be dealing with people for whom it's *very* real and *very* intense."

"Okay, but I still don't understand the purpose of the camera," Monroe said.

"Maybe that's how they warned the others. That might be how the FBI got the email. Somebody was scared, forwarded it, but then shut up," Sloan suggested.

"So are we talking about a cult?" Treynor asked.

"I try not to use that word," Jessica said.

"Why? Is it politically incorrect?" Treynor replied.

"It's both too narrow and too imprecise. It makes you think of people meeting under the moonlight in black robes or someone trying to sell you a personality test on Hollywood Boulevard. What we have to think about is groups with their own personal belief systems, their own code of ethics, and a bond that's so strong that they're willing to break societal norms."

"I think 'cult' works fine," Treynor said.

"The problem is that we should apply it in some places and not in others. If you ask me if I think the MS-13 gang is a cult, I would tell you yes. They have their own rituals, they have their own beliefs, they have special tattoos, they have magical thinking. And they certainly have tighter bonds than what they feel towards society, but we just use the word 'gang.' We're at this point now in society where we call anybody who believes differently than us, any other group, a cult. So I just don't think the word is useful anymore," she explained.

"Okay, but we can all agree that these people believe some very weird shit. They know each other, and some of them are scared?" Sloan asked the group.

"They might not know one another," said Jessica. "We've seen an increasing number of anonymous groups, particularly with the rise of people spending a majority of their social lives online. If you show up someplace and everybody wears a mask, there's a good chance that you're going to recognize their car in the parking lot. But if you're going into a forum and just texting, then you could be talking to a roommate or Russian intelligence operative and never know it."

"So we've got a weird group. Can I call them a coven because of the witchcraft?" Treynor asked.

"Historically, a coven is associated with a group of thirteen members, but it's not exactly a hard rule. And I would be hesitant to try to apply too many labels right now, given we still don't know what's going on. But, as Sloan said, we understand that they may have a high degree of magical thinking, and they are afraid of the group or a group leader."

"And Nia Stratos, Dustin Fonseca, and Radley did something to piss them off," Sloan concluded.

"Or the group leaders *assumed* they did something," said Monroe. "On more than one occasion, cartel revenge killers got the wrong person. But it didn't matter. It still served the purpose of putting the fear into others."

Sloan was reconsidering what she'd said. "Here's the thing, though. These aren't victims who got caught up in cartel business. These are famous, successful people. Whoever did this had to know it was going to attract attention. Whether they want it or not, the bodies would be found. The world would discover that they'd gone missing. So while I agree one hundred percent with Jessica that these killings weren't meant as a message to the rest of the world, the people who committed them had to know we would eventually find out and get curious. And that curiosity would not end until we found out who did it."

Monroe nodded. "There was a case we were helping the DEA with that was wrapping up around the time I started in the Albuquerque office. A small cartel group made up of some former police officers that started getting picked off one by one. There were only about fifteen or sixteen of these guys. Mexican authorities found one of them hanging from a freeway, another one shot in a supermarket, a third one murdered in his house along with his two brothers.

"We assumed it was another gang, the Tarantulas, who were picking them off because the smaller gang, F3, had been trafficking through their corridor, but we were wrong.

"About a week later, F3 went on a killing spree, murdering the higher-ups of the Tarantulas. It turned out they had been planning this for months, and they suspected that several of their own members were going to defect and tell the Tarantulas, so they killed F3 members themselves to protect their plan.

"We ended up with a bloodbath of people shot down in shopping plazas, at boxing matches, and other public places. F3 wanted to make a statement that they were in charge. They even killed two people in the US," Monroe recounted.

"That sounds almost suicidal," Sloan said.

"It was. They got wiped out, but the Tarantulas had been working with insiders in the military to take out F3. F3 found out about it, and so they went for broke and attacked. Not much choice at that point."

"Okay . . . does that mean that Dustin Fonseca and Nia Stratos knew about some big operation?" Sloan asked.

Jessica stepped in: "Not at all. They, and potentially this Radley person, might be weak links—people that know a little bit of information that can connect back to the organization. Killing them ensures they don't speak and serves as a message to other potential leakers."

"Okay, assume you're in our shoes—what do you do?" Monroe asked.

"You need to bring in your best psychologist and get Radley talking, because he knows more than he's going to tell you, but he's scared," Jessica suggested, then thought for a moment. "Whoever's doing these killings, this can't be their first time. Have you guys been looking through old cases, seen anything related?"

"We've got a team back in Las Vegas doing exactly that. Is there anything else we should be looking into?" Monroe asked.

"I can't think of anything, but if you can send us anything you have, we'd like to take a look too. Assuming Callis doesn't have a problem with that," Sloan said.

"Oh, trust us, he'll have a problem. He wants to be the one who catches the Puzzle Master," said Treynor.

"The Puzzle Master?" Sloan echoed.

Monroe sighed. "You see the one boat still out there? That's our evidence-recovery team. Callis is convinced that there's some clue left behind for him to solve."

"Wait, what?" Sloan asked.

"Yeah, he still thinks that the email was sent from the killer. Which, to be fair, we don't know that it wasn't. But he's also hung up on the whole earth, wind, air, fire aspects of the case. He had us spend a half hour yesterday trying to brainstorm ways that you could kill somebody with wind. *Wind.* You can't kill somebody with wind!" Treynor said, exasperated.

"Sure you can. You can pop them inside of a hyperbaric chamber, ramp up the pressure, drop it quickly, and create an embolism," Sloan informed him.

"Well, do me a favor and don't tell Callis that," Treynor said with a laugh.

"So, what's next for you guys? Sleep, I assume," Monroe asked.

"The sooner you can send us those cases, the better. We want to keep looking into this. I'm not sure how well we'll be able to predict what they're going to do next without understanding what has gone before," Jessica told her.

"You mean who they kill next?" Monroe asked.

"Not to sound callous, but I'm not as concerned about who gets murdered next as much as what the bigger plan is. That's what scares me. We might not be looking at one or two bodies found in strange situations. We might be looking at a *lot* of them."

"You were the one who found the bodies of the members of the Red Chain cult, weren't you?" Monroe asked, referencing one of the largest murder-suicides in American history.

Jessica could still see their bodies suspended from the rafters where they'd hanged themselves and hear the cry of the child in the dark who was the only survivor.

"'Cult' is a big word that can mean a lot of things. Sometimes it's not obvious at first. When a popular pastor appeared in San Francisco in the late '60s preaching racial harmony and tolerance, it was hard for anyone to predict that would lead to nine hundred people dead in Guyana. Decades later, when I was pursuing the Red Chain, I had no idea what to expect. What I found certainly wasn't what I thought I'd find. So all I can say is, let's not assume or overlook anything . . . and prepare for the worst."

"You think it could get that bad?" asked Monroe.

"I don't know what to think."

"We'll get the cases over to you ASAP. Are you flying or driving back, by the way?"

"I think we can drop off the rental and catch a flight and save us some time, as well as get a catnap on the way. Why?"

"We tried talking to someone named Robert Ratke. He's well known in online influencer circles. Sets up ad deals and the like. He knew Nia and Dustin. We already have a pretty good idea of where he's been and don't think of him as a suspect, but he's a person of interest. We tried to interview him, but he refused to speak to us without his lawyer. We have an interview set up tomorrow when his lawyer is in town, but you might want to talk to him unofficially beforehand."

INFLUENCE OPERATION

It was late afternoon by the time Jessica and Sloan arrived at Robert Ratke's mansion in Henderson, a large suburb south of Las Vegas. Perched in the McCullough Hills, the home had an expansive view of the city spread across the basin formed between the mountain ranges.

"Maybe there's something to this internet thing after all," Sloan said as they stepped up to the tall entrance leading to a stone path surrounded by water.

Through the front door, a ten-foot pane of glass, directly opposite them they could see a man in his mid-forties, wearing black pants, a black sweater, and no shoes, walking toward them.

"That looks like him," Jessica said.

According to Robert Ratke's LinkedIn, he had worked in the film industry for several years before making the jump to online content in the early 2010s. Realizing that web-based celebrities were gaining popularity faster than traditional actors and musicians, he became a manager and then formed an agency to help connect influencers with brands.

It all seemed a bit suspect and shady to Sloan, but most things tended to give her that impression.

Jessica had called ahead and arranged for the meeting with a clear promise that it was just an informal conversation. Ratke had expressed shock at the deaths but seemed curious and willing to talk to them, with the understanding it was off the record.

"Hello, ladies," Ratke said with a smooth smile as he opened the door to greet them.

They stepped inside the foyer. Just beyond was a living room with two long couches facing each other across a massive coffee table. A glass wall overlooked an infinity pool with a view of Las Vegas stretching into the distance.

"My lawyer said I shouldn't talk to you," Ratke said, addressing Jessica. "But my curiosity was piqued. You're no longer in the FBI, are you?"

He motioned for them to step into the living room and sit down.

"No, I am not," Jessica replied as she took a seat.

"What about you? You said you're a cop in Florida, right?" he said, addressing Sloan.

"Yeah, but I'm only helping Jessica out," Sloan replied.

"Can I get you guys some water or anything? Coffee, tea, soda?" Ratke offered.

"We're good," Sloan replied.

"Okay," said Ratke. "So before I answer your questions, can you clarify for me what your relationship is to all of this? I know that Nia was just found today, Dustin was found yesterday, and now I've heard that this kid, Radley, who I've never met, had a bomb go off in his face. So apparently there's some kind of investigation. Are you two consulting on it?"

"What did you hear about Nia?" asked Sloan. Neither she nor Jessica had mentioned anything about her death to Ratke.

"I tried calling her yesterday after I heard the news about Dustin. We don't talk much, so I wasn't surprised I didn't hear back. And then about four hours ago, somebody texted me the news," he explained.

While they were still trying to recover Nia's body, someone had leaked to the media the fact that she had been found dead. Although there had been no official confirmation, the internet was buzzing with the rumor, and speculation had already begun that there was a serial killer preying on social media influencers.

"I hate to say it, but one of the reasons I like being behind the scenes is that you don't know who's watching you. You still haven't answered my question: How are you guys connected to this case?"

Sloan wasn't sure how to answer. Just about everything else she ever found herself in related to some line of investigation that she was pursuing professionally. However, lately, she'd found herself being pulled into Jessica's orbit with off-the-books cases.

"We were asked in initially," said Jessica, "or rather, I was, regarding Dustin Fonseca and the condition in which he was found. I provided my opinion, and when we became aware of Nia's situation, I asked Sloan McPherson to come assist, given her expertise in that area," she added vaguely, without confirming anything specifically.

"So you guys are officially working with the feds on this," Ratke asked.

"No," Sloan blurted out. "We basically got kicked off. The head of the investigation wanted to try something different. We stuck around out of curiosity and a bit of sympathy for the victims."

She glanced at Jessica to see if she had said too much or something she shouldn't have. Jessica didn't react.

"Okay. I can respect that. If you swear it's the truth, then I can speak a little more freely. Just don't tell my lawyer I said that." He paused. "I just don't want to find out this was some entrapment thing."

"Why are you so concerned about being implicated here? Is there something you need to tell us?" Jessica asked.

"No," Ratke said with a bit of a laugh. "I just don't trust cops. I've had a very bad experience. And, well, you know . . . even having your name connected to something like this can be damaging."

Jessica was trying to parse what he was saying. "Is there something that might come out that has an innocent explanation but might reflect upon you poorly?"

Ratke sat back on the couch and exhaled as he thought it over. "I'm just going to tell you everything that's going to come out, that's already kind of a matter of public record. Nia and I had a relationship early on. It wasn't anything serious, and, well, I don't want to sound like a jerk, but it wasn't really serious for me, if you understand what I'm saying. I was helping her build out her career, and then we went in different directions. There were some words said, we had some fights, that kind of thing, but nothing serious. Eventually, she moved off to LA, and we talked a little bit. That was it," he explained.

"What about your relationship with Dustin Fonseca?" Sloan asked.

"We didn't date, if that's what you're asking. I helped Dustin out. Similar thing: He had a pretty good audience, he was extremely energetic, and I saw a lot of potential there. I helped him out until he cut things off like Nia did."

"So they both stopped working with you. Was this at the same time?" Jessica asked.

"No. Months apart. I don't even know if they knew each other. Probably. It's a small world, but at some point, you start to grow and you think that you can do better than the person who put you there, and you go with new management. It's normal. It's silly, but it's what happens. Some people try to tie up talent into lifetime contracts and that kind of thing. I just don't find it worthwhile. If we work together, we work together. If we don't, we don't. No hard feelings."

"I'm kind of ignorant about all of this. Can you explain to me how this influencer thing works—what you do, what they did, who their audience is?" Sloan asked.

"I've got about a hundred hours of podcast that explains all that. Do you want the short form?"

"That would be nice," Sloan said.

"Okay, here's the thing you need to understand about most of these influencers today. They were theater kids. Remember the type back in high school, always willing to jump onstage, do show choir, whatever. Some of them had dreams, going to go off to LA, become famous, Broadway, whatever. A lot of them just sort of buried those and moved on, did something else. But the internet changed that, because that introverted yet onstage-extroverted kid could sit themselves down in front of a camera and pour their heart out and get an audience. And if they had any kind of talent, then they learned how to cultivate that audience. That's who Nia was, that's who Dustin was, that's who these kids are. They are theater kids who probably have something broken inside of them, to be honest, that they're trying to fill with a bunch of likes and attention." He shrugged.

"And how do you help them do all of this?" Jessica asked.

"So, in the case of Nia, she had been a bit of an aspiring actress but started getting into beauty and modeling tips," Ratke explained. "Now, I don't know if you've ever met her or watched her or know anything about her. She's five one, average build. She's a pretty girl, but nothing a casting agent in LA is putting out a call for, not to sound terrible. But that casting agent in LA doesn't understand the rest of America or kids around the world. Somebody like Nia, who can talk, who can take her average looks and make herself look pretty, is going to be way more interesting to them. And that's how she built up an audience. She was honest, just honestly *Nia*, and that builds trust. I step in because having an audience and having trust isn't enough. YouTube ads alone aren't going to pay the bills. I find brands and sponsors and connect them. It could be some new energy drink or a start-up makeup product. They're trying to build a base too. So what I do is, I find not just a Nia, maybe a dozen versions of her on social media, pair them up with the brand, have them start talking about it, and boom. Their audiences, who maybe are a few hundred thousand each, cumulatively is millions of girls who start talking about a product."

"So you exploit that trust for profit," Sloan said.

"I helped them pay their rent—hell, I helped them buy houses. A girl like Nia, without social media and somebody like me to help her capitalize on that, what happens? She goes to LA for a few years, gets told her dream sucks, that she's not pretty enough, she's not talented enough, whatever excuse they want to give her, and she gives up. Goes back home and spends the rest of her life watching people she wants to be but never being them. Dustin, here's a kid that wants to play video games all day, right? Now, how do you make that pay the bills? Somebody like me. I know this company out of Texas—some former air force veterans who are gamers—who have come out with their own line of joysticks. It's a great little product; it's expensive, it's super niche. How the hell do they sell it to anybody? Well, how about Dustin playing a game using the joystick for twelve hours straight on a live stream? That's worth thousands of dollars to them. They win, Dustin wins."

"Why specifically did things end between you and Dustin and Nia?" Jessica asked.

"They never gave me specific reasons. Like I told you, they said they were going in other directions and pursuing different management," he explained.

"What management did they move to?" Jessica asked.

"With Nia, it's a company called Off the Shelf. They're a spin-off of one of the LA talent agencies, basically taking the model that I tried to pitch them years ago and now doing it in-house. Dustin is with a group called Talent Forge. They focus more on gamers and put together the same kind of deal that I did. They make a lot of big promises to them. Sometimes they come through, sometimes they don't. It's fine. Here's the thing: A guy like Dustin Fonseca does a live stream with 150,000 kids watching him, and it helps me because now there's 150,000 kids with a pipe dream that they can be the next Dustin. Chances are one or two of them are more talented than Dustin, and that's who I look for, the next generation. There's always somebody ready to take your place, and they've been studying you. They know everything about you, and they sell products even better than the previous generation."

"That comes across as a bit cynical," Sloan remarked.

"Maybe, but these kids will knock down their own grandmother for a shot. The funny thing is, the first generation of influencers—your PewDiePies and your MrBeasts—you know, they had to figure it out from scratch. Now it's all out there; they'll even teach you how to do it. So you take a hungrier, sharper kid with a huge head start in knowledge and tech, who can stand on those shoulders, and you can get there faster and bigger than before."

"Were you angry that Nia and Dustin decided to pursue other management?" Sloan asked.

"Like, angry enough to go kill them? No, don't be stupid. I told you, it happens. All the time. You expect it. I would say I was sad because I didn't think they were making the smartest choices. I didn't think they were listening to the right people."

"Off the Shelf and Talent Forge?" Jessica asked.

"Oh, those guys are fine. I'm talking about the other people."

"What other people?" Sloan asked.

"All forms of media, whether it's social or traditional, are bullshit. Everybody knows it. They just don't understand the depth of the bull-shit, and it goes back a long time. Ben Franklin puts out a newspaper. People read it. Why? Because of the comments—letters to the editor. It's back and forth, spicy commentary from old aunties. What's the reality? It's fake. It's Ben Franklin writing it. Both sides. He puts out an article, he writes a rebuttal, he writes a response, et cetera. He invented a controversy. You read it because you had to find out what was happening, who said what, but it was fake. All made up.

"Hypothetically, I've got a young talent—let's say it's Nia, right? She's got an audience. People like what she's doing, but she can't break the algorithm. She's just having trouble building. People who find her like her, but she's not getting recommended outside of that. I take somebody else, you know, maybe they've got ten million followers, they're popular. And maybe they've made enough money and they want to slow down a little—they don't want to be doing five shows a week; they want to take vacations, whatever. Point is, they're in a position where they're worried about relevancy. So I start a feud. I have them disagree over something. One calls somebody else out. Maybe it's about an endorsement, maybe it's about a friend, a guy, some sort of stupid thing. But all of a sudden, those two audiences are aware of each other. People pick up on Nia, and the other influencer's relevant again. We fake it. Now, the good thing is, this stuff often just happens organically because I'm dealing with a bunch of neurotics. So that's one kind of tactic. But there are other things I don't do. You want to build up somebody's numbers? Easy, you pay for viewers and accounts that have a large following." Ratke turned to Sloan. "You want to start a podcast tomorrow? Better yet, you want to start a YouTube channel tomorrow? I can get you three million viewers, three million subscribers, probably within two months' time. I'm going to buy them—not all at once, but slowly. As the algorithm picks up on that, they're going to put you in front of more people. And I keep putting in more paid subscribers, but that keeps putting you in front of more people. So initially, the ratio is going to be a hundred paid fake viewers to every real one. But at a certain point, that flips. Now I've built you into a brand."

"So you do or *don't* do this?" Jessica asked.

Ratke held up his hands. "Within what's legal and ethical. That's what I'm saying. I'll only take it so far . . . because there's a problem: You push too hard, get too much attention, then you find yourself in business with people you really don't want to be in business with."

"What kind of people?" Jessica asked.

"Online gambling, bullshit meme coins, you name it. Everybody realizes there's money to be made here. The problem is, once everybody realizes that, a lot of people show up who you wish hadn't—people in other businesses that aren't anywhere near what we call legitimate."

"I'm curious to know, for somebody who lives in Las Vegas, what you consider legitimate and not legitimate," Sloan said.

"It's funny, I could pull out my phone right now and find five rap concerts this weekend in your neck of the woods in Miami. And I guarantee you the backers behind every single one of them are using dirty money, and millions of dollars are going to be laundered. I may pull some P. T. Barnum tricks to get some attention and build up the brand for my clients. And I can't guarantee you that every ad deal we've taken has been legitimate, but not for lack of me trying to do due diligence. That's the difference. I can only write paychecks with so many zeros. If you're willing to cross the line, then go right ahead."

"I haven't seen everything, but I've looked through Nia's social media. I've looked through Dustin's. There's nothing that looks like that," Sloan said.

"That beauty brand that Nia sells for, besides it being cheap crap made in China—which is fine, you know—what that company is actually known for is selling their customer list to cosmetic-surgery clinics," Ratke said. "When you fill out your body type and your makeup you want, et cetera, they have a list of all your insecurities. That's where the real money is. I tried to warn Dustin. He got asked to pitch a phone app. It's owned by an online gaming company. What they're doing is looking for people with highly addictive personalities. And when they see somebody who is compulsively doing that, and they also know that they're eighteen or have access to a credit card, that person gets barraged with ads for online gambling, tailor-made to the information they gave up in the app. It's a slippery slope."

"Would anybody doing this want to kill Nia or Dustin if they stopped playing ball?" Jessica asked.

He shook his head. "Not the people making those deals. I don't see that."

"Well, then what *is* this wrong type of person you're talking about?" Jessica persisted.

"Call it a Svengali, a Rasputin, a Machiavelli. Eventually, for the more vulnerable who have an audience, somebody shows up, and this person doesn't have an email account with William Morris or work for a Madison Avenue advertising agency. They're something else. They smell opportunity and vulnerability and know how to manipulate it."

"Do you know of somebody like that who got involved with Dustin or Nia?" asked Jessica.

"This is the part where you just might think I'm crazy, but it's fine," Ratke began. "I don't have a name for this guy. Nobody would ever say his name. But I've heard people talk about 'the guy,' 'the person,' things like that. You can call him Voldemort, whatever. Allegedly, there's somebody out there that, like a fixer, does influencers favors. Maybe you can't get rid of an old boyfriend. Maybe you're getting stalked by a fan. The police can't help you. Maybe you don't know who to trust, whatever. That's where he comes in. He solves problems for you. Becomes a shoulder to cry on. You've got an addiction? Gets you what you need. And pulls you in."

"And you think Nia and Dustin were involved with somebody like this?" Jessica asked.

"I know they were. I'll send you the emails when they decided to cut things off with me. They both said the same *exact* thing—copy-paste—about my service not being needed anymore. And when I called Nia, I could hear somebody in the background telling her what to say. When I called Dustin, he didn't take my call. This wasn't talent-agency-switching bullshit. This is somebody in their presence, instructing them what to do, separating them from me."

"Even though you said the influencer business is a small world, you're saying you have no idea who this person is?" Sloan asked.

"Did you see an industrial park when you made the turn up to the road here?" he asked her.

"Yes, there was a company there called Hospitality Logistics. Why?" Jessica asked.

"You probably also noticed the barbed wire fence and extensive security. That's where they physically clean the money that comes through Las Vegas—every coin thrown into a slot machine, every bill put into a cash register. It gets counted and cleaned there, hundreds of millions of dollars a day. The guy that owns that business lives four doors down. He has a key to every lock in that building. If you ask him what he does for a living, he'll tell you he disinfects bedsheets. He's not going to tell you what he really does because the moment he does, he's not safe. His family's not safe. He's got a target on his back. There are hunters out there looking for people like him. This Rasputin I'm talking about, he's one of those hunters. No, I don't know who it is. I know *what* they are—or I think I do—but I don't know *who* they are," he explained.

"Is there anything else? Anything else about him? Or about Nia and Dustin?" Jessica prompted.

"Dustin's father was never around. Nia's father abused her. They're a type," Ratke said. "And I don't know if this is anything, but if you go back and watch videos of Nia before and after she started working with me, that sweet little Christian girl used to always have a cross. A couple weeks before she told me that she was pursuing new management, she stopped wearing it. Could be a rebranding thing. I don't know. But it stood out to me."

❦

Jessica stood by the passenger-side door of their rental, looking at the ground as if wrestling with a thought.

"What is it? You think of something?" asked Sloan.

"No. Not really. My mother lives near here," Jessica explained.

"Oh. Were you staying with her while you were in town?" Sloan replied.

"I haven't seen her since I was a child."

"Damn. Um, and you were thinking about her now?"

"She knows I'm in town. I think she's expecting me to visit," Jessica replied.

"Go talk to her. I'll drop you off and go find a Starbucks where I can read the cases Monroe sent over. If it gets heated, text me and I'll come in and punch her in the face. How does that sound?"

OUTLIER

Jessica couldn't quite explain to Sloan why she felt compelled to visit her mother. Certainly, she'd had other opportunities when in the city, including prior to picking Sloan up. But something about what happened earlier that day, seeing Nia Stratos's body bound underwater, evoked a sense of isolation and loss that still lingered. As she revisited the experience, Nia's face transformed into those of other people she had lost. There was the little girl she used to teach magic tricks to at the hospital—a burn victim. There were the first women killed by the Warlock. All those faces stayed with her, each distinct, yet somehow expressing the same thing.

Jessica sent a text to her mother twenty minutes before showing up so she wouldn't catch her completely by surprise. She had Sloan wait with her at the end of the block before dropping her off. Both were quiet, Sloan having learned to detect when Jessica was in conversation mode versus when she was deep in thought and shutting out the world.

As Jessica walked up the steps, she pulled at the blazer she had put on before meeting with Ratke, suddenly more concerned about her appearance than she had felt in a long time.

The house was in a similar neighborhood to Ratke's, and also quite large. While it didn't have the oversize front entrance and the Las Vegas view, it was a luxury home.

Before Jessica reached the front step, the door opened, and she was greeted by a face similar to her own. She had seen videos and news clippings of her mother and knew there was a striking resemblance. But the similarity wasn't apparent until Jessica became older and her own features began to fully form. Her memories of her mother as a child, on the other hand, were limited and without much detail.

When her mother left her life, it wasn't all at once. She would take trips to visit family back east that lasted first for weeks, then for months, and then forever. Jessica would get phone calls infrequently until she nearly forgot the other woman existed, and she assumed the same was true for her mother.

"My God, you are even more beautiful in person," said her mother as she stared out from the doorway.

Jessica's mother's name was Elise. She wasn't sure how to address her, so she went with her instinct.

"Hey, Mom," she replied neutrally.

There had not been a single moment when her mom was home and then disappeared forever. Instead, she had faded away. How do you react to somebody who faded away? Do you point to some period in time and blame them for that? Do you start at the beginning, or do you pick up at the current moment? By all accounts, she knew her mom was intelligent, and that might have been her plan all along. Never give her a specific reason to hate her, just slowly step away.

"Come in, come in," said Elise as she held the door open and gestured toward a living room. Not quite as large as the last one Jessica was in, but still impressive.

Instead of an infinity pool, the backyard was artificial green grass with a cabana and a traditional swimming pool at the far end. Jessica looked to her right and saw a massive open kitchen with stainless steel appliances. To the left was a corridor that led to what she assumed were bedrooms.

"This is a nice place. Is it yours?" Jessica asked.

She realized that she had a thousand questions for her mother.

"Stephen and I bought this about seven years ago. Then he passed away. It's more his style than mine, but it ain't the worst. Come sit. Do you want some tea?"

"No, thank you." Jessica sat down on the couch. Her mother took a seat just a few inches away from her and studied her daughter closely.

"I'm sure you have questions, and I probably owe you an explanation," Elise said.

"Questions, yes. An explanation, no," Jessica replied.

"I've avoided this for a long time, and avoidance is what I'm good at. I'm sure you hate me, and I completely understand," Elise admitted.

Jessica shook her head. "I don't hate you. I know you had your reasons. I know you were young when you had me. I don't think you understood everything going on in the world around you, and things got more awkward. Honestly—and I don't mean this with any malice—I don't think much about you."

Jessica realized that sounded much harsher than she intended. She was trying to be honest, but it had backfired into cruelty.

"I understand that, but just for my own sake, can I just tell you my version of things—things you probably don't know?"

"Of course," Jessica said, resisting the urge to check her watch.

"How much did your father tell you about my family or how I grew up? I know we never spoke about it over the phone. I wasn't sure what you knew."

"I know your name, that's all I know. And relatives back east—grandparents I never met, cousins I have no idea of."

"My parents were deeply religious. Your grandfather was on a missionary mission to Mexico when he met my mother. They were married. They went back to live with his family in Arizona, where they were a part of a very well-respected family of ranchers. I didn't feel like I fit in, and when I was seventeen, I ran away. I lived with a friend in Los Angeles with the idea that I was going to become a star. I saw an ad in the paper where they were casting assistants for the world-famous magician Jason Blackstar. I'd seen him on television at a friend's house—we didn't have a TV at ours—so I knew who he was. I auditioned. I wasn't a great dancer; I wasn't allowed to do it in school, but I practiced with friends and had a little bit of experience in performing at church. I got the part, which was first for a TV show and then a tour.

"That's how I met your father. He was very shy, but also handsome. LA was so different from where I grew up. Ditto Vegas. Suddenly, I was onstage. People were applauding me. It was amazing, and I didn't want it to go away. I could tell your father liked me, so I pursued him. Part of me knew I didn't fit in; part of me knew that it was just fake glitter. When the tour was over and I moved in, I realized what life was really going to be like, and I missed home. Your grandfather is the most charismatic and disagreeable person I ever met. I'm not saying anybody pushed me away. Nobody did. It was like a restaurant where the music was too loud. Of course, I was pregnant with you. But as you know, your grandfather never had a shortage of young women around, ready to climb inside of a box and be sawed in half . . . or play nursemaid to you. So I felt I could maybe try to find balance. I would go back home. My parents would wonder where I was. I told them a lie. I didn't tell them about you. And I asked myself one day, Was it harder to be in that other world or harder to be back home? And I chose home. But I knew they wouldn't accept me if I brought you, so I made a selfish choice," Elise confessed.

Jessica took all this in silently. While she could have predicted the broad strokes, the details were something else. Her mother's story stung.

After a long silence, Jessica spoke. "My friend who dropped me off here—Sloan—she had her daughter when she was seventeen. Her family's a little bit dysfunctional from what I understand, but they were deeply loving. And accepting. But what I can also tell you about her is, had they not been, it wouldn't have made a difference to her. She was going to do what she was going to do. I can't tell you what I would have done in your situation, but when the people around you are wrong, it doesn't mean you should be too."

Elise nodded. "Everything you said is right, and it took me a long time to realize that. My parents loved me deeply, and maybe they would have accepted that, but . . . I didn't have the strength to stand up to them. I couldn't stand up to your grandfather. I'm not asking you to forgive me. I'm not saying that this makes it okay, because it doesn't. I just need you to know."

Jessica looked around the house, and then back to her mother. "This isn't a farm in Arizona. What happened? Clearly you found some strength at some point."

"I left again, grew up a little bit, went to school, got a degree, met a guy, but that didn't work out; I met somebody else, that lasted a little bit longer. I tried to get away from there again, from the desert, but I missed home, so I moved out here, where it reminded me of home but wasn't home. I found my own faith," she said, touching her hand to the cross at her neck, "and made peace as best as I could."

Jessica looked into her mother's eyes. They were green like her own, but besides the crow's-feet and age, there was something there that wasn't in Jessica's—an incompleteness.

For Jessica, the absence of her mother had been an occasional source of melancholy. She truly didn't think about it often. Her life had been busy, so she'd moved ahead.

But her mother had been haunted by this single choice her whole life.

Jessica had a sudden realization, and her face changed.

"I'll be okay. Don't feel bad," Elise said.

Jessica wiped a tear away from the corner of her eye. "I don't feel bad for you. Like I said, I don't feel anything. I just realized how lucky I've been. You don't know the man you walked away from. I used to think that Dad would invent activities and games to distract me during lean times, or when Grandfather led us into some precarious situations.

"What I realize now is he was distracting me from the fact that you had gone away. He filled that void. I didn't think about you because there was always somebody there thinking about me," Jessica said softly.

"He's a good man," Elise said.

"You don't know the half of it."

"My father hit me," Elise admitted.

"And you still went back . . ."

"You weren't even one before I realized how willful your little personality was. The closest match I could see was your dad's father. I knew where you belonged, and I thought I knew where I belonged. If only I had your strength."

"If only I had the strength people think I have," Jessica said.

"Are you going to have children?"

"That's a personal question the two of us aren't ready to have a conversation about yet," Jessica told her.

A look of relief washed across Elise's face. "There will be other conversations?"

Jessica reached out and grabbed her mother's hands. They were trembling. "Mom, you made what I think were regrettable choices. You were weak. You wounded me. You abandoned me. You hurt me. But I don't think you're a bad person. I don't think you're evil. I have seen evil. You're not it." She squeezed her mom's hands. "I love you. I've always loved you. And I forgave you the first time you said goodbye. Yes. There'll be other conversations," she promised.

Elise burst into tears and wiped her nose on her sleeve. "I wanted to have this conversation with you for so long. I wanted to be a part of your life. Can I show you something?"

"Trust me, my life can get kinda sketchy. I'm not sure if you wanted to be there for all the moments. But please, show me."

Her mother stood up and led Jessica down the hallway to an office.

The wall was covered with printouts of news articles about Jessica, magic posters from her childhood, photographs, and magazine clippings.

"This is quite the collection," Jessica remarked.

"I wish I could tell you that I've been doing this my whole life. I mean, I watched when you were on TV and would read about you, but I was afraid to collect anything about you. When Stephen passed away, that changed. Losing somebody can make you aware of what's been in front of you all along. And this is gonna sound weird," Elise said between sniffles, "but I looked up to you. I still do. How you found your strength, where it came from, I wish I'd had that. Things would have been different. But you made me stronger just by knowing you existed."

Jessica nodded. "We found the body of a young woman this morning. She had been killed and left in a lake. She probably knew she was in trouble but was afraid to say something. I can't understand how somebody could be so scared they let that thing they're afraid of kill them rather than say something."

"I wish I could tell you. I gave up my baby and ran back home to a family that abused me. It doesn't make any sense," Elise said.

"It's what you knew." Jessica noticed the opposite wall was covered with plaques and photographs of her mother and her mother's late husband at various events.

"What are these?" she asked.

"Charities Stephen and I supported. That was really his passion, but I took over for him. There probably isn't a homeless shelter or kitten rescue in Las Vegas we don't send checks to. Not a lot of money, a few thousand here and there.

"I made it a point to get to know the people who worked there and find out what they really needed. The fundraisers want you to write a big check so they can get their cut. But then you find out the ladies working in the food pantry really just want a fan for hot days or an extra freezer to keep food from getting bad," explained Elise.

Jessica smiled, then noticed a buzzing in her pocket. She took out her phone and realized there were several text messages from Sloan. "I gotta go. We'll pick this up again, Mom. I can't tell you exactly when, but we will. I promise."

BURN BOOK

Sloan was parked outside on the street when Jessica stepped outside the house.

"Sorry for cutting you short, but I thought you'd want to know what happened," Sloan said as Jessica climbed into the truck.

"That was the perfect amount of time," Jessica replied as she fastened the seat belt. "What's going on?"

"I just got off the phone with Monroe. Apparently, the search for a clue by the Puzzle Master at Pyramid Lake came up empty-handed."

"And this is surprising why?"

"According to Monroe, Callis is starting to panic. He brought in a lot of backup from DC to show everybody what he's got, and right now he's falling flat on his face."

"So the Home Depot Killer is more than his match," Jessica remarked.

"If that gets out and he finds out we came up with that title, he'll have us both shot."

"Don't worry, I'll make sure you get all the credit," Jessica said.

Sloan checked an address on her phone, then turned onto the highway.

"Something you said back at the initial meeting had one of his agents thinking, and it led to a potential break," Sloan mentioned.

"I can't remember anything I said that would have been helpful. What was it?" Jessica asked.

"When they asked you how Dustin Fonseca could have been murdered like that, you made a comment about laboratory-grade salt," Sloan recounted.

"Yes, you can also get it in different granularities. Did the lab confirm that?" Jessica asked.

"Not only that, they started looking through records of recent purchases of the salt for anything unusual—people who hadn't purchased it before, et cetera. Turns out, if you haven't been buying it for the last ten years, there's not a lot of new people that pop up and decide they need a ton of it," Sloan told her.

"Let me guess. They found a suspicious shipment."

"Very suspicious. It was delivered to a warehouse we're headed to right now. Once they clear the building, Callis wants you and me there—mostly you—in case there's some sort of magic trickery or something. Those are Monroe's words, paraphrasing Callis," Sloan explained.

"But this guy's not a magician. He's just a religious weirdo. Or rather, they are. Does Callis still think it's one person?" Jessica asked.

"So far, Radley has been a dead end. The kid is barely conscious. They're still trying to track down anything that connects him to the others."

"He's our single best lead, and he's all tripped up on morphine," Jessica replied.

"Actually, no. Turns out he had a bit of an opioid addiction while he lived here in Vegas. He told his fans he was going on a meditation retreat but actually spent five days in a clinic in Summerlin before moving back to Colorado," said Sloan.

"So that's going nowhere for Callis."

"Until Radley can speak coherently, I think Callis is open to any suggestion that helps him save face. He pulled in a lot of favors to make this case his and is probably flexible, to an extent."

"I know we didn't have a lot of time, but did you make any headway on the cases Monroe sent you?" Jessica asked.

"I couldn't find any murder investigations that had a cause of death as unique as Nia or Dustin. Nor anything with the witchcraft angle. On top of that, there's been a team of FBI researchers going through the same thing, and as far as I know, they haven't come up with anything either. And Vera Pinellas says the fingerprints on our rental didn't come back with a match."

Jessica thought this over for a moment. "I think I see the problem," she said.

"These are his first kills, or their first ones, done in such a dramatic manner?" Sloan guessed.

"Maybe, but the other ones may not have looked like murders."

"Wait, so you're saying that he might have killed other people before, but they looked like accidents? But they were still killed in the same way you would kill or bind a witch?"

"Maybe."

"What would that look like? Accidentally falling into an industrial salt mixer? Suffocating on too much silver jewelry?"

"You can kill a witch with fire. You can also kill them with conventional means—you just have to bind them afterward," Jessica explained.

"So if he decided to off somebody else, he could have done it through some other way? And then, what, dig up their grave and wrap their body in silver chains or pour salt into the coffin?" Sloan speculated.

"I'm not saying it's a strong lead; it's just a possibility."

Sloan slowed the car when she turned the corner and saw a collection of police vehicles parked in the street in front of an abandoned warehouse. On the opposite side was a self-storage complex that looked older than the city around it.

They parked and walked up to the side of the building where Treynor and Monroe were standing. Monroe held a closed-circuit TV monitor. Both were intensely focused on the screen. Treynor saw Sloan and Jessica and waved them over through the barrier.

"You're just in time; the tactical team is about to go in through the back door," Treynor said.

The monitor showed the POV from a head-mounted camera on one of the members of the tactical unit. In front of him was a man with a battering ram, getting ready to strike the back door.

He pulled the metal cylinder back, then slammed it forward into the area around the doorknob. The metal buckled, and the door flung inward.

"This is why I barricade my door with a steel beam," Sloan mumbled under her breath.

"On your boat?" Jessica asked skeptically.

"I mean, mentally, I do," Sloan clarified.

The tactical team burst through the doorway into a large open space. The cameraman swept his head from left to right, giving everyone watching a full view of the interior. There were three rows of long metal tables in the center. The back wall had giant, empty racks with a half dozen empty spools the size of oil barrels scattered in front.

"What did this place used to be?" Sloan asked.

"They used to make and repair fumigation tents and store them. It closed down about eight years ago and has been sitting empty since then," Monroe explained.

"How do we know the salt was delivered here?" Jessica asked.

"We spoke to the driver who handled it." Treynor pointed to the parking lot in front of the building. "He said he gave it to a man right over there."

"Sunglasses, hat, no other description, I presume," Sloan said.

"Pretty much," Treynor replied.

Callis was in conference with the head of the tactical unit and making intense hand gestures as he tried to explain something.

"He seems tense," Sloan remarked.

"This is kind of it for him," Treynor replied. "He's botched a few career-making investigations already."

"In his defense there were some departmental errors," Monroe replied. "The Las Vegas FBI office was a bit of a shit show. There was a massive reorg, and for three years they had to oversee investigations across the entire state and southern Idaho. They were stretched thin."

The tactical team swept through the building, opening the doors to the offices and bathrooms. The facility looked like it hadn't been used at all in the last nine years. The agent with the head-mounted camera walked toward the front roll-up doors and panned the camera along the edges, showing where dust and insulation fragments from the ceiling had fallen and collected.

"It doesn't look like those things have been opened in ages," Sloan remarked.

"Did the driver see the guy go into the building?" Jessica asked.

"Negative," Monroe replied.

"For all we know, he could have waited for him to leave and then loaded it into his own box truck and taken it somewhere else," Sloan noted.

Monroe stared at the empty warehouse on the screen and replied, "I think we're all coming to that conclusion right now."

Jessica stepped away from the group and looked at the street and the faces of the observers who had stopped to see what was happening. She then scanned all the buildings in the vicinity.

She heard somebody swearing and glanced over at Callis, red-faced and clearly frustrated by what had happened. The other FBI agents he had brought in were gathered in a huddle, staring at the monitor and coming to the same realization.

He locked eyes with Jessica and started to stomp over to where she was standing.

"Well, that was a goddamn waste of time," he snarled, not at her, but at the situation.

"It was a worthwhile lead," she allowed.

"They could have picked it up here and driven it all the way to Reno, for fuck's sake," Callis muttered.

"Why not just have it dropped off in Reno?" Jessica asked.

"That close to the scene of the crime? I don't think that makes much sense at all," Callis said.

"'Close' is a relative term," Jessica said.

"Yeah, well, maybe."

"When somebody tries to pull off something elaborate like this, or a precision bombing, you don't want to spend any more time than you have to traveling back and forth with whatever suspicious materials you have. It increases the likelihood of an encounter with the police, increases the likelihood you're going to create a trail. And sometimes physical distance isn't as important as legal distance," Jessica explained.

"Thank you for your observations, Ms. Blackwood, and what the hell do you mean by 'legal distance'?"

Jessica felt silly explaining it to a man who had been in the FBI even longer than she had been. "I can get a search warrant for a suspect's PO box, but I can't look a millimeter to the right or left or up or down because those are owned by entirely different people. I can get a search warrant for an email account that sits on a server on a hard disk where their zeros and ones and somebody else's zeros and ones are literally butting up against each other. That's what I mean by 'legal distance.' Sometimes you don't have to separate things physically in space to make it difficult for us. We had a hell of a time with the tribal police because we were in protected waters when we were trying to find Nia's body. Whoever did that probably understood the site would create a complication."

Callis glanced over at the other agents brought on to the investigation. He was wrestling with his ego and determination to solve the case. "Can you expand on that a little bit, please?"

"Do you ever do any construction projects around the house?" Jessica asked.

"Yeah, that's why my weekends suck. My wife has no shortage of projects she wants done. The only thing I look more forward to than the end of the workday on Friday is going to the office on Monday."

"What was the last project you did?" Jessica asked.

"You ask odd questions. I don't know—I had to repair a toilet in the guest bathroom," Callis said.

"How many trips to the hardware store did that take?" Jessica asked.

"I don't know. I bought the valve, but it was the wrong size. Then I realized I was missing a gasket, and one of the screws from the seat came off. It's probably three times, give or take. Actually, four. I made four trips that day to the hardware store."

"So, imagine you're trying to encase somebody in a ton of salt and make it look like a statue, or find the right kind of silver chain to trap somebody underwater, or build a nail bomb and detonator that works exactly like you want it. Is that just one trip to the hardware store? It's probably a hundred.

"One of the strongest pieces of evidence the prosecutor used in court against the Warlock was his collection of Home Depot receipts. He was meticulous about using untraceable debit cards and paying in cash and wearing disguises so he wouldn't be seen, but, being a bit anal-retentive, he kept every receipt. They taped them all together and stretched it across the courtroom and out the door," she said. "The people behind this probably haven't gone through that much trouble, but they've gone through some."

"It's been a long day, Blackwood. What's your point?"

"You talk that way to everybody who's trying to do you a favor?" said Sloan, who had been listening in on the conversation.

"Please, I apologize. Just explain it to me like I'm five," Callis said.

"Mind if I try?" Sloan asked.

"Please do," said Jessica.

"We think the people behind this probably have a Las Vegas connection because that's where Dustin was last seen. Nia Stratos had roots here, and it turns out that Radley did as well. Vegas is the nexus. You knew this. It's why you took the case on, at least I assume it is. So our killer's probably based around here. And if you're planning a criminal operation, you don't want to get stuck in Las Vegas traffic any more than you have to," Sloan explained.

"So they probably used a building close by," Monroe stated.

"Very close by," Jessica cut in. "In fact, I think it's very important that you just keep looking at me right now. I'm going to tell you something, and we'll figure out how to deal with it. I'm willing to bet if we look through the rental agreements for the facility across the street, we're going to find one or two suspicious ones. But given the fact that we found a camera aimed right at Nia Stratos's crime scene, there's a good chance we're being observed right now. So I don't know if I would send my tactical team in just yet," she warned.

"We don't even know if this salt delivery was connected to Dustin Fonseca's case," Callis said. "It's one thing for me to send in a tactical team here, but if you're telling me that we've got to be worried about booby traps and spies watching us right now, I think you're the one making this way more complicated than it needs to be."

"But we are here right now, and I think it's a very good lead. A little caution wouldn't hurt."

Callis mulled this over for a moment, then glanced again at the team from headquarters he had brought in. "It's not your neck on the line, Blackwood, it's mine. Time is something I don't have. Thank God Radley is alive, but I can't say the same about the next person. We have to move now."

He motioned at one of his lieutenants and met him in the middle of the street, spoke for a moment, then the two of them started walking across the road toward the other storage facility. The management office was near the sidewalk. Sloan could see someone working behind the counter through the large street-facing window.

"At least he takes you seriously about the other location," Monroe offered.

"Yeah, but it's the other—"

Sloan's voice was cut off by the sound of a massive explosion from the storage facility where Callis was headed. A cloud of black smoke shot out from one of the units, blowing the metal doors against the opposite row of storage units.

Callis and the other FBI agent dropped to the ground as the building shook and glass shattered. The manager of the storage facility threw himself to the ground in the office.

"Get your camera phones out, record everybody around here!" Jessica screamed as she dashed toward the crowd of onlookers with her phone up in front of her. "Get every face. Hold everyone!" she shouted to the local police.

OPPORTUNIST

Agent Callis, unharmed but deeply shaken, was sitting on the curb next to an ambulance as the other agents surrounded him, discussing in loud voices what had happened a half hour earlier. The smoke had cleared, and while part of the storage section was completely torn apart and windows were broken, nobody had been seriously injured.

Agents Monroe and Treynor were working with the Las Vegas Metropolitan Police Department officers to collect as many photographs and videos as they could of the crowd that had gathered around the crime scene.

"What a fuckup," said Sloan.

She and Jessica were observing the chaos from the safety of their rental car. They had their windows rolled down but their air-conditioning turned up because of the intense Las Vegas heat dome that persisted into the evening.

Sloan nodded at Callis. "Do you know what the worst part is for him?"

"Having your investigation literally blow up in your face," Jessica replied.

"That you told him not to go there, and everybody heard it," Sloan said.

"Was I supposed to let him go?"

"Of course not, you did the right thing. You were quick. If it had been me, I probably would have run across there and kicked in the door myself. The point is, he asked for our help, specifically your help, because he was on the verge of . . ." Sloan paused. "And now, God knows what happens next."

"If I had to guess, they're going to appoint somebody from the Los Angeles office or DC. They can't just hand it to the next person in line at the Las Vegas FBI office, because this was too much of a disaster," Jessica speculated.

"Why not Monroe? She's smart," Sloan suggested.

"Callis already effectively demoted her, and even though he's screwed up, he's headquarters' boy. They're not gonna elevate her. They're gonna swap somebody else in. He'll catch hell for this, to be sure, but they'll protect their own."

"So, what does that mean for the case?" Sloan asked.

"They're going to double the number of people working on it, and they're going to take twice as long. So in the long run, they'll probably figure it all out. But will that be before it's too late?"

"What does your gut tell you?" Sloan asked.

"They blew up a storage facility to cover their tracks, which tells us two things," Jessica said. "They're afraid we were going to find something there, maybe even fingerprints. But on the other hand, they knew there was going to be an entire forensic investigation; every fragment, every particle of dust is going to be sent to the FBI lab. All they did was gain time, and that's what scares me."

"Time for what?" Sloan asked.

"Exactly. Time to do something so important that they don't care if we figure out everything after the fact."

"Like, the kind of thing where they don't expect to be around afterward?"

"Yeah, the problem is, by not being around, do we mean they think that they're gonna end up on some beach in Tahiti, or in heaven, or Valhalla, or whatever the hell they believe?" Jessica wondered aloud.

Sloan started rapping her knuckles on the dashboard. "Tick tock, tick tock," she murmured.

"We don't have any interesting forensic evidence on Dustin. Ditto Nia. Radley's doped up and not talking. We had one lucky lead that led us here but then turned unlucky because that idiot Callis couldn't shut the fuck up and listen," Jessica recounted.

"If this was your case, what would you be doing right now?"

"Pumping Radley full of adrenaline, getting him coherent, and grilling the hell out of him to find out everything he knows."

"Well, we could go to Boulder."

"I don't know anything about how to do that. If Theo were here, it would be a possibility—completely unethical and morally repulsive, but doable."

"I was kind of joking about us going to Boulder to do that," Sloan admitted.

Jessica made a wry smile. "I know your limits."

"What does that mean?" Sloan asked.

"You still carry a badge, you still have a reputation, which is good. I, on the other hand, exist in the not-caring-anymore category."

Sloan sat quietly and watched the flickering of the police lights through their dirty windshield.

"So this kid, Radley, he's a drug addict, right? And he lived in Las Vegas," Jessica said. "And he met our mystery man here like the others did. Then he goes to rehab, presumably gets cleaned up, moves to Boulder, but that's not good enough, and they try to take him out."

"Ratke's Svengali theory. I keep thinking about that," Sloan remarked.

"Let's talk to him," suggested Jessica as she pulled out her phone and dialed his number.

"I'm assuming that's you guys I'm watching on the news right now. Please tell me nothing I told you caused that to happen," Ratke said.

"No, but when the FBI comes, you better have a really good lawyer, because they're gonna want somebody to blame, and you're the only one they know who knew both Nia and Dustin," Sloan warned.

"Yeah," he said with a sigh, "and they'll be barking up the wrong tree."

"It's just Sloan and me here, and I'm going to ask you a question, and there are two ways you can answer it. If you feel uncomfortable, one, you can just tell me the truth, the affirmative. Or if it's the affirmative but you don't want to say it, just hang up and end the call, and we'll understand. Trust me, that won't be admissible," Jessica said, making a shrugging gesture toward Sloan, not sure if that was true.

"Let's hear it," Ratke said.

"Did Nia or Dustin have a drug problem that you knew about?" Jessica asked.

"That's the question? No, Nia, maybe two glasses of wine and she got a buzz, and that was it. Dustin was on Adderall like every other gamer kid. Maybe the occasional recreational, as far as I know. There are people around them that did it, but that wasn't them. It's why they were reliable."

"What are you not telling us about Nia?" Sloan asked.

"I'm not sure what you mean."

Jessica was watching Sloan carefully, realizing that she had picked up on something she had not.

"I can tell that you were vibing on her. I assume there was something more to it. She was probably impressed and taken aback by you," Sloan said. "But there's something else."

"Yeah, well, fuck it, here goes. It's gonna come out and it doesn't involve me, so I don't care, but I don't want to be the guy talking about this. There was talk that she had a sex tape an ex-boyfriend made. She's still considered kind of a 'good girl' brand, and while if she wanted to turn baddie, that wouldn't hurt, it really wasn't how she wanted to be perceived," Ratke said.

"Who was the ex-boyfriend?" Sloan asked.

"A little prick named Reggie Pinewood. A wannabe influencer but compulsive starfucker and drug addict."

"And where is he now?" Jessica asked.

"Last I heard, shoplifting from Target, getting a hit, and crawling through the tunnels of Las Vegas, where he's living."

"He's a mole person?" Jessica asked.

Sloan hit the mute button. "What the hell is a mole person?"

"There're a few hundred miles of drainage tunnels, mine shafts, and utility corridors under Las Vegas, and several hundred people, maybe as many as a thousand—99.9 percent of them drug addicts—living down there," Jessica explained.

"Apparently, Reggie burned through all of his friends several times over. They're a pretty forgiving lot, but even then, he ran out of friends and screwed over some other people that he shouldn't have, and he's been hiding down there ever since," Ratke explained.

"Do you have any idea where we could find them?" Jessica asked after unmuting.

"How much do you know about mole-people culture?"

"I know the meth heads and the heroin addicts don't like to mix because they intrude upon each other's vibes. Other than that, not a lot."

"The last Reggie Pinewood sighting I heard about was two weeks ago near Caesars Palace. As far as I know, there's five or six tunnels there, one of them a pretty long one, and I think that's where the meth heads are. But it's bad territory. You could suggest to the FBI that maybe they just stake somebody out there and wait for him to pop his ferret head out and bust him. I saw an article the other day that said some of the tunnels were being controlled by Guatemalan gang members, basically charging rent."

"Goddamn gentrification," Sloan quipped.

"Why didn't you tell us about Nia's sex tape earlier?" Jessica asked.

"As burned as I felt by her, I still liked the kid. She'd been through a lot," Ratke said.

"And Dustin?" Jessica prompted.

"I never got into the specifics. I know his dad wasn't in the picture, but you have to understand, for most of these kids, there is a reason that they want to sit in front of a camera and pour their heart out 24/7, and that's because they're not getting something at home," Ratke told them.

Jessica was watching the flared tempers among Callis and his team members. "As a piece of advice, have your alibi straight and proof of where you've been basically every minute for the last year when they call you in to talk, because they're going to want somebody to call attention to."

Jessica hung up, sat back, and stared blankly at the lights of the dashboard. She turned to Sloan hesitantly but said nothing.

"I'm armed, and I have a flashlight, if that's what you're wondering," Sloan said.

"I knew you were packing. I was pretty sure you had a flashlight. I just wasn't sure if this is what you'd signed up for," Jessica said.

"What, two incredibly hot women venturing into a dark, dangerous, drug-infested tunnel controlled by violent gang members? That's *exactly* what I signed up for."

"It might not have to be the two of us. Chances are, we can probably get a guide," Jessica said.

"Who do you have in mind?"

"I'm going to ask my mother," Jessica said.

"Wait, what?" Sloan exclaimed.

"No, not to go into the tunnels with us. While I was at her house, I saw that she had written checks to a ton of different Las Vegas charities. I'm sure there are a couple that try to help the people down there. If we want to find Reggie Pinewood tonight, I think she's the person to call."

UNDERGROUND

Reverend Jack was a tall man in his mid-sixties, wearing dark pants, a dark turtleneck, and a dark blazer, who seemed completely oblivious to the Las Vegas heat as he waited by the trunk of his beat-up Honda Accord in the Target parking lot.

The sun had fully set by the time Jessica and Sloan had arrived, but it neglected to take the heat with it. Jessica parked their rented SUV next to Jack's car and exited.

Reverend Jack ran a charitable organization called the Lighthouse, which provided assistance to people living in the tunnels, such as opportunities for rehabilitation, medical help, and even spiritual assistance, if they wanted. He had a reputation for being fearless and able to navigate the different subgroups that lived below Las Vegas. Jessica had only a few minutes to look him up, but he seemed like the right guy—well, at least the only person willing to meet them on such short notice.

"Darlin', if I didn't know who you were, I'd know exactly who you belonged to from one look at you," Jack said as he greeted Jessica.

"You look like your mom?" Sloan asked.

"There's probably a bit of resemblance," Jessica admitted.

"So, your mother wasn't too specific about the details. I was still trying to process the fact that she had a daughter she never told me about. But I understand you two are both police officers," Jack said.

"I'm a former FBI agent assisting on a case. McPherson here is active duty with the Florida Department of Law Enforcement, on an assist with the Las Vegas FBI," Jessica explained.

"I just need to know that you understand what you're getting into here. This is a place where the police don't go if they can avoid it," Jack said.

"It's kind of an emergency. We're trying to find somebody named Reggie Pinewood and understand that he might live in a tunnel near here," Jessica said.

"That's good enough for me. If you've got your flashlights, let's go. I'll explain the rules to you on the way."

Jack led them to the end of the parking lot, where the concrete ended in a two-foot-high barrier. Beyond was a concrete canal that led into a dark tunnel running under the freeway.

"Rule number one is don't shine your flashlight in anybody's eyes," he advised. "While most of these people come out at least some part of the day, usually right about now, others have been down there awhile. Either way, be courteous. Don't touch anybody's stuff, and by 'anybody's stuff,' it could be anything—a tin can on the ground. Some of these people can be very territorial and will stab you over a shoe. That said, you're polite, they're polite. Unless we run into one of the gangbangers. Then there could be an issue."

"Is there a lot of violence down here?" Sloan asked.

"A lot more than ends up in the newspapers. People down here have a habit of covering things up and keeping bad things out of the public eye. If somebody finds a body, the mayors are more than likely to push it down deeper where it won't be found than let the cops know, because if the cops know, then that means cops down here—which is not what anybody wants," Jack explained.

"The mayors, who are they?" Sloan asked.

Jack stood at the entrance to the tunnel. "Every section has its own leader. Nobody moves in without their permission. Something happens, they decide how to deal with it," he explained.

"Why do you come down here?" Jessica asked.

"We all have our causes." He lowered his voice. "We got a lot of troubled girls. They get addicted. They sell their bodies. And one thing nobody will talk about is there are a lot of babies born down here, but there ain't no children."

The implication of what Reverend Jack had said hit Sloan like a punch to the face. She turned to look at Jessica.

Jessica showed no reaction, but Sloan knew to look into her eyes, and there she saw everything she needed to know.

They turned on their flashlights and aimed the beams at the concrete floor of the tunnel. Garbage was littered everywhere—tin cans, ripped-up pieces of fabric, broken shoes, plastic shopping bags. It was as if someone had swept all the garbage off the streets and shoved it where it couldn't be found.

It reminded Sloan of the animal nests she would find in the swamps, except it wasn't animals that had dragged this debris down here.

Jessica aimed her flashlight at a black armchair on its side.

"That'll be gone in an hour. Sometimes people up top leave things down here for the people in the tunnels," Jack said, aiming his flashlight deeper inside. The light hit something metal.

"They put up barriers so when the cops come and shine their flashlights in there, they can't see what's beyond. Now, the police know what's going on, but if they can't see anything, then they don't have to say they saw anything," Jack explained.

"That's a convenient arrangement," Sloan remarked.

"Well, you have to understand from their point of view: If they see somebody shooting up and they arrest them, that person's going to be back down here in a few hours. All it does is waste gas."

"How often do the police come here?" asked Sloan.

"Not enough to do any good. Sometimes to look for fugitives."

"Have any FBI agents been down here in the last few days?" Jessica asked.

"FBI? No. We had someone from the Nevada Department of Public Safety a week back. She was doing a fugitive roundup with a few detectives," Jack explained.

"Did they find who they were looking for?" asked Sloan.

Jack shrugged. "I don't know."

As they drew closer to the barrier, a blue glow was visible beyond, and they could hear the sound of a movie playing.

"Is that *Die Hard*?" Sloan remarked.

"*Die Hard 2*," said a voice on the other side of the barrier.

Beyond the obstruction was a couch with no cushions and two very skinny, clearly addicted men watching a laptop resting on top of a milk crate. "Hey, it's Reverend Jack," said the gaunter of the pair. He had a black eye, and his companion a swollen, broken nose.

"That's Ahmet on the left and Wayne on the right. Gentlemen, these are my friends. This is Miss Jessica, and this is Miss Sloan."

Ahmet stood up and said, "Ladies, nice to meet you," then sat back down.

"I would get up, but I hurt my knee," said Wayne. "My apologies."

Sloan looked down and could see where his pants had been ripped away below the knee. There was a large bandage, soaked in blood, stuck to his leg with duct tape.

"What happened to you guys?" Jack asked.

"The Guatemalans raised the rent," said Wayne.

"And you poor fellows didn't have the money to pay," Jack commented.

Wayne pointed toward an empty area next to the couch. "They took my fridge."

Sloan was no stranger to the impoverished conditions people lived in, sometimes literally beneath everyone's feet. But it still didn't make her feel any less sad. She knew hundreds of people like Ahmet and Wayne. Outside of the drug addiction, they could be anybody—a waiter, a father, your daughter's best friend.

She wasn't looking at hardened criminals. She was looking at two people who were separated from most people only by an unfortunate situation that led to an addiction or a too-strong chemical response to methamphetamines.

"Ahmet, do you mind showing the ladies your back?" Jack asked.

Ahmet stood up, turned around, and lifted his shirt. Scars reached from his rib cage to his spine, indicating burns and massive skin grafts.

"What happened?" Sloan asked.

"An IED in Afghanistan took out the driver and killed two of my friends. I was stuck in my seat when it caught on fire. I was the lucky one," Ahmet replied.

Sloan knew the story too well: After the surgeries and the prescriptions run out, the pain continues. At first, a lot of people try to numb it with alcohol. When that doesn't work, they move on to harder drugs. While there are opportunities for vets to get treatment, results can vary. Sometimes the addiction is too powerful, the victim too stubborn, or the trauma too strong.

"I'm sorry that happened to you," Sloan said.

"Don't feel bad for me. I'm alive. I'm sitting here watching *Die Hard* with my buddy Wayne here. Comparatively, life is fine."

Sloan had to admit that Ahmet was more upbeat and at peace with himself than many of the people she knew. That didn't make his situation any less tragic. In fact, his ability to deal with it made her even sadder.

"We're looking for somebody named Reggie Pinewood. You know him?" Jessica asked.

"That little prick," swore Ahmet, "is the one that told the Guatemalans about my fridge. I had it hidden under some boxes, and you can't even see the electrical cord plugged into the conduit. No, I haven't seen him. He knows not to come through this entrance."

"He's back there in Chud territory," Wayne said.

"I don't think you want to go there, though; the Guatemalans are collecting," said Ahmet.

"Unfortunately, we don't have a lot of time, and it's important that we find him," Jessica said.

Wayne pointed deeper into the tunnel with his thumb. "Just keep going until it smells bad, and when it gets even worse, make a right."

They left Wayne and Ahmet to their movie and passed a ripped tent and a pile of boxes with a door cut into it, surrounded by shopping carts and other clutter.

"That's Ahmet's tent. That's Wayne's apartment," Jack pointed out.

Through a hole in the cardboard boxes, Sloan could see where Wayne had fastened a plastic shelf to the wall. Resting on it were several torn paperback books and plasticware. Piles of clothing shoved into plastic bags littered the area around the stained twin mattress he slept on.

As they probed deeper into the tunnel, mounds of debris popped up. Sloan had a hard time telling if it was just random garbage or somebody's house. Jack explained that many of the people who lived here were aboveground at the moment. Some were dumpster-diving, some were scoring drugs, others prostituting themselves. Their lives were more complicated than just sitting around in the dark, shooting up.

Sloan heard squeaking and skittering in the dark. She was no stranger to rats and other nocturnal animals and wasn't particularly startled by their presence. She also understood that this place was crawling with spiders and scorpions escaping the heat.

"Somebody's following us," Jessica said in a low whisper, "and it's not Wayne or Ahmet."

Sloan kept her flashlight forward but turned. There was a silhouette of someone standing there.

"Looks like we woke up a zombie," Jack said.

"Just don't let him bite us," joked Sloan.

"Oh, I'm not joking," Jack replied. "The Guatemalans have some new weird drug that's half between a high and a coma, and then you just flip out. We probably just woke him up. He has no idea where he is."

"Still glad you came?" Jessica asked Sloan.

She shrugged. "It's this or alligators and poisonous snakes. It makes no difference to me."

"So what's the procedure here?" Jessica asked.

"We just keep going. He'll probably sit back down and fall asleep. You don't want to get too close. It's like waking up a sleepwalker."

They continued deeper into the tunnel, and the smell certainly got worse, as Wayne had told them. Sloan wasn't sure if this was just merely the bad smell or the awful smell.

The sound of footsteps and traffic was coming from up ahead.

Jack pointed his flashlight at the ceiling. "We're getting close to one of the casinos. You'll be able to look right up through the sewer grate and see the people passing by. Every day, hundreds of thousands of people walk right over this. No idea what's down here," he told them.

Twenty meters later, Sloan and Jessica looked up at the light coming from the streetlamps and bright neon above.

"Did you know this was down here?" Sloan asked.

"Not when I was a little girl coming here, but later on, yeah, I heard stories. Crazy ones too," Jessica said.

"Oh, you heard about the real mole people," Jack replied.

"Wait, what?" Sloan asked.

"You should have asked Ahmet or Wayne, but there are tunnels under these tunnels, and some of these drains go even deeper. And you talk to people who've been living here a long time, they'll tell you there are people living here even longer, people who've never even seen the sun."

"This would make an incredible ghost tourism attraction if it wasn't for all the hepatitis," Sloan noted.

"I know you're kidding, and I consider myself a pretty rational person, not one to take the stories of literal drug addicts too seriously. But you start to wonder, and I see things down here. Some people talk about bad vibes, bad spirits. I don't know if the devil would be more at home up there with the slot machines and all that greed, or down here with all this sorrow."

"Do you know what the first permanent settlement was here?" Jessica asked.

"Yep," said Jack. "The Old Mormon Fort. They built it here because it was halfway between Los Angeles and Salt Lake City. But people have been coming through here for thousands of years before. Some people say when they went to go build the storm tunnels, they found older tunnels already there."

"Get that light out of my fuckin' eyes!" somebody shouted from the tunnel ahead.

"I think we ran into the rent collectors. We should probably head back," Jack suggested.

Jessica stepped in front of Jack and Sloan. "No, I think we're going to continue on." She told the figure, "I'm looking for Reggie Pinewood."

She kept her flashlight aimed at the ground but could see a stocky man wearing jean shorts, a white T-shirt, and arms covered in tattoos just above the beam.

"Gangbanger," Sloan whispered under her breath for Jessica.

"I don't know no Reggie Peckerwood. You better get the fuck out of here, or you fuckin' tourists are gonna be in a lot of trouble," said the man as he gestured toward the butt of a gun tucked into his waistband.

Jessica kept walking forward. "Maybe one of your friends could help us."

"Ain't nobody here but me, bitch," he replied as he stepped almost directly in front of her.

"Are you the one who hurt Wayne and Ahmet?" Jessica asked.

Sloan had her hand at her hip, ready to pull the gun hidden under her loose outer shirt. She caught a flicker of a glance from Jessica, telling her to stay back.

"I fucked them up good, and bitch, I'm gonna fuck you up real good," he growled, glaring at her.

"That sounded like a physical threat," said Jessica.

The man grabbed the butt of his gun with his right hand and reached out with his left for Jessica.

But he was too slow. Jessica brought her right fist to his temple, smashing into the socket protecting his eye, then grabbed him by the throat with her left and slammed him against the ground, hard, bashing his head into the pavement.

It happened so quickly, Sloan could barely get her gun drawn. She prided herself on quick reflexes, but Jessica was on an entirely different level.

Jessica looked up at her. "Don't worry. I broke his fall. He'll have a headache, but no brain damage. At least . . . no more than he already had."

She pulled the gun from the man's pants, removed the slide, tossed it aside, did something to the firing pin, ejected the magazine, and pocketed the bullets. Finally, she smashed the frame on the pavement, rendering it unusable.

Sloan was speechless, but Jessica could see her eyes boring into her.

"Theo and I spend our vacations in some interesting places," she said, then turned to Jack. "What happens when he wakes up? Should I put some zip ties on him?"

"I'll tell his capo he was out of line," Jack said.

"His boss? Is he down here too?" Sloan asked.

"The guy he works for?" Jack said. "He lives in a nicer house than I do."

"So you would say this was out of character?" Jessica asked.

"Absolutely. It's one thing to throw each other around, but when a couple of tourists come down here for something other than buying drugs, it's 'yes ma'am, no ma'am, this way to the exit.' The last thing they want is dead tourists," Jack explained, "because that's when the police come down, and they come down hard. At that point, nobody is going to be listening to me or the other advocates."

Jessica carefully reached into the man's pocket and pulled at the visible edge of a plastic baggie, then held it up for Jack. Inside was a small amount of white powder.

"Meth?" he asked.

She put her light behind the bag. "Looks like cocaine. You don't see much of that down here, I suspect."

"No. But I know the gangbangers are into it. Although these guys aren't supposed to be carrying while working."

"Maybe. But that depends on who they're working for," said Sloan.

Sloan was aiming her flashlight along the walls, peering into crevices. She stopped when the beam hit an eighteen-inch round tunnel that connected to some other part of the underground.

"It looks like that may have been a bribe," Sloan said. She knelt near the entrance to the pipe and aimed her light inside.

"Reggie Pinewood, I presume," she said.

"I will do anything and everything you ask me to as long as you keep that crazy Amazon away from me," a voice echoed from the tunnel.

PRAYER GROUP

Sloan thought Reggie looked like what would happen if you stranded a member of a boy band on an island with nothing to eat except for a pack of Twizzlers and a case of Diet Mountain Dew. His boyish good looks were betrayed by the dark circles under his eyes and hollows beneath his cheekbones. Although he still had all his teeth, they were yellow, and he smelled like someone who had spent a lot of time crawling through a sewer.

Jessica had grabbed him by the wrist and yanked him out onto the concrete floor, where Reggie skittered backward like a crab until he had his back against the wall and stared up at her in terror.

Jessica held up the tiny bag of cocaine she'd pulled off Reggie's bodyguard, who was still lying on the concrete, passed out. "This must have cost you a bit. Who are you afraid of?" she asked, her voice sharp and demanding.

"Who are you guys?" Reggie asked, visibly trembling.

"We're not here to hurt you," Jessica replied.

Reggie looked from face to face as if searching for someone familiar. He stopped at Jack. "I've seen you. You're the guy that helps people."

"These two are okay. I know her mother," Jack said, nodding at Jessica.

"Is her mom mean like her?" Reggie asked.

Jessica made a thin smile. "You haven't seen me mean."

Reggie kicked a foot in the direction of his downed bodyguard. "Tell that to him."

"I'm not here to threaten you," Jessica repeated. "We're here to find out what happened to Nia Stratos."

"I don't know who that is," said Reggie.

"Come on, son. Don't be stupid and waste everybody's time," Jack told him.

"Everybody knows you two dated. You're not jeopardizing yourself by admitting that," Jessica assured him.

"Are you guys cops?"

"I used to be one. Now I help people. She still is, but in Florida. We don't work for the Las Vegas Police Department. We're trying to help out with an FBI investigation. We need to know what happened to Dustin Fonseca and Nia."

Reggie began to relax, and the tension eased from his body as he fell into more of a slump than a defensive posture. "I know she disappeared and they pulled somebody out of a lake. I kind of figured it was her. First it was Dustin, then Nia."

"And you think they're after you?" Sloan asked.

"I don't know. I don't know who they are. I know you don't fuck with them. I've been hiding from them for a while."

"If you don't know who they are, why are you hiding from them?" Sloan asked.

"Why would you hide from a vampire or a werewolf? I've never fucking met one, but if I thought one was after me, I would certainly hide, wouldn't you?"

Sloan squatted, mirroring Jessica's posture. "Is that what you think killed Nia and Dustin? Is that what's after you?"

"I don't mean literal vampires and werewolves, lady. I am saying these people are not to be fucked with. And if they have your name, it is not good news."

"Let's back up a little bit here, Reggie. What do you know?" Jessica asked.

"Where do you want me to begin?"

"Let's start with when you first became aware of these people."

"I don't know, a year or so back, Nia and I had this on-and-off-again kind of thing going on. And then we were working on stuff. We had plans. She was getting tired of this asshole, Ratke."

"He was working with her on branding, right?"

"I guess that's one way to say 'wanting to sleep with her.'"

"He has a rep?" Sloan asked.

"Yeah, any cute girl with more than a hundred followers, he's all over 'em, promising branding deals, exposure, et cetera. He's just an LA perv that preys on innocent girls like her." Reggie shrugged.

Sloan wondered if Reggie and Ratke were both describing younger and older versions of themselves.

"So what happened?" Jessica asked.

"Nia started ghosting me. At first I thought it was because of Ratke. Then it turned out to be something else. I'd run into her from time to time, and I'd ask her, you know, why we weren't hanging out. And she said she was busy . . . except one time she made a comment that was kind of weird."

"What was that?" Jessica prompted.

"I'm pretty used to people's personalities changing, like, every six months, but she had a *radical* change," Reggie said. "When I met her, she was this sweet, Jesus-loving Christian girl. And it's not like she got, like, gothed out and tatted up and started saying, 'Hail Satan.' It's just, she stopped wearing the crucifix. There used to be a Bible on her shelf; it wasn't there anymore. Gone from her live streams. When I asked her what she'd been up to, she said she'd joined a new prayer group. Well, that's the first and last time she ever mentioned that. It seems to me, if you're in a prayer group, like the ones I was in as a kid, you tend to get, you know, more religious, not less."

"Did she say anything else about the prayer group or anybody she was hanging out with?" Jessica asked.

"No, and when she said it, she acted like she'd slipped up, but . . . she just seemed a lot more serious."

"Like in a cult?" Sloan suggested.

"Maybe. It wasn't like she just started spouting off a bunch of weird bullshit or something or tried to recruit anybody. But she felt like a different person than the one I'd met."

Jessica stood up and stared at the ground for a moment in thought. "What did you do then?"

"I moved on. It's what you do, you know? Sometimes it just doesn't work out, and . . . you carry on with your life."

"That's what you want to tell yourself you did, but what did you really do?" Jessica asked.

"Are you, like, a psychologist or something?" Reggie asked.

Jack cleared his throat meaningfully, and Reggie lowered his head.

"No, but you seem like the kind of person to cling a bit and not easily let go. What did you find out when you followed her?" Jessica asked.

"I'm not some kind of stalker," Reggie protested.

"I'm not saying you were. You cared for her; you were probably worried about her," Jessica pointed out.

"Yeah, so because of the projects we worked on, I'd set up all of her electronic devices—her phone, her computer, and all that—and I'd accidentally left on one of the tracking applications," he explained.

"It happens," Sloan said.

"Well, I noticed that she spent a lot of time up in northern Las Vegas, out by the mountains, kind of the boondocks," Reggie explained. "But it was odd because I would see her dot on the map, and then it would blink off for, like, four hours, five hours, sometimes an entire day, and then it would pop back on. But never in the same spot. It was weird."

"She was shutting off her phone," Sloan said.

"Yeah. But not at the same spot, not like a routine. It was kind of random, because there wasn't one pattern."

"How many times did this happen?" Jessica asked.

"Six or seven. And then the tracking thing never came on again. I saw her at an expo in San Diego a few months after. And I think I asked her, like, 'Hey, you still hanging out with your friends in North Las Vegas or whatever?'"

"And how did that go over?" Sloan asked.

"She freaked the hell out. I mean, like, she didn't make a scene, but she looked at me with death eyes and said, 'I can't talk about that.' And she told me I should never talk about her again. She told me if I did, she was gonna make up some shit about me," he added hastily.

"Like the story about the sex tape?" Jessica asked.

"What the hell is a sex *tape*?" Reggie said, emphasizing the word "tape." "We're a couple; we did some stuff on our phones for, like, private, but it wasn't a big thing."

Sloan stared at him. "That's nothing to be ashamed of."

"Is that all?" Jessica asked.

"Yeah. That was pretty much all I needed to know. Other people have been getting kind of weird too. Not in the obvious way; they just start ghosting, you know? And a lot of times, it's just the fame going to their head. You're there for people, you're their friend, help them out, and then next thing you know, they don't want you in their life."

"So there was nothing else, really, to the sex tape—or video—or whatever you call it," Jessica clarified.

"No, why? What did you hear?" Reggie asked, a hint of suspicion in his tone.

"What did you do on it?" Jessica asked.

Reggie's eyes got wide. "Nothing, nothing. We just—it was kind of a crazy idea I had, and she was into it. And then she ghosted me and wasn't into it." He paused. "Oh, yeah," he added. "That was another thing. When I last saw her, she told me I had to, like, erase it all. Because apparently, she didn't realize how much of it was being logged. She pretty much told me that if I didn't, the people were going to come after me. But, like I said, she was vague."

"She wanted you to erase the 'project' you were working on?" Jessica asked.

"You have to understand, it was her idea, mostly, pretty much," Reggie said. "We were talking about how people have career arcs. You're young. People see you a certain way. Then you mature a bit, and how it's kind of rough for, like, women, because, like, you know, you hit thirty and then whatever, you know? And she was saying how much that sucked. And then I thought about something, like how hot Sigourney Weaver, you know, that lady from the *Alien* movies, was. And like, too bad she didn't do porn when she was younger, because I would have loved that."

Sloan was struggling to keep her mouth shut. Jessica, on the other hand, displayed zero reaction.

"So what did you do? Make a video for posterity's sake?" Jessica asked.

"No, no, nothing like that. I made a digital avatar of her. We took a bunch of photos, and then we created a 3D model, and then I recorded her voice. So, like, you could talk to her online. It's kind of, like, the big thing in porn, and some influencers are starting to do it, you know? There're OnlyFans where it's just literally AI chicks," he explained.

"No job is safe," Sloan said.

"Well, you can look at it that way," Reggie replied, not realizing she was making a joke, "but it's just another revenue stream."

Sloan had followed the trends in social media, especially after their run-in with the cult leader who was using AI and social media apps to manipulate young people. But the willingness for some people to try to commodify themselves in every conceivable way still astounded her. Sloan had grown up believing that sexually exploiting yourself for financial gain was something you did as a last resort.

"So when you last saw Nia, she wanted you to, what? Destroy the videos and the photographs?" Jessica asked.

"Yeah, of course. That said, I mean, it's hard to truly destroy anything these days. It was more like letting me know that if those ever got out, there'd be hell to pay . . . for me. It wasn't an overt threat, and she didn't talk about the people she was with, but I kind of understood. I felt like I was talking to a Mafia princess. But the thing she was really worried about was the AI avatar."

"Why?" Jessica asked. "Risk of deepfakes?"

Reggie shook his head. "No. Anyone could take three minutes of her YouTube stream and create a new one of those. It was the other thing—it was that the AI learned to talk like her."

"The clone of her voice," Jessica said.

"No, you can, like, do that in ten seconds with somebody's voice that you just get off of a video. I meant the one that we trained on our email and our text messages and all that—it learned how to talk like her, answer questions she'd know the answers to, stuff about her past, whatever. So a fan could have a deep conversation."

"A virtual Nia," Jessica said.

"Right. See, I found software that made it easier to train it. What you basically did was let it scrape your text messages and phone calls, other kinds of stuff, and generally pay attention to things you said, how you said 'em. So instead of you having to sit down there and answer, like, a thousand questions, it's just actively trained on your digital history. The thing is, it's like I let it keep running for a while," Reggie said, his voice trailing off.

"So you could spy on her," Jessica said.

"Not exactly . . ."

"Did she ever talk about the people she was with?" Sloan asked.

"No. And get this, I tried asking her avatar—the virtual version trained on her digital footprint—and it said it didn't know what I was talking about. To be honest, I talked to it a few times, but that was it. It just made me miss the real Nia," he said with a shrug.

"Could we talk to this avatar?" Jessica inquired.

"You can't anymore. I deleted it," Reggie replied.

"Bullshit. Is this thing in the cloud, or does it sit on a phone?" Jessica asked, taking a step closer to him.

"It's a cloud thing," he said quickly. "I'll show you the QR code. You can log in with it. I haven't given it to anybody else, just so you know. Like, I was legit terrified after she warned me." Reggie pulled his phone from his pocket and pressed a code in. "Here you go," he said as he turned the screen around, showing Jessica a QR code. She took his phone from his hand, removed her own, and snapped a photo, then placed both phones into her pockets.

"I'll have Jack give this back to you later tonight."

Reggie was clearly shocked at her brazen theft of his device. "That's my phone!"

"You'll get it back after you have a talk with Jack and find out the ways you can get cleaned up when you decide it's time," she assured him.

"Jesus Christ, lady, you are the worst thing that ever happened to me."

She nodded. "Tell me more about Nia. Did she have any interesting beliefs? Any interesting hobbies? Anything you found weird or unusual?"

"Typical girl stuff. Astrology. My God, she paid so much attention to that bullshit. She was into angels, even when angels really weren't that popular anymore," Reggie said. "I made fun of her for that." He thought some more. "You know, true-crime stories. She was . . . and this was after she started getting kind of obsessively into any kind of true-crime stuff involving, like, religion or cults. That Warlock guy—I don't know if you've ever heard about that case. She was fascinated with him. Yeah."

Sloan noted that Jessica's face didn't move a millimeter while Reggie talked about a case that nearly killed her.

"Why do you think she liked angels?" Jessica asked.

"If you want my opinion, it's because she knew devils were real. Her dad was a real piece of work. And I think she got fixated on the idea that there had to be special, really good people out there. I tried talking to her about it, but it was kind of just a little bit wishy-washy; she couldn't make up her mind about angels being something you could see around you. But I know she took that shit seriously. I found out she was still into it but was hiding her books. She didn't want me to know. Didn't want anybody to know."

"I'm going to give you a phone number you can call if you need help," Jessica said.

"Yeah, there's only one problem with that . . ."

"I'll give it back to Jack before we leave. In the meantime, think about whether you want us to find someplace safe for you, or if you want to stay here. To be honest, I don't know which one's safer right now."

Sloan was about to protest that leaving him here in this horrific place couldn't be better. But then she understood what Jessica had already realized. They knew nowhere else where Reggie would be safe. Because they still had no idea who'd killed Nia and Dustin.

AVATAR

Jessica was standing next to their car with a black box plugged into Reggie's phone that downloaded its contents to an internal drive.

Reverend Jack had returned from the Target Superstore carrying two bags of groceries purchased with money Jessica had given him to benefit the men in the tunnel.

"You always carry that in your purse?" he asked.

"Some people use fingerprint kits and magnifying glasses; I look for the zeros and ones," Jessica said.

"You have one of those?" Jack asked Sloan.

"I'd need a search warrant, and I wouldn't even begin to know where to find one. Although I have a suspicion it might be one of a kind."

"Two of a kind," Jessica corrected her.

A green light flashed on the box. Jessica unplugged it and handed Reggie's phone back to Jack.

They could see the young man across the parking lot, hiding at the edge of the tunnel, just outside the glow of the streetlamps on the road above. He was still too terrified to leave what he considered his safe place.

Jack turned and held up the phone. Reggie gave him a thumbs-up.

"You have my contact info. If the kid decides he wants treatment, let me know. We can take care of it," she told Jack.

"I think this one's still in too much denial for that," he said.

"You're probably right. The offer still stands. And, you know, if there are special cases you need help with, let me know."

"You take after your mom," Jack said. "She's got a big heart too."

"I'm learning," Jessica said with a smile.

After he left, Sloan held up the iPad on which she had logged into the site Reggie had provided. "You ready to watch this?"

"Let's take a look," said Jessica as she climbed into the passenger seat.

Sloan rested the iPad on a stand in the middle of the console so they could both see. On screen was a slightly pixelated image of Nia. Below was a button labeled "Start Conversation."

"Is this like Jules, where we just talk to her, or are we going to be type-chatting?" Jessica asked.

"I think there's an option here to do either. Do you have a preference?"

Jessica mulled this over. Hours ago, she had been face-to-face with Nia's corpse.

"I guess it might be helpful to hear her voice, although I don't know how much the AI will convey that," Jessica said.

Sloan pressed the "Start Conversation" button. Electronic static filled the screen with a glitch effect. Then, a slightly pixelated, shiny version of Nia's head and shoulders appeared.

"What's up? It's me, Nia. What do you want to talk about?" her avatar asked.

"I guess this is voice mode," Sloan said aloud.

"That's right. You can ask me anything or text. It's up to you. And for a few extra dollars a month, I can SMS you during the day, tell you things, send you photos. Wink," Nia's avatar said.

The avatar said the word "wink" as it winked.

"I think that's a programming glitch," Sloan said.

"Do you like to program? That's cool," Nia's avatar replied, assuming it was being spoken to.

"What can you talk to us about?" Jessica asked.

"Anything you want! You can learn about me. We can talk about your favorite movies, your crushes, who you have a secret crush on. Wink."

"Tell us about yourself," Jessica prompted.

"Well, for starters, my name's Nia. Well, technically, I'm Nia's avatar, her virtual version," it explained. "But I've been programmed with millions of conversations with Nia, so talking to me is probably like talking to her—except, don't tell her, I have a better memory. I can give you some beauty tips, tell you about my favorite brands, and give you advice."

"Tell us about your friends," Sloan said.

"Being an influencer is pretty busy work. I don't have as much time to hang out as I'd like to. But when I do, I love to go on vacations with my friends Annalise, Shada, and Daniella. You probably know them from their Instagram."

"Those are all influencers," Sloan whispered under her breath.

Jessica nodded.

"Where do you live?" Sloan asked.

"I spend part of my time in LA and part of my time in Las Vegas, where I love the music and concert scene. If you're visiting there, you should check out Resorts World," Nia's avatar said.

"Where did you go to school?" Jessica asked.

"I went to Deckerville Public High School. While I wasn't the best student in class, you might say, I did love choir and drama class. Surprise, surprise," it told them.

"Who was your favorite teacher?" Sloan asked.

"High school was a little bit rough at times. I didn't get along with everybody else. I kind of marched to my own beat. But I had a teacher,

Mrs. Keel, who was always there for me, especially when I didn't have anybody I could talk to at home," Nia's avatar explained.

"So it seems this might be a little bit deeper than scraping all of her Instagram posts," Sloan whispered.

"What's your Social Security card number?" Jessica asked.

"Ha ha, not so fast. A girl's gotta have some secrets," Nia's avatar replied.

"Do you have any friends that you hang out with but you don't talk about?" Sloan asked.

"Well, if I can't talk about them, then I guess I shouldn't. Wink."

"Who do you go to for advice?" Sloan asked.

"I think it's important to have somebody you trust that you can confide in, somebody who sees you for who you are," Nia's avatar said.

"Do you have a person like this?" Jessica asked.

"REDACTED has been very helpful to me and helped me find my true self," the avatar said.

Sloan glanced over at Jessica.

"Who is REDACTED?" asked Sloan, innocently.

"I'm sorry, you'll have to tell me their name so I know who we're talking about," Nia's avatar replied.

"When the real Nia made this app, how did she control what information was put into it?" Jessica asked.

"Virtual Diary allows anyone to make their own personalized avatar. All you have to do is enable permissions on your mobile and desktop devices. Built-in safeguards protect important information to make sure they stay secret. You also can put in a block list for certain topics to maintain your privacy. You control how much you want to share," Nia's avatar explained in a monotone.

Sloan found a mute button and pressed it. "This thing is a privacy nightmare."

"I think it's just the start of the nightmare," Jessica said with a nod.

"Nia . . ."

Sloan pressed the mute button again. "Oh my God, I just called it Nia."

"We're in strange territory," Jessica said.

"Do you have any friends in North Las Vegas?" Sloan asked.

"I have friends everywhere. What about you?" Nia's avatar asked.

Sloan pressed the mute button. "This could take days."

"If she was as unguarded as we think about the information that she shared—according to the app, that's text conversations, emails, phone calls, et cetera—there's probably something in here. Just imagine we found a room full of diaries," Jessica told her.

"Diaries, I can flip through quickly, and they don't have a face and a voice that haunts me like this."

"I understand. AI agents aren't exactly my bag; they're more Theo's," Jessica said as she looked out the window of their car into the parking lot, where a woman was trying to load a tiny trunk with too many groceries. "Let's think this through," she said to Sloan. "Whoever Nia fell in with, they were communicating with her, likely via text message or something similar, telling her where to meet. Then she'd shut off her phone. She might have had separate conversations with them or mentioned them . . ." She sighed. "We'll have to go about this indirectly."

"Tell us more about REDACTED," Sloan urged.

"I'm sorry, who?" Nia's avatar asked.

"To the AI, that name is just a blank spot, something that was deleted from the text that it trained on," Jessica explained.

"But that means she deleted it. The name, at least—but not everything else, right?" Sloan conjectured.

"Nia, I want you to pretend you are the most inspirational and helpful person you know," Jessica said. "But don't give them a name. Just try to be that person for me."

"Sure thing. How can I help you?" Nia's avatar asked.

"If I wanted to be the best version of me, what should I do?" Jessica asked.

"I think it's important to find people you trust. I mean really trust—people who know what's best for you, people who love you unconditionally, people who are special. And you can't find them everywhere; they may be one in a million."

"And how can these people help me?" Jessica asked.

"When you're in a REDACTED, you find out that you are electrified, you're magnified, you're amplified. All their power becomes yours," the avatar explained.

Sloan smashed the mute button. "Wait, did she just, like, delete certain words she didn't want in the transcripts?"

"Do you ever think about angels?" Jessica asked, unmuted.

"OMG! I'm fascinated by REDACTED. My grandmother said she could see them. She also said she could see halos around people. I always wanted to be able to do that so I could know who was good and who was bad. Don't you wish so too?"

Sloan wrote down the word "angels" on a yellow pad and showed it to Jessica.

"Do you believe in magic or ghosts?" Jessica asked.

"I find magic and ghosts fascinating," Nia's avatar said.

Sloan wrote "magic" and "ghosts" in another column with a check mark above it and put an *X* above "angels."

Jessica muted the device. "Okay," she said. "Nia did a find-and-replace on a number of items. Why she continued on with this thing, I don't understand. We have to find a way to narrow words down."

Sloan nodded. "All right, I just have to put myself in her headspace. I've met somebody charismatic, someone interesting, some group of people. I know you don't like the word, but let's just call it a cult, for expediency's sake. And clearly, I've passed some sort of initiation. I'm part of them, still clinging to some parts of me. I don't want to delete this, maybe because I've put a lot of effort into it. Maybe . . . Hmm. Maybe deleting it felt like killing herself."

"I thought about that too. To us, it's just a thing, but to her . . . it's a reflection. Or a twin." Jessica unmuted the device. "Do you believe in God?"

"I feel that God is in all of us," Nia's avatar replied.

Sloan wrote "Spiritual advisor name" in the X column.

"Nia, how would you define a spell?" Jessica asked.

"A REDACTED is a wish you make that has a real effect on the world around you," the avatar explained.

Sloan added "spell" to the X list.

"What about witches and demons?" Jessica asked.

"I don't like to talk about REDACTED and REDACTED. Let's change the topic," Nia's avatar told them.

"I want you to channel the most inspirational, spiritual person you know. Just say yes if you can do that," Jessica said.

"Yes," it replied.

"I want you to stay in character. I want you to think about everything you know about this person, the things they've told you about their life, the advice they've given you. You're no longer Nia; you're this person. Understand?"

"Yes," Nia's avatar replied.

"What is the best advice you would give Nia?" Jessica asked.

"Trust nobody except the people in your REDACTED," the avatar said.

Sloan hit the mute button. "Damn it!"

"Don't worry; the AI doesn't know that it didn't say that. It's still having the conversation or whatever it's doing." She unmuted the app. "How important are secrets?" Jessica asked.

"Secrets are the most important things we have," Nia's avatar said. "The more we share them, the less valuable they are."

"Tell me an important story about your childhood," Jessica said.

"I felt like an outsider. I didn't fit in. Everybody around me was different. I knew that Brotherhood was not where I was destined to find my true self," the avatar explained.

Sloan whipped out her phone and googled "Brotherhood." She turned the device to Jessica.

"Did Nia ever live in Idaho?" Sloan asked.

"Nia has never lived in Idaho," it replied.

Sloan pressed the mute button.

Jessica read the screen. Brotherhood was a religious community in Idaho, an offshoot of excommunicated Mormons.

Jessica unmuted the app. "Tell us about Brotherhood," she said.

"I think it's a place in Idaho, but I don't know. You would have to google it," Nia's avatar said.

Jessica muted the app again. "I think there might have just been one reference—some bit of conversation that got captured."

"Do we think that's where one of the cultists is from?" Sloan asked.

"I want you to repeat these names after me. Only respond with the names Aaron, Ammon, Brigham, Hiram, Nephi, Moroni, Ezra, Alma, Lehi, and Mosiah," Jessica instructed.

"Aaron, Ammon, Brigham, Hiram, Nephi, Moroni, Ezra, Alma, REDACTED, and Mosiah," replied Nia's avatar.

Sloan wrote the name "Lehi" and drew a circle around it.

"Now repeat these names: Ada, Eliza, Soraya, Hannah, Abigail, Emma, Lucy, Naomi, Dina, and Clara," Jessica instructed.

"Ada, Eliza, REDACTED, Hannah, Abigail, Emma, Lucy, Naomi, Dina, and Clara," replied the avatar.

Sloan wrote the name "Soraya" and circled it.

She pressed the mute button. "Do you think these are members of the group?" Sloan asked.

"Maybe, but I don't think he would use his real name. I think that he would have had a new identity, assuming we're talking about a male and he's a leader of whatever it is that she was involved in," Jessica said.

"Then who're Lehi and Soraya?" Sloan asked.

"They might have been names from a story he told that Nia repeated to somebody else. Either way, she felt it important enough to delete them. There are probably a few dozen other Mormon names we could try," Jessica suggested.

Sloan reviewed the list. "So she's deleted 'angels,' 'Lehi,' 'Soraya,' 'witches,' 'demons,' and 'spells.'"

Jessica unmuted the iPad and nearly shouted, "Tell me about Dustin Fonseca."

"REDACTED is a podcaster, live streamer, and gamer."

"Tell me about Michael Radley," Jessica said.

"REDACTED is a podcaster, live streamer, and gamer."

Sloan hit the mute button. "How does she—pardon me—*it* know who we're talking about if it just says 'redacted'?"

"I think the part of the AI that understands us converts our words into tokens, and the part of the AI that speaks to us isn't allowed to say them," Jessica explained.

Sloan unmuted the app. "Nia, I want you to describe the perfect guy to me."

"I like guys who are a little bit older, more mature. There's something about somebody who knows what they like. I like guys that read a lot. I don't mind a little bit of a bad boy, somebody who's had some life experience. As far as looks go, tall. He doesn't have to be conventionally handsome; he just has to know who he is. Dark brown eyes, thick hair, flecks of gray—a voice, a low voice that you have to listen closely to hear."

"Do you think that's a description?" Sloan asked.

Jessica shrugged.

Sloan pressed the mute button again. "I think I'm getting a sense of why we found her dead. Because they were afraid Nia would talk. Like she did here."

"Where is a good place to meditate and think with other special people?" Jessica asked the avatar after unmuting the conversation.

"I like to be out with close friends in the desert."

"Do you know anybody who grew up in a town called Brotherhood?" Jessica asked.

"I think my REDACTED was from Brotherhood. He mentioned it a few times, but I never asked."

"Your guardian angel?" Jessica asked.

"Yes. My REDACTED is very special to me," Nia's avatar replied.

"How did you know he was your guardian angel?" Jessica asked.

"I heard the most beautiful music in my ears, and he had a glow about him. I could tell he was special, and he showed me that I was too."

"I think the poor girl got roofied," Sloan said in Jessica's ear.

"Did your guardian angel have a favorite movie or book?" Jessica asked.

"He said books and movies are ways to control us and limit who we are."

"What about the Bible?"

"He said it had been adulterated and twisted and turned," the avatar explained, "and you had to talk to somebody who really knew what it was about—a guide."

Sloan muted the app. "So this is from her text messages, some conversations, recordings—probably her version of 'dear diary.' But she tried to clean it up by removing names. What else could be in here that could tell us more about who this is or who they are?" she pondered.

"Reggie said she would turn off her phone at different locations, which sounds like she got into somebody else's car, where they made sure that all of her devices were off or left back in her own vehicle."

"Assuming that car always took her to the same place, she probably earned enough trust to know where it was," Sloan said. "Which means it's in here, but there are hundreds of thousands of addresses. Even if we narrow it down to the street names, it's thousands."

Jessica took out her phone and started typing. Satisfied, she clicked it off and unmuted the app.

"Have you ever been to 44 Lucky Star Road?" Jessica asked.

"I've never heard of REDACTED Road," Nia's avatar replied.

"What was that?" Sloan asked.

"At the same time as the warehouse explosion today, this ranch caught on fire," Jessica told her.

"Are you thinking they torched it?" Sloan asked.

"What are the odds that this out-of-the-way ranch in northern Las Vegas caught on fire today at the same time? Arson investigations are a slow process."

"Do you think they know about this?" Sloan asked, gesturing at the app.

"I doubt it, but I think they thought Radley, Nia, and Dustin were loose ends, and they didn't want to take any chances."

"What do we do now?" she asked Jessica.

"Let's call Monroe and go check out the ranch."

INNER SANCTUM

Special Agent Monroe was already waiting for Jessica and Sloan at 44 Lucky Star Road, standing at the front gate and speaking with a Las Vegas Fire Department inspector. The charred ruins of the structures were visible behind them. Sloan could smell burnt wood before she even opened the door of their vehicle.

"Is it okay if we have a look around?" Monroe asked the fire department official.

"Just be careful where you step. I gotta do some paperwork, then sit on this and make sure nothing reignites," he explained.

It wasn't uncommon for an extinguished fire to start again as burning embers reached new sources of combustion. His job was to babysit the fire until they were satisfied it didn't pose a threat. Sloan could see a thermal imager on his dashboard . . . Hmm. It so happened that she had a thermal-imaging attachment for her iPhone.

"Just give me one second," she told Jessica and Monroe before heading back to the vehicle.

"No problem. I'll catch up Agent Monroe here on why the hell we're out here," Jessica said. She had texted Monroe and Treynor, saying it was urgent that they send somebody out to the ranch.

"It's a little bit complicated," Jessica explained, "but we ran into Reggie Pinewood in the drug tunnels."

"Did he tell you about this location?" Monroe asked.

"Not quite," Jessica said.

Jessica and Sloan had decided not to tell the FBI yet about Nia's AI avatar. They had some questions about the way the case was being run and were afraid that somebody might decide to take it down from the server before they had a chance to ask more questions.

While it was a risky decision, they both were confident that the FBI team was in no place to make headway with it and would never have found it themselves.

Jessica decided to fudge the details a little bit, ensuring it wouldn't cause Monroe to think too poorly of her later when she found out the rest. "Reggie was a bit stalker-y and had taken to following Nia's location data. This is the approximate location of her activities."

"Approximate," Monroe repeated.

Jessica knew the woman was smart and wasn't going to try to push it any further. "Let's just leave that for now. We think there's a high probability this property is connected to the warehouse bombing."

Monroe flashed her light across the burned-out structures. "All right, we'll have a look. You might be interested to know that a preliminary analysis indicates the explosives used to blow up the storage unit matches the nail bomb that nearly killed Michael Radley."

"Well, that's a hell of a connection," Jessica remarked.

"So that connects Dustin's salt delivery to the Radley bombing," Sloan stated. "And we have the photo connecting Dustin and Nia, along with the close timing of that with the explosion."

"This will make a really beautiful tight loop on our crime board at the office," Monroe remarked. "The only problem is, other than the victims, there are no suspects."

"Who's in charge of the investigation now?" Jessica asked.

"A committee at this point," Monroe told her.

"That's not good."

"It gets worse. There were some complaints about Callis. While I had my issues, some of theirs sounded a little more unfounded. There were questions about his professionalism and the overall way the Las Vegas office handled the case."

"From who?" Sloan asked.

"I don't know. They were made anonymously. I know lots of people are upset, but someone has been griping to headquarters. We've got about forty different law enforcement officers working on this."

"That seems a bit unprofessional," Sloan replied.

"Callis is connected. Someone could be afraid of reprisals. Unfounded or not, it just makes the investigation look sloppy," said Monroe. "Not that it's a well-oiled machine. But this isn't the time for all that."

Sloan aimed her flashlight at the first structure. "Sorry to hear that. Let's just see what we can see."

"I didn't get a chance to look at this on Google Maps. What's the layout?" Monroe asked.

Another pair of light beams cut across the property. They turned around to see a van with the Nevada Department of Public Safety logo pull up.

"I think that's Vera Pinellas," Monroe told them.

Pinellas exited her state police vehicle, turned on her flashlight, scanned the beam across the compound, and stopped at a corral.

"Jesus Christ, please tell me there weren't any horses here," she said.

"I don't think there have been horses here for a long time," said Jessica.

"Are you a rider?"

"When I was a little girl, I used to ride up in the Hollywood Hills near the Hollywood Sign. I haven't done a lot since then, but you can smell when there have been horses, even if a fire has burned through everything else."

Pinellas took a deep breath through her nose. "Yeah, that checks out. I was at the office giving an update on all the footage we'd been collecting. We checked every gas station between here and Pyramid Lake and the Sheldon Refuge."

"I guess it's too early to expect anything," Monroe said.

"You never know. Not every camera is visible in some of these stations, and it stands to reason somebody will have to refuel at some point and get recorded. I'm sure we got them on a camera somewhere. Of course, it's going to be a few hundred people we have to narrow down," Pinellas said.

"Not to mention all the footage we have from the storage-unit explosion," Monroe added.

"Yeah, there's that," said Pinellas, "but if this guy's planting cameras with transmitters and the like, I can't imagine a saboteur being anywhere near there."

"Maybe, but the question comes down to when they rigged it to explode," Monroe suggested.

"That is outside my area of expertise. I understand, though, that they were able to connect those explosives to the ones in Colorado."

"Yeah, some of the dots are starting to connect," Monroe said.

"Keep the faith. What can I do to help?" Pinellas asked.

"Well, a lot of this ranch has been burned out, but there still might be something here. We're looking for another staging area or really any signs of habitation."

"Habitation?" Pinellas asked.

"I don't know how else to put it, but what did whoever lived out here *do*?" Jessica asked.

"Certainly not breed horses," Pinellas cracked.

"Take a look at this," said Sloan. She was standing about twenty meters away, with her flashlight aimed at a building that was still about sixty percent intact, although completely charred and smoke-stained.

She stepped through what would have been a doorway and aimed her light at a pile of charred wood and roof that had collapsed on top of workbenches and a large tool chest.

"This looks like a workshop," Monroe said.

Sloan stepped over several burnt boards and pointed at a metal winch. "I think that's used for motorcycle engines," she said.

"So this guy rode bikes. Interesting," Pinellas remarked.

"Might have repaired them. Did you guys do a Yelp search?" Monroe asked.

"There were no businesses here. Fifteen years ago there was a stable, but then property records changed hands," Jessica explained.

"Who owns it now?" Pinellas asked.

"Treynor looked it up while I was on my way over. Apparently, an overseas holding company. Surprise," Monroe said.

"Data Dynamics. They've owned it for fourteen years," Jessica said.

"Did the fire inspector get a description of the owners from the neighbors?" Sloan asked.

"What neighbors? All the homes around here are effectively abandoned," Monroe answered. "People just hold on to them for their property values. I'm sure we'll find somebody who knew someone, but right now, it seems like whoever lived here chose this place exactly because there were no prying eyes."

"Somebody saw something," Pinellas said. She squatted and used the end of her flashlight to push a board aside.

Sloan walked through where the back wall had been, aiming her flashlight at the ground to avoid nails and sharp objects, then turned the beam onto the landscape that lay beyond. Fifty meters away, there was a small trailer parked near a pile of tires and dry trees.

"They didn't torch that," Sloan stated.

"Ten bucks says it's a sex dungeon," Pinellas said.

"I'll take that bet because I think technically it has to be underground to be a dungeon," Sloan shot back.

"You guys check that out. Blackwood and I are going to have a look around the main house," Monroe said.

Sloan had her flashlight aimed at the ground directly in front of her. It was hard to see anything at night, but she wasn't going to miss an opportunity to find something unexpected.

Pinellas kept pace about four meters away from her, doing a parallel sweep of the ground.

"This would be a lot easier during the day," Sloan remarked.

"You're telling—" Pinellas exclaimed. "Fuck!" she screamed as she tripped and vanished into the weeds.

Sloan twisted her light in Pinellas's direction. The woman was lying face down, and her legs weren't visible.

She ran over as Pinellas was picking herself up. She had stumbled into a large hole filled with rusty springs, rocks, and twisted pieces of metal.

She wiped away ash and broken glass from her palms. "I hope to God I'm all caught up on my tetanus shots."

Sloan helped her to her feet.

"Can we leave that part out of the official report?" Pinellas asked.

"If I had to leave in all the times I tripped or fell or landed ass-backwards into something in my reports, they'd be twice as thick," Sloan remarked. "I once got stuck trying to climb up the side of a building when I fell into a pile of rotten crates and had to bribe some car thieves to help pull me out."

"Yeah, but you're a tough cookie," Pinellas said.

"I have plenty of scars, that's for sure. You okay?" Sloan asked.

Pinellas dusted the ash off her slacks. "I'm good. What do you think we have here?" she said, changing the subject.

They aimed their flashlights into the pit, probing the debris for anything out of the ordinary.

"My guess is it's a fire pit," Sloan said.

"I think you're probably right. Let's go check out the sex dungeon," Pinellas said.

When they reached the trailer, they found that it was secured from the outside with a padlock. The windows had plywood blocking the interior.

"Looks like we may not be able to settle that bet," Pinellas said.

Sloan pulled a small pry bar from her pouch and wedged it between the hasp and the doorframe. She gave it a swift yank, and the lock fell to the ground. "Can't be too sure with a fire. Could be something combustible inside," she advised.

"Efficient. I like the way you think."

Sloan reached for the door handle and was about to open it, then hesitated.

"What is it?" Pinellas asked.

"I didn't learn anything from earlier, did I," Sloan said.

"What do you mean?"

"Special Agent Callis, running in like Custer at Little Bighorn and falling flat on his face," Sloan remarked, "literally."

Pinellas turned her flashlight around the trailer, then stepped back. "Ah, I get it. We don't want anything to go explode-y."

"If it was that important, they probably would have torched it, right?" Sloan asked.

"Unless he was in a hurry and forgot," Pinellas said.

"Goddamn it. Do me a favor. Would you step back about, I don't know, a hundred feet?" Sloan put her flashlight under her armpit and reached into her pouch, pulling out a spool of fishing line.

Pinellas watched with curiosity as she tied a loop on one end, carefully slid it over the door handle, then walked back to where the police officer stood.

Sloan gave the line a good yank, and the door flew open. The two of them waited, bracing for an explosion.

"I think we're good," said Sloan as she started reeling in her line. "Let's leave this out of the report too."

"My lips are sealed."

Sloan pointed her flashlight inside the interior of the trailer. The floor was wooden; the only furnishings were several benches along the walls. In the center, there was a metal pan filled with charcoal briquettes.

"And this would be a sweat lodge," Pinellas stated.

"That or a really inefficient smoker," Sloan remarked.

"Let's see if they fared any better," Pinellas said.

They found Jessica and Monroe standing at one corner of the burned-out main structure. Jessica was aiming her light at a section where the roof had caved in.

It was bouncing off something reflective.

Sloan shifted her light to a different angle and stepped up onto the concrete that was the only part of the building not covered in debris. "Is that a refrigerator?" she asked.

"Brand new. The appliances too," Jessica remarked.

"But check this out," said Monroe as she shined her flashlight through the skeletal structure to an area beyond the garage.

"What am I looking at?" Sloan asked.

"Nothing. We've got a fully equipped kitchen. We've got an extra garage with tools and motorcycle parts. But you know what we don't have?" Jessica asked.

"Any vehicles?" Pinellas asked.

"That would be traceable. We mean what's not in the laundry room."

"There's no washer or dryer," Sloan noted.

"Some people still do it the old-fashioned way," Monroe noted, "but not when they have expensive refrigerators and a hundred thousand dollars' worth of tools laying around."

"So nobody lived here," Sloan remarked.

"It doesn't look that way," Jessica said.

"This is like an office," Monroe suggested.

"Or one hell of a man cave," Pinellas added.

"So what the hell was this place?" Sloan asked.

"The Warlock had a warehouse, which is where he tested everything he did. It was like a movie studio inside, but he was careful to keep anything personal out of it. You could find everything about the criminal, but nothing about the man," Jessica told them.

"We do have a lot of eccentrics out here," said Monroe. "Guys with a lot of money, a lot of odd hobbies." She turned her flashlight back toward the garage.

"You mean like where somebody killed time on the weekends?" Sloan asked.

"Maybe, but there's the other thing," Jessica said, turning her beam away from the structure and across the yard toward a dark-green electrical box.

"Were they going to wire that up for a residential neighborhood?" Sloan observed, noticing the size of the transformer.

"I think it was for this," Jessica said, turning her light on a row of four electric meters.

"Was this a grow house?" Sloan asked, suggesting that the extra electricity might have been used to power the lighting for cannabis cultivation.

"I don't think so." Jessica stepped onto the concrete pad and walked through a burned-out doorway, shined her light at a concrete wall with a large rectangle missing. On the opposite side, an industrial air-conditioning unit lay on the ground.

She then turned her light toward rows of empty shelving that had been knocked over, apparently by the firefighters. Copper wire and burnt cables were spread across the ground.

"What was here?" Sloan asked.

"If I had to guess, it was a Bitcoin mining operation," Jessica said.

Sloan stepped through the rubble over to the wall with the electrical meters and pointed her flashlight at a metal plate underneath one of them.

"2017? Damn, they got in early," she remarked.

"Assuming it was Bitcoin," Monroe said.

"What else could it have been?" Pinellas asked.

"I don't know. Maybe porn?" Monroe suggested.

"I only see one cable connection out here. I think you would need fiber optic for that, but I could be mistaken if you wanted to run a bunch of network servers," Jessica said.

"So we have a crypto millionaire who likes to ride motorcycles and sit in his smoke lodge. If this was any other city besides Las Vegas, I would say that narrowed it down, but Jesus Christ . . ." Sloan shrugged.

"Yeah, I might as well arrest every sunglasses-wearing, sunburnt asshole sitting at the high-stakes poker table for all the good that does," Monroe said.

"Agent Monroe?" called out the fire inspector, who stood at the end of the driveway. "Can I speak with you for a second?"

"Give me a moment," Monroe said, excusing herself.

She went over to confer with him, then said thank you and headed back.

"The good news is, when they were looking for the source of ignition, they found a 9 millimeter pistol under what was left of the couch," Monroe said.

"And the bad news is they couldn't get any prints?" Pinellas said.

"Actually, he said the Fire Investigations Division got a partial. They're running it through right now." She checked her watch. "This thing could get wrapped up any time now."

"Assuming," Sloan said.

"Assuming what?" Monroe asked.

"Well, we don't know how many people came through here. We don't know who started the fire. It could be our guy; it could be somebody he hired," Sloan said. "Or his worst enemy. We're still not sure who tipped us off about Nia's murder."

"Is one minute of positivity gonna kill you?" Monroe asked.

"You're right. That's great. I don't think there's much for us to do right now, except wait and see," Jessica said.

🦋

"I've never seen you that upbeat," Sloan remarked after getting back into their vehicle.

"I'm not. That was an act. Sometimes I do that."

"What's going on?"

"I'm trying to decide if I need to tell them or just let things sort themselves out. Maybe let them have their distraction," Jessica said.

"I'm still a little punchy and jet-lagged, and that's not even counting how much brain damage I've suffered over the years. What's going on?" Sloan asked.

"The gun is going to have Robert Ratke's fingerprints on it. He's going to realize it was stolen out of his house a day ago or a while ago, and they're going to haul his ass in. He's going to look suspicious because he's got money; he's the kind of guy that might be into crypto, et cetera. Assuming, you know, they don't actually shoot him while arresting him—which I doubt—his alibis will check out; he'll be exonerated. But for the next week or more, he's going to be their guy. The DC team's going to go back home, Callis is going to skulk off to wherever he goes, and all the Las Vegas law enforcement people are going to go back to their normal routines, patting themselves on the back. And then it'll turn out that it's not him," Jessica responded. "The problem comes when the other shoe drops."

"Like all of that just went through your head in two seconds," Sloan remarked.

"Not really. It's just that there's two kinds of patterns: the obvious one and the not-so-obvious one. Eventually, the not-so-obvious one begins to be obvious. The kind of killers I went after, and Theo went after, were ones that were smarter than the average cop. They knew how to think like a police officer; they knew how investigations worked. They understood that what you're really trying to do is outthink the way criminal justice worked, not necessarily how logic or reason functioned," Jessica explained.

"That's a cynical thought," Sloan said.

"Do you know why we had to invent RICO laws? Because you couldn't prosecute the Mafia any other way. There are too many people in between. We have a justice system that's based on giving firsthand testimony. But when the guy calling the shots and the person pulling the trigger are separated by several layers, that doesn't work. We literally had to rewrite our legal system to go after people like that. And they weren't particularly bright. They just sort of adapted," Jessica replied.

Sloan let out a long sigh. "Yeah, can't blame a girl for wishing. So why not tell Monroe and them anyway?"

"It would make zero difference and possibly complicate things for us," Jessica told her.

"How do you mean?"

"The camera we found at Pyramid Lake, the storage unit blowing up, this place catching fire . . . these people are following this case. They're watching the news. Probably have cameras we haven't even seen. We search the premises out here and find something. They have all our faces. If the bad guys think the investigation's been derailed, then that'll make things a little easier for you and me and what's next," Jessica said.

"And what's that?"

"I'm gonna take a trip to Brotherhood, Idaho, and see if I can't find this Lehi and Soraya," Jessica said. "And for you, I have a side quest . . . if you're up for it."

BROTHERHOOD

Jessica Blackwood was parked one mile outside the town limits of Brotherhood, Idaho, in her third rental car in as many days. It was a tiny religious community at the southern end of the state, where farmland began to give way to desert.

Knowing that time was critical, Jessica had hired a charter flight to take her there. She spent the three hours of flight time sending emails to anybody she could find online who might be able to give her more information about Brotherhood.

The first person to respond was Drayden Lindelman, a professor of sociology at Boise State University. He was cohost of a podcast that covered Mormon politics and history alongside a friend of his, Gabe Newberg, a former member of a Mormon sect, who joined him on the line.

"Where are you now?" Drayden asked.

"A mile outside of town," Jessica replied.

"You probably heard about the police department there, I'm assuming?"

"I know they're all members of the Sons of Joseph, but other than that, not a whole lot," Jessica said.

"Well, that kind of says it right there," Drayden continued. "They are polite but firm. The town likes its tourists. Their antiques and dried goods sell pretty well with the hipsters. They put on a show, but you gotta be careful."

"They still practice polygamy, right?" Jessica asked.

"Officially, no," Drayden said. "But if you keep track of how many women are sharing the bed with the elders, it's pretty apparent what's going on."

"About thirty years ago, there was a child sex abuse scandal when Prophet Philip came under fire," Gabe explained. "The rest of the elders could sense how the times were changing and acted swiftly, excommunicating him, providing just enough witnesses to implicate him and only him, and let the state win that round."

"The reason a number of these communities have survived is they've learned how to navigate the court systems," Drayden added. "If you don't have a record of a marriage, it's hard for them to prove it's polygamy. All they're going to do is accuse your women of being loose, which even Idahoans are hesitant to do. That was the mistake other sects made—they kept records."

"That'll get you," Jessica affirmed.

"The last time a prosecutor started to make noise, they hired a highly respected law firm, and their attorney asked the judge handling the inquiry what the difference was between a group of Mormons who practice their faith as they originally believed it to be and a free-love community. The answer came down to the clothes and the magic underwear," Drayden explained.

"There's also the ratio of the men to the women," Gabe pointed out.

"You were kicked out of your community at sixteen, weren't you?" Jessica asked.

"On paper, I was a runaway," Gabe said. "The reality was, they just kept piling more and more chores on top of me and shunning me until it was apparent there was no place for me."

"I can't imagine what that was like," Jessica said.

"It was lonely," Gabe agreed.

"I am trying to track somebody down who may have been in a similar situation. How often has that happened in Brotherhood?" Jessica asked.

"If you look at census records and voter registrations, quite a lot. Officially, not at all. But when you walk around, you're going to notice there are going to be a lot more women than men. I would say in the last ten or twenty years they've gotten a bit smarter about it; they wait till they're eighteen. They encourage boys to join the military—and not come home," said Drayden.

"I know I'm going to sound naive," Jessica said, "but it still shocks me every time I find people who wrap themselves in spirituality and act so reprehensibly."

"You have to understand, the men in my community thought they were the chosen ones. They literally felt this was a privilege granted to them by God. What you and I thought was aberrant behavior was them acting out in the most Christianly manner they thought they could," Gabe explained.

"Still sounds pretty shitty," Jessica remarked.

"If you read between the lines, Moses and Solomon really weren't stand-up guys either," he noted.

"Anything else I should know before I head into town?" Jessica asked.

"The chief of police there is named Matthews," Drayden said. "He's their Prophet Isaiah's son. You'll find out that they'll use different last names to make it less apparent that there are only three last names in the town. Just assume whoever you talk to is the son or the sister of the next person."

"Beware of any friendly women," Gabe warned.

"Why is that?" Jessica asked.

"They're not your friend. They've been sent to find out who you are, why you're there. These people are extremely paranoid," he emphasized.

"They've predicted end of days three times in the last forty years. They stopped announcing it, but that doesn't mean they don't have a date in mind," Drayden said.

"Wait, they believe in the Rapture and all that?" Jessica asked.

"Every prophet they've had has said it was going to happen within his lifetime," Drayden noted. "Isaiah's in his eighties now; I'm not sure what he's waiting for."

This struck Jessica as interesting. Right now, their single best theory was that the man behind the group that had committed the murders had rebelled against his faith and struck out on his own. But she was beginning to wonder how far he'd strayed after all. Even her own mother had made a comment about wanting to leave the desert but ending up in the desert.

"Gabe, this may be too personal a question, but what's your faith?" Jessica asked.

"Am I still a Mormon? In a lot of ways. Do I still believe in God? Yes. That was the only thing that gave me hope. And you know, it might be a bit of brainwashing, but some people say your religion wasn't chosen for you but you were chosen for your religion," he told her.

"Dumb question: Do the Mormons in this group go out on missions?" Jessica asked.

"Are you asking if they proselytize and try to bring people into the fold? The answer is no. As I said, you look at the census data; it's very clear. It's a bunch of perverted old men who've been perpetuating a system for a century that benefits them and only them and victimizes the women around them," Drayden explained.

"Last question. How media-savvy are these people? I don't want to sound full of myself, but would they know who I am?" Jessica asked.

"These people aren't the Amish, Ms. Blackwood. The moment you set foot there, somebody's going to grab a photo and google you.

They'll pretend they don't know who you are, but they will," Drayden assured her.

Jessica was glad she asked the question. She had thought about going in with a cover story, claiming to be a novelist curious about their culture. But if they already knew who she was, then that would immediately mark her as a liar and decrease the chances of them talking to her. She didn't know what she was going to tell them, but she had to figure it out soon.

She thanked the men for their help, then hung up and drove toward town. A half mile from the exit was a billboard advertising the Brotherhood Antiques and Preserves shop—the tourist-catering that Gabe and Drayden mentioned.

If she was going to play the coy undercover tourist, that would be the first place she would stop. But given what she understood about the town and their paranoia, she decided the best thing to do was confront things head-on and go straight to the police station.

At the back of her mind was a troubling thought. Although Drayden had said the members of the community didn't proselytize, they did believe in an apocalyptic vision. Was the man who killed Nia and Dustin doing so in defiance of the faith he was raised in or in accordance with some mission he had been given by the religion's elders?

Jessica took the turn that led to Brotherhood. High above the farm-land and scattered houses stood the Prophet's Tower, a six-story white building that loomed over the area for as far as the eye could see.

SAFE SPACE

The sun was just coming up as Detective Erdman from the Las Vegas Metropolitan Police Department pulled up in his unmarked car behind Sloan McPherson in front of a two-story villa-style house located inside an upscale community in the town of Henderson.

Sloan had spent the night going through the case files Monroe and the FBI team had passed on to her involving suspicious deaths. Rather than focusing on ones that investigators had decided were murders, she was interested in the ones they'd ruled accidental, because she and Jessica thought it an untapped area of inquiry.

The best case she could find was the death of Tyler Kulos. He came from a wealthy family that owned several shopping malls in Las Vegas. He was thirty-four years old, physically fit, but was found underneath the crawl space of his house, where he died of heat exposure.

"Thank you for meeting me out here," Sloan called to Erdman as he got out of his car.

He was wearing tan pants, a button-up shirt open at the collar, and had a goatee and stylish sunglasses that seemed a little out of place on a law enforcement officer. But it made sense if he also did undercover work. If she'd seen Erdman in a casino or supermarket, she wouldn't have immediately thought *cop*.

"Not a problem. This house is actually on my way to work, so it's not an inconvenience. What do you want to know?"

"I read the report, but if you could just kind of give me the CliffsNotes version," Sloan requested.

"Tyler was a trust-fund kid," Erdman said. "A little bit of gambling, a little bit of drugs, nothing major. Didn't get in too much trouble. Hung out with some people that liked to party. His family wasn't too thrilled about that and wanted him to take over the business. He went missing for a week and we were called in. He was known to take vacations in Bangkok, and at first his family thought he had just gone away. But when they hadn't heard anything from him, they called us and we did a preliminary search of the house, found nothing—no sign of any struggle. But we came back a few days later with a cadaver dog, in case something had been buried in the backyard. And he started barking near a closet."

"And that's where you found the crawl space," Sloan said.

"Yeah, I wasn't at the scene at the time. One of the officers and a forensics technician pulled open the hatch and could smell him right away. He had been slow-cooking down there. It had been a very hot summer," Erdman explained.

Sloan nodded to the for-sale sign. "I take it they've been having some trouble with this house on the market."

"It stinks in there. We'll take you in if you want to go, but I think we're better off out here."

"According to the case file, initially there was a suspicion of foul play, but then you all decided that wasn't the case. Can you walk me through that?"

"At first, we thought maybe he got trapped, but I went down there and had no problem opening up the door. So we're left with a question: What the hell was he doing there? One thought was that it might have been an impromptu panic room. He could have been afraid. He's got money; he hangs out with some weird and sketchy people. And you get home invasions from time to time. Somebody follows a person from the casino, someone barges in with a gun and takes whatever cash, jewelry, drugs, et cetera they got. That was theory number one—that he might have been trying to hide from some people trying to rob him."

"What was the problem with that theory?" Sloan asked.

"We found several thousand dollars' worth of cash in his nightstand and a collection of expensive watches in his closet that would have been easily found. The other question was, Why didn't he come back up? We did forensics on the carpet above the crawl space to see if an object had been placed there, but we couldn't find anything," Erdman explained.

"Was he chasing an animal?" Sloan asked.

"We found where rodents had been living, but not recently. It's possible he could have heard something under the house. But he was dressed in designer clothes . . . That's why we thought he decided to hide because he was afraid of somebody in the house," Erdman explained.

"What about drugs?" Sloan asked.

"Trace marijuana, but that was it."

"Did he hang around any social media influencers, like YouTubers?" Sloan asked.

"Not that I'm aware of. He had a pretty tight social group—some people he went to high school with. Their parents were well off too. They would take vacations, like I said: Bangkok, Mexico, whatever. He just seemed to be living the good life."

"Do you know if he was involved in, like, cryptocurrencies or Bitcoin at all?"

"Not that I heard. He didn't even like to gamble; his family had money. He was just kind of a good-time guy."

"But you seem reasonably satisfied that this wasn't foul play."

"I think we have a pretty good understanding of what happened here," Erdman said. "We explored a lot of different options, you know, considering the money involved, but everything ended up going to a charitable trust and nothing was missing."

"So what happened?" Sloan asked.

"Tyler's family wasn't up front with us," Erdman said. "One of the first questions we ask is if somebody has a mental health condition. And in their situation, they lied. It turns out that he had had periodic bouts of schizophrenia."

"He *was* hiding, then?" Sloan asked.

"He spoke to a psychiatrist, and he had said that since he was a child, when he felt threatened or attacked by whatever imaginary things he thought were out for him, he used to hide in his closet. I don't think his parents realized there was a crawl space there," Erdman told her.

"Did anything else lead you to that conclusion?"

"Normally, we ask the neighbors for any surveillance footage from their cameras," Erdman said, pointing to a house diagonally across the street from Tyler's. "We couldn't get hold of the gentleman over there. It was a vacation home. When we finally were able to reach him and get the footage, we could see that Tyler entered his house, and nobody stopped by until police did a wellness check.

"When we spoke to his friends, we found out they had been covering for him too because Tyler was terrified he was going to be disinherited. He had been having some emotional outbursts and that night got into an argument with them and accused them of using him for his money," Erdman said, "which was ironic, because most of them came from wealthier families than his."

"And nobody wanted to tell you that they argued with him the day he went missing," Sloan said.

"Exactly. Now, am I one hundred percent positive that's what happened here? No. But it seems like it's just a sad story. He was dead by the time anybody realized he was missing," Erdman said with a shrug.

Sloan looked at the printout. "All right, well, thank you for that."

"I'm sorry if this wasn't what you were looking for."

"I'm gonna put an asterisk next to it, but it was the best fit I had so far."

"What kind of cases are you looking for?" Erdman asked.

"Suspicious deaths, people with either money or prominence, maybe connected to influencers. Something accidental or incidental that could have been murder," she tried to explain.

"Sorry, I can't help you there. I can think of a couple of tragic deaths, including some guy with money but not a lot of common sense," he said.

"Who was that?" Sloan asked.

"Alexis Weissnott, a forty-six-year-old electrical engineer, built himself an indoor sauna, got his piping wrong, and managed to burn himself to death."

"Burned to death?" Sloan asked.

"He was using propane to heat up the rocks, but he had a leak and didn't know it. Went in there one night, lit a match—poof," Erdman explained.

"And no foul play was suspected?" Sloan asked.

"There was no reason to. The house is still on the market because he had done all of his own electrical work and none of it was to code. Truth is, I'd choose that grave over what this one smells like," he said, pointing at Tyler's house.

"Where did he live?" Sloan asked.

"Spring Valley." Erdman checked his watch. "Want to see it? It's about ten minutes from here. I'll call the Realtor and get the code for the lock."

WELCOME CENTER

The town of Brotherhood was mapped out in concentric rings, radiating from the prophet's temple at the center.

One paved road led from the highway to a cul-de-sac a hundred meters away from the park that encircled the massive white building. The rest of the roads were covered in gravel. Jessica could spot a few pickup trucks parked next to houses, but other than that, there weren't any personal vehicles.

Although the town wasn't closed off to visitors and had a general store and small museum available to the public, everything felt like a facade.

Whereas cult leaders like Warren Jeffs were able to conceal their activities behind the gates of a private ranch, the people of Brotherhood projected the semblance of openness with nothing to hide. A carefully crafted veneer, according to Gabe and Drayden.

She parked on the street at the edge of the cul-de-sac. To her right was the general store, complete with old-timey writing on a wooden sign. The overgrown grass around it was filled with antique farm equipment, crates of milk jugs, and metal sculptures.

Directly ahead was the Visitor Center, an old two-room house that had been converted into a museum. Jessica found a photo diary online that detailed all the exhibits, which added up to a highly edited telling of the town's history.

To the left was the town's municipal building, which housed the police station and the post office. Brotherhood was too small to justify several government buildings, especially given the fact that the real power lay in the six-story building directly ahead.

There was only one other car parked near the general store—a Volvo with a bumper sticker for a middle-school soccer team. Through a window Jessica could see a man walking around with a child on his shoulders as he browsed the curios.

When Jessica turned around, she saw two young men in their twenties wearing khaki police uniforms. Despite the cold weather, they were in short sleeves with no jackets.

They looked like brothers, with the one on the left appearing to be maybe five or six years older and having darker hair.

"Hello there," he said with a broad smile full of white teeth.

Jessica grabbed her bag, slung it over her shoulder, and closed the car door. "Hi. I'm looking for Chief Matthews."

"You found him, ma'am. How may I assist you?" Matthews asked.

He was exceedingly polite and seemed filled with sincerity, but Jessica had no idea what lay behind the mask. Her first reaction was that he looked too young to be a police chief, but then she realized that the politics in this town weren't like everywhere else. He was appointed, and that appointment likely came because he was somebody's favorite—more likely than not, Prophet Isaiah's. And to be a favorite in this town meant he was probably one of his legitimate sons and not a bastard.

The young man to his right had sergeant stripes on his sleeve and the same chin and nose as the other. They could have been brothers. But Jessica also knew that in a town with a small gene pool, that wasn't always the logical assumption. Likely brothers genetically, but not on paper.

That was one of the problems with cultures that practiced first-cousin marriage or discouraged marrying outside the community. Given enough time, even second cousins would share more genes than fraternal twins.

Jessica remembered sitting in a college class when a professor explained how the genetics of polygamy and incest worked. One of the students raised their hand and said that it was mathematically impossible to inherit more than fifty percent genetic material from one parent because there are only two sets of genes to inherit, to which the professor explained to the class you couldn't think about polygamy linearly. What happens when your father is also your grandfather and your great-grandfather on both sides of your family? To which the students responded with a collective *eww*.

To Jessica's eyes, Chief Matthews appeared healthy, as did his brother. Although genetic defects could manifest themselves in nonobvious ways, ranging from food allergies to a shortened life expectancy.

"I'm Jessica Blackwood. I work for an organization that tries to track down missing children," she explained, knowing she had to stick with the truth, or at least *a* truth. Since leaving the FBI and meeting Theo Cray, the two had spent plenty of investigative energy assisting in cases involving missing children.

The police sergeant, whose name badge read JEFFERSON, responded, "I think all of our children are accounted for."

"Well, this is actually an old case, and I'm not so much looking for the child as much as a person of interest. I was hoping you could help me out. Is there somewhere we could talk?"

"Yes, ma'am," said Matthews as he opened the door to the police station and held it for her. "Luke, do you mind grabbing another chair from Miss Cathy's office?"

The front area was divided into two sections. To the left of the entrance were two desks, the American flag, the Idaho flag, and a corkboard filled with wanted posters and notices.

To the right was another set of desks, behind two of which sat women in white blouses buttoned up to their necks.

They each appeared to be in their thirties. A woman with short, dark curly hair looked up and greeted Jessica with a smile, then turned back to her computer.

Matthews pulled his chair out but stood by it and waited until Luke returned from a back room pushing another chair.

"Thank you," Jessica said.

The two men waited for her to sit before taking their own seats.

At least their manners were impeccable. Jessica wondered how much of that was due to the constant surveillance. It was obvious that the two women were pretending to work as they listened.

"About how far back does this go?" Matthews asked.

"This is a person of interest connected to an ongoing investigation, and I don't have much to go on," Jessica said, "but I would be grateful for any help you have."

"When you say 'ongoing investigation' . . . are you working with a law enforcement agency?"

"I'm a former FBI agent. I do consulting, occasionally teach at the academy, and provide assistance in certain cases," she explained.

"That's a little vague," Jefferson remarked.

"I apologize for my colleague here. He is a bit impetuous," Matthews said.

Jessica ignored the distraction. "This gentleman might have left here when he was in his late teens. All I have right now are two names, one of which might be his, or possibly that of his parents."

Matthews picked up a pen and grabbed a pad. "What are the names?"

"Lehi and Soraya," Jessica told him.

Matthews set the pen down and grinned. "Unfortunately, Ms. Blackwood, that doesn't exactly narrow it down. Lehi and Soraya in this town? Well, it's kind of like looking for a Chin in a Chinese phone book."

"I don't believe that's politically correct," Jefferson said in a half-mocking tone.

"Okay," said Jessica, "but if that was the name of his parents and we're talking maybe a few decades ago, there has to be some records. There couldn't have been that many pairs with those names at that time."

"Did you try the county records office first?" Matthews asked.

"No, I figured I'd go straight to the source, but that's next on my list."

"Unfortunately, this is all before our time," Matthews said.

"But fortunately, this isn't that big of a town; there's got to be somebody to call or ask. How many young men would have up and left around that time?"

"There aren't a lot of prospects out here if you're not into farming, so more than you might realize," Jefferson told her.

She nodded. "I've heard that a lot of young men end up leaving. It makes me wonder: What's the ratio of men to women here?"

Jessica caught a reflection in the window of the woman with dark curly hair looking up from her desk and glaring at her.

Damn it, she thought. *I pushed too far.*

"You're welcome to go outside and count. The nice thing about our town is you won't have trouble telling the women from the men," Jefferson said.

Matthews's face reddened. "Please excuse Officer Jefferson, ma'am. His pronouns are 'dumb' and 'dumber.'"

"He uses that joke about once every other day," Jefferson fired back.

"'Cause it never gets old," Matthews said with a smile.

Jessica pointed at the old-fashioned rotary phone sitting on his desk. "Maybe the person who was chief before you knows. Could you give him a call?"

"Chief Jeffords is a bit of a cranky man and doesn't like to be bothered. Some would say he was ill-suited for the job to begin with," Matthews explained.

"That's unfortunate, but I could really use your help." She wasn't sure how much she was being stonewalled specifically or if this merely showed their general distrust of outsiders. Either way, she needed to figure out a way to break through it. While these men were tightly bound to their community, they also had badges on their chest and the American flag on their shoulders.

"From one cop to another cop, help me out here," she urged.

"You don't wear a badge anymore," said Jefferson.

Jessica turned and stared into his eyes. "Do you want to see the bullet scars?"

"Maybe I—"

"Shut up, Jefferson," Matthews said, cutting him off. "I'll make a call. In the meantime, why don't you have a look around? Maybe grab a coffee at our general store. It's not Starbucks, but it's not bad."

MR. FIXIT

Alexis Weissnott's property took up half a block in a quiet Spring Valley neighborhood. Sloan noticed that while all the other homes had fences, Alexis's fence was tallest. The only things visible on the other side of the brown stonework were tree branches.

"He sure liked his privacy," Sloan remarked as Erdman typed in a code on the gate.

"By all accounts, he was what they would call an odd duck."

The gate made a beeping sound and then unlocked.

Erdman held the gate open for Sloan. She stepped into the front yard, which was mostly dry dirt, dehydrated trees, and some stonework forming paths going to the house and around the back. A dry pool with a cracked lining lay to the left.

"Odd in what way?" asked Sloan.

"The neighbor said he was a man of varied tastes," Erdman explained. "I guess that's what you would say. He would have parties, but people wouldn't show up until real late, real, real late. High walls kept their music in. And I looked up to see how many complaints there were, and there weren't any. So nothing too out of control. But these were sleepovers, if you know what I mean."

"Like swinger parties?" Sloan asked.

Erdman shrugged. "I don't know. I didn't get the invite."

Weissnott's home was a pueblo-style ranch house of at least three thousand square feet, by Sloan's estimate.

Erdman walked up to the door, entered in a code, and unlocked it. "I don't think the power's on."

He stepped into the doorway, flipped the switches, then said, "Nope. Still want to look inside?"

Sloan pulled a small flashlight from her purse and turned it on. "We're good."

The entrance was lined with Spanish tile. Just beyond lay a sunken living room covered in thick shag carpeting.

"I take it he wasn't the original owner," Sloan remarked, noticing the antiquated decor.

"I take it there's not a lot of shag carpeting in Florida?" Erdman asked.

"Only if you like mildew." Sloan did a turn through the empty living room, then walked over to the kitchen. Except for the shag carpeting and paneling, the house was empty. "What about the furniture and his belongings?"

"He had a sister in California. She inherited it all. She sold or gave it all away, maybe burned it. I don't know. And she's been trying to sell the house ever since."

There was an empty spot where the refrigerator had stood. The range was still in place, an older model with spots of rust and chipped paint.

Sloan thought the place had a bachelor vibe. It was more about physical space than anything else. She couldn't imagine the furniture had been anything more than functional and convenient. God knew what stories the shag carpeting could tell.

The dark interior reminded her of the style she'd seen in ads from the '70s. Everything felt like a cave made of wood and leather.

"What did Weissnott do?"

"He was a security contractor," Erdman said. "He installed camera systems in businesses, hotels, casinos, supermarkets."

"Did he work for somebody else or a company?"

"He had his own company, Mesa Surveillance. At one point he had five crews working for him. I understand he sold the trucks off and just went solo. Too much headache."

"Did you speak to any of his clients?"

"No, we got reports from the neighbors, spoke to a couple of friends, and that was it."

Sloan walked down a long hallway connected to the kitchen. The fourth door led to a guest bathroom. The second door opened into a small room that could have been an office. At the far end, she could see the master bedroom, with the sunlight glowing through thick beige curtains.

A brass-colored chandelier hung from a hook on the ceiling. Sloan noticed there was no electrical cable going to the chandelier. She pointed her flashlight up at it.

"I don't need to ask, do I?" Sloan said.

"I think the sister hung that up to hide the fact that there was a suspicious hook in the ceiling in the bedroom," he told her.

Sloan entered the bathroom. It was exceptionally large, but the vanity was covered in dark Formica chipped at the edges. There was a combination bath and shower next to a toilet missing the lid to the tank.

"It looks like he did zero work on this place," Sloan remarked.

"He redid some of the electrical and built the sauna; I know that," Erdman said with a glint in his eye.

"Where is that?"

"Other end of the house. I'll show you."

Sloan followed him through the hallway and kitchen to the other side of the house.

He stopped at a wooden door and said, "This whole part of the house had smoke damage. If you look closely, you can see it's just a cheap coat of paint. Firefighters had to bust down the door. This was put in afterward.

"Thankfully, this place is built like a brick oven, so the only thing that burned was the sauna. All the wood's been yanked out. It should be just bare concrete right now," Erdman explained.

He opened the door to the room and showed Sloan the painted concrete.

Sloan splashed her light around the interior. It was completely dark except for a six-inch hole at the top that must have been some kind of ventilation system.

"I take it she painted this too."

"Did the bare minimum," Erdman said.

Sloan stepped inside the sauna, surveyed the room, and tried to imagine what it had looked like before. The doorway was only a few feet away. "And he couldn't get out?"

"Fire inspector says he was probably knocked out and suffocated. Maybe he hit his head but didn't really have a chance. Screwups like this are why we have building codes."

"What about his friends? Anybody stand out?"

"I went through his Favorites list on his phone; it was kind of sad. It was mainly just bartenders and some cocktail waitresses that barely knew him—the kind of people that'll show up at your birthday party, drink your booze, but not bother to wish you a happy birthday. Vegas is full of them."

"So you searched his phone—nothing odd or weird?"

"Nope. He didn't even keep it locked."

"What about photos?" Sloan asked.

"There weren't any on the phone. He might have had another one, I don't know. But since this wasn't a murder investigation, there wasn't really much reason to try to get those records."

"Who found him?" Sloan asked.

"The neighbors across the street are the ones that called the fire department. It was the firefighters."

Sloan's mind was searching for connections. The sauna had originally stood out to her because of the improvised sweat lodge she'd found at the burned-out ranch. But that wasn't exactly a smoking gun. If it were, everyone in Finland was a suspect. She did sense a similarity between the two places: Both could be described as man caves.

Sloan stepped back into the hallway and pointed her flashlight at a doorway at the far end. "What's that?"

Erdman opened it. "Storage room, I think. He kept some of his work tools here."

The floor was bare concrete. A closet with no doors stood at the opposite end. Cinder blocks filled the space where sliding glass doors would have gone.

She tilted her flashlight up at the ceiling and a large ventilation duct. "What kind of tools did he keep here?"

"I'm not sure. I think there may have been some electrician's tools and spare materials that were accounted for in the inventory."

Sloan shifted the flashlight to the opposite wall and saw a 220-volt outlet, then another one a meter to the right.

"Why don't I take a look outside." She walked out the front of the house, past the empty pool, and stopped at the exterior wall of the room she had just been in.

"What is it?" Erdman asked, coming up behind her.

Sloan was staring at a row of electrical meters, exactly like the ones she had seen at the torched ranch.

"How often do you see that much electrical power for one room?" Sloan asked.

"That's more than enough for a grow house. Maybe for his power tools?" Erdman said, clearly realizing that it sounded stupid.

"Did his sister mention anything about Bitcoin?" Sloan asked.

"She said that he dabbled in it and spoke to her about it, but she really didn't understand it. At one point, she thought he had bought a trucking company."

"Did he?" Sloan asked.

"No. She said it was a mining rig," Erdman replied.

"That's a computer you use to generate cryptocurrencies. Do you recall any computers in the inventory?" Sloan asked.

"An old laptop that wouldn't turn on and an iPad with a cracked screen," Erdman noted.

"But no desktop computers? Because that's what a mining rig is. With this much power, there'd be a lot of them."

"Are you saying they were stolen?"

"Not necessarily, but if they were there, they had to end up somewhere. Did his sister mention anything about friends, acquaintances, or business partners?"

"Just one guy. He had been working with him on what she thought was some sort of online venture, but they had a falling-out."

"How acrimonious was it?" Sloan asked.

"Weissnott mentioned it to her once or twice, then stopped talking about it. She got the impression it was more of a personal betrayal."

"Did she mention a name?"

"Now you're making me do work," Erdman said, putting his hand to his temple as he started to concentrate. "While we were still waiting for the fire inspector's report, I had her on the phone a couple of times. She mentioned a guy who called himself John, I believe. It may have been the same person as Weissnott's business partner. But then she said he used another name . . . or was it her brother who'd used the name? Sorry. I'd have to go look back at my notes. It may have been the same guy and just a different name."

"If you find out, that might be helpful."

"I'll go back to my notes, and . . . oh, I got it! It was a funny Mormon name: *Lehi*," he said at last.

"Lehi?"

"Yeah. Now I remember," Erdman said. "I was asking her if she knew any of his other friends we could get hold of because everybody in the Favorites list on his phone was barely an acquaintance. But she remembered Weissnott calling her up one night, a little bit drunk, ranting about somebody named Lehi. Now, her brother had had a business partner named John, as far as she knew. She only made the connection later that they were probably the same guy."

"You have no other details on this John or Lehi from her?"

"No. Like I said, once the fire inspector came back with their report, it wasn't a murder investigation; it was just a tragic death."

"Okay, one more question. Did the neighbors ever describe anybody coming here? Maybe a young girl in her early twenties? Can I show you a photo?" Sloan asked as she took out her phone and showed him a photo of Nia.

"I can email this to them and ask. If I had more time, we could go door-to-door, but a lot of people are gonna be at work right now."

"I might do that," she said.

"We asked the neighbors about who came and went, and two different people told us about seeing a tall white guy, dark hair, bits of gray, always dressed in black, like he was Johnny Cash or something."

"Do you know the last time they saw this guy?"

"They said he stopped coming around a few weeks before Weissnott died."

"Interesting," Sloan said.

"Yeah, I can tell by the look on your face. Now you have me thinking that I missed something. What are you not telling me?"

"I think that man was Lehi, and I think Lehi murdered Alexis Weissnott," she told him.

"For the Bitcoin mining rigs?"

"Sort of. You can store a billion dollars of Bitcoin on a piece of paper. You steal the Bitcoin mining rigs to hide the fact there was ever any Bitcoin to begin with."

Sloan already had her phone out to text Jessica. While they still didn't have a clear ID on Lehi, the possibilities had narrowed considerably.

THE TOWER

Jessica wasn't in the mood for coffee or a trip to the Visitor Center. Instead, she decided to take a walk along the path that encircled the Prophet's Tower.

The six-story structure had long, dark windows that stretched from floor to floor and ended in overhangs that resembled a fantasy castle. Each corner had a spire, and on top of the building, a ziggurat of white steps ended in a gold statue of an angel blowing a horn.

Jessica knew a little bit about Mormon architecture and recognized this as a mishmash of styles and probably whatever pleased the original architect.

The jumbled nature of its appearance didn't make it any less imposing. Anyone stepping out of their house would be greeted by this tower. She searched her mind for a cinematic analogy and realized one had been lurking there all along: the Eye of Sauron atop Barad-dûr from *The Lord of the Rings*.

In Brotherhood, the current holder of the title "prophet"—presently the police chief's father, Isaiah—served as God's vessel on earth. His word was the Lord's. So of course it was appropriate that he would live above everyone else, close to God—or as a god.

Two young girls, one of whom appeared to be about ten, the other twelve, both wearing traditional dresses, walked past Jessica and gave her polite smiles.

"Morning, ma'am," they said in unison.

"Hello, ladies."

Jessica looked to where the girls had likely originated their walk. A woman was hanging clothes on a line in front of a white wooden house that was an exact copy of every other house. Although the woman seemed focused on her laundry, Jessica had the feeling that she was watching everything and the girls had been sent to greet her. Maybe not as spies, more like . . . *mascots*—that was the word for it. Like costumed characters at a theme park, dispatched to entertain the guests. Except here, they served to convince visitors that this was a perfectly happy place.

While the ratio of women to men she'd observed so far wasn't scientific, it appeared to be at least three to one. But there was another tell that Jessica suspected even town elders weren't aware of that gave away their unofficial policy of polygamy (aside from the lack of genetic diversity). When she'd first arrived, the lack of cars had been obvious. The only vehicles were pickup trucks.

These pickups were parked all over the small town. But you never saw two of them in front of adjoining houses. Women weren't allowed to drive in Brotherhood, so a parked pickup meant a man was staying in that house. And while a man's pickup might pull into different driveways each night, those houses would always be within their "territory," for lack of a better word.

Jessica understood why Drayden, the sociology professor, found these communities so fascinating. You could probably create a complex social graph by looking at time-lapse footage of which trucks parked where. Theo would have been all over that.

Earlier that year, Jessica, Sloan, and Theo had investigated a series of seemingly unrelated incidents of juvenile violence. All connected back to a strange community on an island in Washington. They went searching for a man they believed was using social media apps and other technologies to manipulate young minds. What they didn't expect was to find an entire community of former runaways and disenfranchised people living in a small town centered around this man.

Jessica noted the contrast between that man and Prophet Isaiah.

The cult leader on Cap Island was a master at both manipulation and finding those susceptible to it. He lived in a simple house similar to the ones everyone else lived in. He wasn't interested in controlling their bodies, or even their beliefs. They were more like prior experimental subjects he'd grown attached to and cared for.

Prophet Isaiah and the prophets before him were a different kind of manipulator. They had to *breed* their subjects and create an imposing culture around them.

What would keep those girls trapped inside this community, despite the lack of gates?

For one, unlike other Mormons, these girls were not educated outside the home and had no practical experience of the world. Everything outside the safety of the Prophet's Tower was unfamiliar and frightening.

With a healthy replacement rate, you didn't have to punish rebelliousness. You just kicked it out.

"Good morning," said a voice from behind Jessica.

She turned around to see a blond woman about her age, wearing blue jeans and a puffy ski jacket.

"Hello," Jessica said.

The woman walked alongside her. "My name's Angela. What's yours?"

Jessica wanted to reply *You already know* but held her tongue. "My name is Jessica," she said.

"I can imagine this place seems pretty weird at first."

Jessica returned the feigned ignorance. "Oh, you're from here?"

Angela pointed toward the girls in the distance who had greeted Jessica. "Yeah, we don't all dress like that. We can wear whatever we want. But, to be honest, I miss wearing it sometimes. I had to learn to dress a little fancier when I went to college."

Jessica had been around dozens of different cult groups, ranging from the Scientologists who politely greeted you on the Hollywood Walk of Fame and offered a free personality test to the dark-web weirdos who spent months doing background checks before meeting you in a coffee shop.

Like the two little girls, Angela's job was to portray a sense of normalcy. She was their version of the modern independent woman who gets to go to college but chooses to come back because this is the best place on God's earth.

According to Drayden, a select number of women, generally Isaiah's daughters, were allowed to go to local colleges and universities. But even then, they were chaperoned by a sibling or cousin—which effectively made it the same as here.

"It all seems very nice and quiet here," Jessica said.

"Oh, we have our drama. Every small town does."

Jessica noticed how Matthews, Jefferson, and Angela referred to their community as a "town." They never used the word "religion" or "church."

"What did you study?" she asked.

"I studied nursing."

That made sense. If this town really wanted to hide in plain sight, they needed to control both the police and the medical clinic—because that's where many of their secrets were born and died without anybody knowing.

One of the telltale signs of a community that's practicing plural marriage, aside from wedding photographs featuring a groom and twelve brides, is the infant-mortality data. Since pregnancies are never officially recorded, in a town like this there was no way to know what percentage of pregnancies were carried to term—or how many children were born and allowed to survive. Some places had a cruel way of dealing with birth defects.

It was likely that Angela had practiced midwifery before she went to college. She might have a personal interest in making sure what happens in this town stays in this town.

"How about you, Jessica? You're very pretty. Are you an actress?"

"No, I was a police officer, then an FBI agent."

"Oh my God, that's so badass! Did you, like, get to carry a gun?" Angela asked, using language not normally heard on *Veggie Tales*, eyes wide with excitement.

"Guns weren't my favorite part of the job," Jessica admitted.

"How about now? Are you still in the FBI?" Angela asked.

"No, I decided that really wasn't for me."

"Are you married? Have any kids?"

"Not married. I have a guy I'm fond of."

"I've got five," Angela replied.

The sarcastic part of Jessica wanted to reply, *Five guys or five kids?* but she knew, of course, how things worked here.

"Five kids. You and your husband must be exhausted," Jessica remarked.

"I'd kill for a frozen yogurt shop, or a Lululemon. But the upside of a small town like this is, knock on any door and you have a babysitter," she said with a smile.

"That's so convenient."

"Speaking of which, I've got to go pick up my littlest from Grandma's, but I'll see you around."

"Yeah, that'd be nice. Do you want to exchange numbers? I can let you know next time I'm here. Maybe we can grab coffee," Jessica suggested.

Angela patted her jeans. "I left my phone back at the house. If you want, just write down your phone number and leave it at the country store. I can get it later and text you."

Jessica didn't doubt that she had a phone but suspected that, given the strict nature of the belief system here, it was probably locked away in her house like a firearm and only used for important situations.

A group like this was anything but egalitarian. You had Prophet Isaiah on top, his brothers acting as elders, his favorite sons below him working as the enforcers, a favorite daughter or two being indulged and spoiled. Like Angela. For everyone else, it was hand-me-down sack dresses and statutory rape.

Angela made a beeline for a house on the other side of the park. Jessica watched her retreat, trying to figure out what information she'd been dispatched to retrieve.

It was possible Angela had intercepted her out of boredom. But there were no coincidences here.

She walked back to the municipal office. Chief Matthews was waiting outside, leaning on the railing where she first saw him.

"What'd the ex-chief say?" Jessica asked.

"Sorry, ma'am," Matthews said. "He said he doesn't recall anybody that fits that description."

They were trying to shut her down. Either they were afraid they had something to hide, or they knew they did.

Jessica shook her head. "Well, that's kind of weird, because a little while ago you were telling me there are so many Lehis and Sorayas and teenage boys that headed off for greener pastures that it'd be hard to know which one I was talking about. Now you're saying nobody meets that description."

"I apologize if I gave you a mistaken impression, ma'am."

"No, I'll be honest with you. I'm just bummed out that I missed the miracle."

Matthews gave her a bemused look. "I'm sorry, what miracle is that?"

"The resurrection of Chief Jeffords, because according to the newspapers, that man died three years ago. So how you talked to him is beyond my understanding."

"Ma'am, I'm sorry. I think you may have misunderstood me. I apologize if I miscommunicated to you," he said again.

Jessica could tell he was getting flustered, caught between a rock and a hard place. She had known back at the station that he was going to call Chief Jeffords. He failed to tell her who he'd really spoken to. Which was ridiculous, given the six-story phallus parked in the middle of the town.

"It's fine. I don't really need to deal with the middleman, do I? I think I should just go talk to Prophet Isaiah myself," Jessica said as she turned around and started walking briskly toward the Prophet's Tower.

Matthews was caught off guard, unsure how to react. "Ma'am!" he shouted.

Jessica kept going.

Matthews jogged beside her. "Pardon me, but you can't go there."

Jessica pointed at the Visitor Center. "There's a sign there that tells people to take a walk and enjoy the park."

"But, ma'am, you . . . you just can't," he stammered.

Jessica stopped and turned to him. "I think I'm within my rights here," she said, then continued walking.

"No, ma'am, you are not. This is trespassing."

Jessica pointed at the ground. "I thought this was a public park."

They were almost at the steps, and Matthews was sweating. "Miss, this is all church property. You are trespassing."

"I'm sorry, clarify something for me," Jessica said. "I see the badge and I see an American flag patch on one shoulder and the Idaho patch on the other. Do you work for the town of Brotherhood, or do you work for the church?" She now stood in front of the massive white wooden door. "Which is it?"

"I'm authorized by the church to enforce the town's rights, just as I would yours if you were a citizen of Brotherhood," he recited.

"Great," said Jessica as she started knocking on the door. "Let's see if Prophet Isaiah can clarify that for me."

"Ma'am, there's nobody there," Matthews said.

Jessica could see the security cameras aimed in all directions from the building, and the two trained right where she was standing. "Are you telling me God's not home?" She didn't let him answer. "Mr. Isaiah," she called loudly, "you need to know one of your own is about to commit a terrible act. And if you don't help me out, it will lead back here, whether it was your fault or not. And when the TV cameras show up, they can either be talking about how you helped or how you didn't."

"Ma'am, I don't want to have to arrest you," Matthews told her.

"Then don't. Tell your dad that the next time people come here, it's gonna be with battering rams. You may have fooled some of the people, but you haven't fooled everybody. It won't last."

She turned and walked toward her car, leaving Matthews standing by the door.

She counted her steps, trying to estimate how many she had to take before she could make a run for her vehicle. She'd reached the edge of the park near the path by the Visitor Center when she saw Jefferson come running out of the municipal building toward her.

"Oh shit," she muttered.

SCION

Jessica turned around. Matthews was jogging toward her too.

"Hold up. Hold up," he shouted.

Neither cop had drawn a weapon, but that didn't mean they didn't wish her harm. She was out in the open and they didn't want to risk a scene, and while there was only one tourist car nearby, other tourists might be watching.

Jefferson was still running and had put his hand to his hip where he had his handcuffs.

"It's cool, it's cool!" Matthews yelled.

Jessica turned her body sideways, ready to move in either direction. She had a gun tucked into the belt behind her back, but she wouldn't use it unless she absolutely had to.

"Prophet Isaiah says he'll speak with you!" Matthews shouted.

"What in the name of . . . ?" Jefferson came to an abrupt stop.

"Go back to the station," Matthews told him, then turned to Jessica.

"Ms. Blackwood, I apologize for my miscommunication. If you would follow me," he said, waving her over.

Jessica looked at the Prophet's Tower. The tall door she'd been pounding on a minute earlier was open. A gray-haired man in a black suit and tie stood outside, holding it open.

She recognized him as Elder Schilling, one of the leaders of Brotherhood.

The interior of the temple was dark, and she couldn't see well inside. Matthews was ready to lead her in, his head bowed respectfully.

"People know I'm here," Jessica told him.

"I wouldn't doubt that," Matthews replied.

"Ms. Blackwood, it's a pleasure to meet you," said Schilling as he greeted her by the door.

"Elder Schilling," she said, letting him know she knew who he was.

He responded with a curt smile. "This way," he said.

Her eyes adjusted to the interior. A large wooden staircase covered in a cerulean-blue carpet stood before her. Directly above was a chandelier hanging from the third story. The walls were wood with golden trim. On either side of the staircase were velvet ropes that looked like they led to a theater.

"Let's take the elevator. I don't think my knees are ready for the stairs right now." Schilling pointed to an ornate golden elevator. He pressed a button, and the doors opened.

Jessica stepped inside but kept her hand near her gun. She saw no buttons on the inside of the elevator.

"Are we going up or down?"

"Today, we're going up," Schilling said.

The doors closed with a soft chime, and the elevator began to ascend smoothly, the walls reflecting the golden trim in the dim light.

"Not a lot of visitors get to see the inside of the prophet's temple, let alone meet the prophet himself," Schilling remarked.

"Aren't I a lucky girl."

The elevator came to a stop. The doors opened.

The top floor was a wide-open space with wood floors and glass windows on all sides that let in natural light. At the center was a gold-trimmed dais, and in the middle of that was an old man sitting on a simple wooden chair.

Jessica could only speculate about the contrast between all this grandeur and the man at the center of it all, resting his ass in a chair from Cracker Barrel.

He stood up with the help of a cane as she entered.

He had the older face of the man she'd seen in online photos. While he wasn't a complete recluse, and visitors to Brotherhood had claimed to speak with him at the country store or in the park in the evening, Isaiah shunned publicity—which is highly advisable when you're rumored to have seventeen wives.

"I'll bring you a chair," Schilling said.

Isaiah waited for her to take her seat before he sat in his own.

These perverts sure like to make gestures of chivalry, Jessica thought. Would it be too much to hold a door open for a woman and not expect her to support child marriage?

Her eyes were drawn to a dark-blue curtain in the back sealing off part of the chamber. She wondered if it was only the three of them here . . .

"Ms. Blackwood, I believe you have questions about somebody we may know," said Isaiah. His voice was deep and smooth and didn't betray his age.

"I don't know how much you follow the news, but two young people were murdered and a third one nearly killed. The situation was peculiar, and while investigating the case, some names came up that led me here," she told him.

"And what would those names be?"

Jessica felt like telling him the same ones Matthews had already told him but decided not to be antagonistic. "Lehi and Soraya."

Isaiah made a small nod and looked over at Schilling, then back to Jessica.

She wasn't sure if she was going to be walking out of here like a breeze or with a gun to the old man's head and her hand around his chicken neck.

These people were a hard read.

Well, here goes . . .

"We believe the murderer was somebody who lived here around forty years ago and ran away or was kicked out. I don't really care about the details. And those names might have been his parents', his friends', I don't know. But we're reasonably sure that he was born and raised here. And I'm also pretty sure you have an idea who he is. And anything you can tell me would be very helpful."

Isaiah nodded. "I know exactly who you're talking about. His name is Lehi."

"What can you tell me about him?"

"Lehi is my nephew," Isaiah said. "He was very bright, very inquisitive, very passionate about belief. But he had different ideas."

"What kind of ideas?"

"I know you're not a fool, and you've probably learned something about us, or at least what people on the outside think about us."

"Not as much as I'd like to. But I think I know," she confirmed.

"Some of us are chosen because we have visions," Isaiah said. "I sit in this chair because of the things that I saw. Sometimes those visions are meant to test us, but also help us." He pointed at Elder Schilling. "His father sat in this chair before me. When he was forty years old, he looked up into the sky and heard a voice tell him that there was a great danger coming.

"He rang the church bell and told everyone to go into the shelters. Twenty minutes later, a tornado tore through here. It killed seventeen people in the town east of us and twenty-two people in the town west of us. Do you know how many people died in Brotherhood?"

"None, I'm guessing."

"I was a young man when that happened. I had questions about faith. I had questions about visions, and after that I understood what they meant," Isaiah explained. "You don't ask for them; you don't tell God, 'Give me a sign.' He chooses you. Some of us are selected; some of us are not. My Lehi very much wanted to have visions. He hoped to one day sit where I am sitting."

"But he didn't have visions."

Isaiah chuckled and nodded to Schilling, who made a small laugh. "Oh no, Lehi had visions. Every day, a new one. We used to call him Cry Wolf. He was determined to be an instrument of God, but he wasn't chosen."

"So he left."

"I wish it was that easy, but we had to ask him to leave," Isaiah said. "Lehi saw where I and the elders sat, and he felt great envy. But he didn't see himself as a shepherd. There was a cruelty about him."

"The man I'm looking for murdered two, maybe three people, and almost killed another. Do you think Lehi is capable of this?"

"Any man who mistakes his own voice for God's is capable of that and much worse," Isaiah affirmed.

"Was Lehi charismatic? Could you see others following him?" Jessica asked.

"The last we saw my Lehi, I wouldn't say that he had the skills to gather a flock, but charisma can develop late in our family, so who's to know what kind of man he became?"

Jessica could tell that Isaiah was dancing around something, not necessarily withholding, but trying to avoid.

"What was the vision he had that made you realize he had to leave?"

"I was warned you were a very astute woman." Isaiah smiled. "The last time I spoke to him, he had interrupted a meeting of the elders, held right here, and he stood almost where you are now," Isaiah told her, "pointed at me, and told everyone that they were fools, that he'd had a vision, and that it was his duty to see God's will be done."

"What was the vision?" Jessica asked again.

Isaiah's face turned serious. "He said he saw our temple in flames and me burning inside of it as a voice called out from the heavens, 'Kill thy false prophets. Suffer them not to live.'"

"I can see why that would get you voted off the island."

"And I should tell you something else," Isaiah said. "I had a vision of my own—that one day he would return, and there would be flames and great death. But I am relieved to know that's not going to come to pass."

"Great. Well, I need a description, photographs, and I need the names of anybody else from here that he might have stayed in contact with," she told them.

"I think we can help you with the photographs. As far as anybody he would have spoken to afterward," Isaiah said, "we excommunicated him completely."

"Yeah, well, just in case. Let me know who his friends were."

"Elder Schilling will see to it. Is there anything else we can do for you?"

"You can tell me what's under the temple."

Isaiah made a thin smile. "I don't think so."

As Schilling escorted Jessica to the elevator, she glanced back and caught Isaiah looking at the curtained-off section. He appeared to be nodding.

When she exited the building, Chief Matthews and his henchman Jefferson were nowhere in sight.

She kept looking over her shoulder because she felt like she was being watched—but caught no one.

Jessica waited until she was two miles out of the city limits before she pulled over and took a deep breath. When she checked her messages, there was already one waiting from Schilling. She immediately called Sloan.

"How'd it go?" Sloan asked over the speakerphone.

Jessica was looking in the rearview mirror, afraid she'd see police lights. "Spooky as hell. Next time, *you* go. I've had my fill of these cults."

"So we're back to calling them cults now?" Sloan replied.

"Give me a second. They just sent something about Lehi. Clearly this was already prepared," she explained.

Jessica reread the message because she was rattled when she read it the first time.

"They're cooperating," she said.

"That's good. You get my text about the guy who died in the sauna fire?" asked Sloan.

"Yeah, that jibes with what they told me about Lehi. He was too nutty even for them. I'm sending you a photograph of him when he was seventeen and a list of some of his friends from when he was here. A number of them no longer live in Brotherhood," she pointed out.

"I'll get this over to the FBI. I think we got him."

"I hope so. Tell Monroe or whoever to pressure one of the casinos to let them use the gray database," Jessica told her.

"What's that?"

"They have been keeping track of every person that gambled or worked in a casino, going back decades."

"Oh, for card cheats?" Sloan asked.

"That and other reasons. Point is, they have extensive records. If Lehi's been within fifty feet of any casino in Vegas, they'll have a photograph and know something about him."

Jessica hung up and checked her rearview mirror one more time. She couldn't quite place her anxiety. She realized that it wasn't Isaiah or his minions coming for her that had her spooked.

No, what was putting her on edge was the violence of Lehi's vision.

COUNTERINTELLIGENCE

Sloan McPherson was waiting in her rented SUV in the parking lot in front of the lounge at Henderson Executive Airport when Jessica came walking through the doors.

She set the computer that was sitting in her lap on the center console and stepped out into the sweltering heat. "Hey, Jessica!" she called, waving to her.

Jessica spotted her and climbed into the passenger side and placed her backpack in the rear. "What's the latest?"

"We ran the photo through the gray database, then sent it with the casino's results to the FBI. They came back with a match for the photo and a legal name change."

"I take it he doesn't go by Lehi anymore?"

"No, John Kaufman, and he's been living in the greater Las Vegas area for the last twenty years," Sloan replied.

"Doing what?"

"He's run through a couple different companies. The last one was vending machines," Sloan said.

"What's the status of the search?" Jessica inquired.

"It's a full-on manhunt. They took it seriously. They sent out an all-points bulletin with all the data. They've got police in front of his businesses and house. Check this out: He lived three miles away from the man cave up north."

"Why doesn't that surprise me?"

"They're working on getting a search warrant right now for his business and his home," Sloan said. "Of course, the problem is, given the bombing at the storage facility and the fire at the ranch, it's not like we're going to be rushing inside anytime soon. We're going to have to send in a bomb squad."

"That will take forever."

"Yeah, but the good news is he's on the run, not on the attack."

"Maybe. Are they sure he's not holed up inside?"

"No vehicles, so unless he was walking around Las Vegas, they don't think he's home, and they have the place surrounded."

"Did they know anything else besides vending machines? Because I don't think that's what he was doing."

"No, I think he got into the crypto thing, or rather found Alexis Weissnott and decided there was more money in that. There have also been a surprising number of robberies in the area in which people had their crypto wallets stolen at gunpoint and had to turn over keys. This has been going on for six years, so it's possible he's connected to that," Sloan explained.

"It's probably not a bright idea to brag on Instagram or Twitch about how much money you've made from selling people Ponzi schemes," Jessica noted.

"Yeah, that's part of it. Some of them aren't too eager to go to the feds because in the cases where they have, they've been told there's no chance of getting their property back and then asked questions about how they're paying their taxes."

"This crazy world, stealing zeros and ones . . ."

"I read your email, but what the hell happened up there?" Sloan asked.

"This Lehi, or John Kaufman, is a real piece of work for sure," Jessica said. "But Lord knows, if I'd grown up in that Looney Tunes town, I'd probably be just as crazy. I can only imagine the anxiety for a teenage kid there, wondering if on their seventeenth birthday they're going to be told they've got to get out. And don't get me started about what it's like for the women. It's not a good place."

"That bad?" Sloan asked.

"Yeah, the worst part of it is I realized something," Jessica continued. "It's a town where the ratio of women to men is off the charts."

"Ugh. How often do the women get out?" Sloan asked.

"A few here and there, but not as much as the men."

"What do they say about Lehi?"

"I spoke to Prophet Isaiah himself. He referred to Lehi as his nephew, but at least once or twice, he referred to him as 'my Lehi.' I have a feeling . . ."

"That Prophet Isaiah is Lehi's father?"

"I wouldn't be shocked. That old bastard's probably got sixty or seventy kids."

"Jesus Christ."

"According to the prophet—who I wouldn't consider the most reliable witness—his son had his eye on the throne and was not subtle about it."

"So that's why they kicked him out," Sloan said.

"That, and he apparently interrupted a meeting of the elders to tell them about his prophetic vision, which involved their entire tower burning to the ground and Prophet Isaiah dying with it."

"Okay . . . So help me spell this out," Sloan said. "Lehi, born into the worst version of *The Handmaid's Tale*, gets too big for his britches, makes some threats, talks big. They tell him to leave. He goes on to change his name legally about three years later.

"After that, we can't find anything for twenty years. Then he pops up in Las Vegas, first working at a welding company, then doing AC repair work, and finally he saved up enough money to buy a vending machine business. But that's only what the business permits and the driver's licenses tell us. Who was he, really? Who *is* he?"

"That's the mystery," Jessica agreed.

"Well, let's look at what else we know. Somewhere along the way, he developed a personality, became somewhat charismatic—at least enough for Nia, Dustin, and Michael Radley to fall under his spell. Why them? Why YouTubers, streamers, and influencers?" Sloan asked aloud.

"I asked Isaiah if Lehi was charismatic, and I got kind of a neutral answer," Jessica said. "But we could chalk that up to jealousy. Lehi was certainly persuasive enough to get those kids into his cult."

"Makes you wonder why he didn't just buy a trailer park somewhere and set up shop like old Dad," Sloan remarked.

"Some people are charismatic from afar but fall apart up close. Other people are the opposite. Cult leaders often have an inverse kind of charisma. L. Ron Hubbard sounds like he'd be a redheaded Cary Grant. But when you see him in recordings, he's a homely guy with nicotine-stained teeth. Lehi might be persuasive one-on-one, but not from the pulpit," Jessica replied.

"Or not on TikTok," Sloan added. "Maybe he was hoping Dustin and the others would rub off on him? Like a church adding a rock band."

"Yeah, but when the rock band is more popular than the priest, you have a problem. Maybe, but I don't know," Jessica said. "Perhaps we're reading too much into this. He ran from Brotherhood."

"Yeah, hold on a second. You made a comment about your mom going back to the things she knew in order to get away from them. As I understand it, groups like this have their guy at the top, but then they have their elders, right?" Sloan said.

"Yeah, Prophet Isaiah was the leader, but the visible work of the Brotherhood was done by a small group of men—more than likely his brothers or half brothers."

"So that's Lehi's organizational model. You have a strong leader at the top, who kind of sits in the shadows, then a group of lieutenants publicly growing the church."

"I hadn't thought about it that way," said Jessica. "It kind of makes sense: Lehi grew up with a model, but he wanted to change it. So he created the kind of organization he wanted."

"Yeah, but witches, spells, and necromancy? That doesn't feel very LDS," Sloan remarked.

"Actually, it's very Mormon. Joseph Smith, Brigham Young—they believed in magic, amulets, scrying, astrology, all of that. While the main Mormon church gave that up around the same time as bigamy, that doesn't mean everybody else did. I don't know what they practice over in Brotherhood. Such things wouldn't surprise me."

"So he wanted to turn Dustin and the others into his PR team?" asked Sloan. "But none of them were overtly religious in their live streaming—as far as we saw."

"Of course not. The religious turn would have the most dramatic effect if it happened later," said Jessica.

"Later than what?" asked Sloan.

"That's the big question."

"I think I understand why he killed them like witches, but I don't know why he killed them in the first place," Sloan said.

"He might have cultivated them for outreach, then found he had a mutiny on his hands. Perhaps he told them the real inner secrets, and it turned out to be a guy with a rubber mask on and a smoke machine, and they weren't impressed. Could be any number of reasons, but I believe he thinks his visions are real. I believe he thinks he's acting on behalf of God, and when you tell God no, you're not forgiven." Jessica shrugged.

"Maybe it was kind of hard to take seriously a demigod whose day job was shoving Twix bars and Sour Patch Kids into vending machines," Sloan joked.

"Jesus was a carpenter, but I get your point. Remember the secrecy. He may have kept that part of his life completely away from them. There was the ranch house, which is different from where he lived—a place where he's at his most magnetic."

"He's wearing Dockers by day and Dolce&Gabbana at night."

Jessica laughed. "Maybe, but I will tell you this from my brief experience at the Prophet's Tower in the town of Brotherhood: They are all about presentation and intimidation via subtle psychology. He grew up around that; he understood it. The AI version of Nia was in love with him," she pointed out.

"And he's also rich. I forget that he's got all that crypto. Do you think he's even still in town?" Sloan asked.

"It wouldn't surprise me. We don't know if there's anybody else on his kill list, and guys like that think they're invulnerable, which also means that they don't go down easy."

"Speaking of the slightly delusional, what's the latest with Robert Ratke?" Jessica asked.

"He is probably your number one fan right now because they were in the process of interrogating him when you sent the confirmation on Lehi's identity," Sloan said. "You called it."

"I'm pretty sure he's somebody I do not want doing me any favors." Jessica thought something over. "Who's handling questioning him?"

"Monroe, I believe. Why?"

"We should text her and ask if Ratke knows a John Kaufman."

"Ah, damn, I didn't think of that." Sloan thought for a second. "I was at the office earlier, and I don't have a lot of confidence in that operation . . . Hmm."

"Spit it out, McPherson," Jessica urged.

"I think I know a way we can catch him—at least get him to show up somewhere. The rest of it, we're going to have to use your tricky brain to figure out. But you made a copy of Reggie's phone, right? Which means you could make calls from it," she said.

"Yeah, but there are two problems," Jessica said. "Number one, we don't know how to get hold of Kaufman. Second, Reggie doesn't know him, only *of* him. Kaufman would smell a trap right away."

"Aha," Sloan said, holding a finger in the air. "This is what we like to call in my family one-dimensional tic-tac-toe."

"Sounds simple," Jessica said.

"Can you check your clone of Reggie's phone to see if Kaufman's number is in there?"

Jessica reached in the back and pulled out her black box, flipped over a panel, and started typing on the screen. "Huh. What do you know?" she said, showing it to Sloan.

> John Kaufman (crypto dude)

"That sounds like Reggie-speak for our guy," Sloan said.

"I think we might be able to pull this off," Jessica agreed.

"So what do you do? Use a voice changer and have a conversation?"

Jessica held up her device. "I can make a phone call from this and go straight to voicemail and play an AI version of Reggie's voice saying whatever we want."

"But how do you make it compelling to Kaufman? I don't think the two are buddies."

"I'm going to leave a message in Reggie's voice where he's yelling at some friend—not John Kaufman—about why he hasn't been picked up," Jessica explained.

"And Kaufman will either ignore it, send somebody else, or show up in person," Sloan said.

"Maybe. It's a stretch. But Kaufman might think Reggie is too high out of his mind to realize he made a potentially fatal mistake. The smart thing would be to ignore it."

"But Lehi thinks he's invulnerable, on a mission from God."

"Yeah, that's the thing you have to think about," Jessica said. "He may be crazy, but he's not stupid. We'll have to be careful."

RICOCHET

Agent Monroe looked at the dark entrance to the tunnel and murmured, "Jesus Christ."

The sun had set, and the only illumination came from a flickering streetlight.

"Don't worry, it gets worse," Sloan said as she shifted a duffel bag over her shoulder.

"You couldn't get anybody else to come?" Jessica said.

"Special Agent in Charge Nowitz thought it was a stupid idea and gave the chance of success one in a trillion," Monroe said with a shrug. "He's a numbers guy."

"You know, it was my first day on the job as a police officer that I realized I was a police officer," Sloan told her as they headed into the tunnel.

"I would have thought you'd learn that on the first day of police academy."

Jessica laughed. "I know what she means."

"Thank you, Blackwood. My point is that we grew up conditioned: When you're in trouble, you call for help, but then when you become a cop you realize you *are* the help."

"Have you ever heard of backup?" Monroe asked.

"That's the funny part about it," Sloan said. "You're our backup. Who's yours?"

"Ah, I see," Monroe replied.

"We need to move a little bit faster because if he does show up, it's gonna happen sooner than later," Jessica urged.

"And what about the civilians?" Monroe asked.

"Our friend who looks after them says they're out shoplifting, buying drugs, and stealing from tourists right now," Jessica said. "You know, working."

They entered the tunnel, and Sloan used a one million–candlepower flashlight to illuminate the interior.

There was less trash and filth than in the tunnel where they'd found Reggie.

"This is the outer suburbs for tunnel people, so it doesn't get used as much," Jessica explained.

"Good to know the next time my husband's parents are in town and I need to put them up somewhere," Monroe remarked.

Jessica froze and held her finger to her lips with one hand. With the other, she reached out and flicked the light off on Sloan's flashlight.

"Footsteps," Jessica whispered.

"How far away?" Sloan asked quietly.

"On the sidewalk over the entrance," Jessica said.

Sloan knew Jessica had all kinds of tricks that bordered on the supernatural. She'd have to ask her how she'd acquired echolocation some other time.

"Three meters ahead and to your right, there's a side tunnel. Go wait there," Jessica said as she slid the duffel bag off Sloan's shoulder.

"I can't see shit," whispered Monroe. "Your fucking flashlight blinded me."

"Sorry," Sloan replied as she grabbed the other woman by the arm and pulled her to the side tunnel. "Just stay close."

"What about her?" Monroe asked.

"She's at home here," Sloan assured her.

Sloan could hear the muffled sounds of Jessica opening the duffel bag and pulling out items.

After they had formulated the rough sketch of their idiotic plan, Jessica had called her father to pick his brain for a few minutes. They then drove to a theatrical supply store, where the owner knew Jessica and her family. She let Jessica have the run of the warehouse as she sprinted around grabbing various items and tossing them into a duffel bag.

Sloan heard a metal pipe hitting the ground near Jessica, followed by her quietly cursing. While it was comforting to be reminded that her friend was human, this wasn't the time for that.

Jessica's movements stopped. Sloan cocked her head to listen, like a cat. A shuffling sound came next—like sliding down a concrete drainage ditch.

"Someone's coming," Sloan whispered to Monroe.

"I hope it's fast, because I think a spider is crawling across my foot," she responded.

"You hope it's a spider."

"What the hell is that supposed to mean?"

"Sorry. How far away is backup if we need it?"

"Not long. We've got every available officer on the street right now looking for Kaufman," Monroe said.

"Good to know."

"Whatever reassuring is, you're not it," Monroe whispered.

Sloan pushed her ear closer to the edge of the wall. She could hear Jessica moving again, but this time much more quietly. She could also hear the heavy footsteps of someone approaching.

Slowly, she pushed her head out to take a look.

The end of the tunnel was a tiny postage stamp–size yellow glow, in the middle of which Sloan could make out the silhouette of a person standing in the entrance.

Assuming it was Kaufman, every impulse in his body must have been screaming: *It's a trap!* In a moment, he would almost certainly turn on a flashlight so he didn't stumble his way through the tunnel.

That's assuming he chose to enter.

The sound of faint footsteps on gravel came from Jessica's position. They then faded.

Jessica's voice spoke softly behind Sloan's right ear. "I'm right here."

"Warn a person next time," whispered Monroe. "I almost screamed."

"Everybody stay put. I think he's wearing night vision," Jessica said.

"Is that going to screw things up?" Sloan whispered back.

"I hope not," Jessica murmured.

Sloan felt a delicate touch on her shoulder as Jessica walked toward the center of the side tunnel.

The footsteps grew louder. It was either a man or a very stocky woman, Sloan decided.

The footsteps stopped.

Sloan saw Jessica with her back against the opposite wall of the tunnel now. She was staring at some point in the distance.

"Reggie, it's John. I got your message. Are you there?" Kaufman called into the dark.

Sloan could see that Jessica was holding her phone behind her back and tapping the screen.

"John, we both know this is a trap. Can we talk?" Jessica asked.

"The balls on this woman," Monroe said under her breath.

Sloan heard the man's feet swiveling and walking away.

"There are two snipers waiting for you at the entrance," Jessica called. "You can talk to me or take your chances with them."

The footsteps stopped. Jessica moved from the wall to the center of the side tunnel.

"I can see you like it's daylight," Kaufman said.

"I know," Jessica replied, holding her hands up. After a brief silence, she said, "Can you put the gun down for a moment?"

Sloan heard a flick, and then a green laser dot appeared in the center of Jessica's chest. If only she could see where Kaufman was standing.

Sloan felt Monroe start to get up. She put her hand on her arm and held her down. "Let her handle it," she whispered.

"If my finger moves another millimeter, you're dead. How does that make you feel?" Kaufman asked.

"I feel nothing," Jessica said.

"And why is that?"

"Because I don't think this was part of your vision."

"Who told you about those?" Kaufman asked, a hint of curiosity in his voice.

"Your father did. This morning."

Sloan watched as the green dot wavered.

"My father? What do you know about him?"

"Not much, but he told me a lot about you."

"Really?"

"I saw what Brotherhood is like. I stood in the room where you told him about your vision."

"And what did he say?" Kaufman asked, his voice hesitant.

"He thought you were crazy."

"Yeah, well, he's the one sitting inside that white prison."

"And where do you think you're going to end up?"

"That's for God to decide."

"You haven't seen it yet, have you?"

"I haven't had that vision yet," Kaufman confirmed.

"Why don't you set your gun down and surrender? God can still come to you," Jessica suggested.

"I don't see anything around you," Kaufman said, confused.

"I get that."

"You're like a void."

"We can go talk about it somewhere else."

"I don't like it down here either. You know, when I first came to Las Vegas, I used to come down here to these tunnels to try to help these people."

"That was kind of you."

Kaufman laughed, but the gun didn't move. "You have a gift like mine, lady, that's for sure. You're always calculating the right thing to say."

"I could see that your father had that too."

"Some of us want to speak, and some of us want to be spoken to," he said.

"Why don't you set the gun down."

"Do you know why I stopped preaching down here?" he asked.

Sloan speculated that the smell probably played some role.

"Because these people were already in hell," Jessica said.

"Yes," Kaufman said after a long silence.

"This is going on too long," Monroe whispered.

"I can see the shadows of your friends moving," Kaufman said.

Sloan realized that with the night vision, things looked completely different. The green dot moved from Jessica's chest to her forehead.

"Half a millimeter," Kaufman said.

He started to walk toward Jessica. Although Jessica had given Sloan firm instructions, it was taking all her energy not to leap into the tunnel and start firing at him.

Kaufman stepped a foot closer, almost within arm's reach of Jessica. Then came a flash of brilliant light, and Jessica was gone. Sloan's eyes adjusted, and she could see her standing behind the man with her gun pointed at the back of his head.

He dropped his gun, a broad smile on his face as he whispered, "A fucking miracle."

He put his hands behind his head and got down on his knees.

A flash of chrome, then Jessica clapped his wrists into handcuffs faster than Sloan could blink.

Monroe leaped to her feet to help Jessica.

"Watch out," Jessica warned her.

Sloan turned on her spotlight, catching the entire scene in bright blue light.

Jessica pushed Kaufman flat on his chest. His head was turned to the side as he stared straight at the large portable mirror angled toward the side tunnel.

"Perfect," he whispered.

AFTERMATH

Jessica and Sloan were in a conference room filled with FBI agents and other law enforcement as they watched a screen showing Kaufman confessing to everything inside an interrogation room located at a different part of the building.

"Why was Dustin encased in salt? Weren't you all paying attention? Haven't you studied your Bible? Lot's wife," Kaufman said. "She was instructed by God not to turn back and look at Sodom, but she did. She couldn't resist. Dustin kept falling back into his temptations. Sure, we argued over biblical interpretations, but that's fine. I loved a good debate. Ultimately, he betrayed himself, and he betrayed me."

Nowitz, the agent now in charge of the investigation, asked, "And you did this by yourself?"

"I didn't do anything. God did it."

"God and the two tons of laboratory-grade salt you had delivered to a warehouse across from where your storage unit was," Nowitz pointed out.

"The salt had to come from somewhere."

"And how did Dustin's body end up in Sheldon Wildlife Refuge?" Nowitz asked.

Kaufman looked up to the ceiling as if staring into the heavens. "You'll have to ask God that."

"This fucking guy," Sloan growled.

"Is this going to be his entire shtick?" asked Agent Running Deer. "Admit to everything, but say it was done by God?"

"What a crock of horseshit," another agent said. "He is the worst actor ever. Zero stars."

"I don't think he's acting. I mean, he knows he's bullshitting, but he genuinely believes that these were acts of God," said Jessica. "The technical connection to him—and he will *not* say this—is that he's the hand of God."

"Well, he's going to feel the wrath of God soon. I think we have enough evidence to tie him to all the murders and bombings," Monroe said.

Jessica nodded. "We'll see."

"What, you don't think so?"

"Maybe. I'm just not sure we know what his whole vision is."

"For all we know, his plan is to get us to lock him up with nine hundred poor sons of bitches that are going to have to listen to him all day long," Monroe joked.

"My money says he gets shivved before first light on day one," Running Deer predicted.

"Look at Agent Balvin over there," said Jessica.

"What about him?" Running Deer asked.

"He hasn't looked at Nowitz once. He can't figure out Kaufman's deal."

"I don't think any of us have figured out Kaufman's deal," Running Deer said.

"As much as we hate to admit it, he's charismatic in the way he speaks. He holds your interest," Jessica pointed out.

"And what about Nia Stratos?" Nowitz asked Kaufman.

"Poor Nia," Kaufman said. "Poor, poor Nia. Her magic was powerful—really powerful—but it had to be contained."

"By drowning her," Nowitz said.

"No, it's the silver chains that matter," Kaufman said. "They bind you. If you put a witch underwater, bound in silver chains, then that contains the forces they brought into themselves." He turned to Agent Balvin. "That's the thing. People forget, magic doesn't come from us. It either comes from Him or the guy below, and sadly for Nia, it wasn't coming from the man upstairs."

Jessica noticed how Kaufman adapted his speaking style to whoever was around him. At the moment, he seemed to be channeling the Dude from *The Big Lebowski*, trying to make himself likable, affable, but deeply spiritual: a surfer who saw the face of God.

"Seriously, this guy is like all the worst youth ministers I ever had as a teenager. It's why I married a Jewish girl," Running Deer told the others.

"But that's just it. You've seen this shtick before; other people haven't. If it's the first time you've heard it, it can be compelling," Jessica explained.

Sloan felt that she was out of her depth trying to understand the motivations of the religiously inclined, but a question gnawed at the back of her mind, so she leaned in and asked, "Why is he talking?"

"I don't know," said Jessica. "He's trying to tap-dance around the fact that he did it. He's taking credit, but not giving enough details for conviction. But he's got to know that's not going to matter."

"I understand your father is quite an impressive religious figure. Do you have a following of your own?" Nowitz asked.

"That's one way to put it. 'Impressive religious figure.' What was the thing they said when that Islamic extremist terrorist died? 'An austere religious scholar'? That describes my father too. A following? No, that's not for me. I couldn't get away from there fast enough, but spirituality is part of everyone. I'll talk to anybody who wants to know, and a few that don't," Kaufman said, agreeably.

"All right, did he act alone or not? What do you think, Blackwood? You're the expert," Running Deer said.

"I don't know. One person can pull it off, but that doesn't mean that one person did it," Jessica said.

"Have you guys made any progress with any of his contacts or friends?" Sloan asked.

"Nope. Shocker—he was a loner who kept to himself," Running Deer said.

"But clearly he wasn't. He had a very deep and emotional relationship with three famous influencers. There's a side to him that he's kept concealed," Jessica remarked.

"The call logs, the surveillance tapes—it's all in the other room if you want to have a look at it. Right now, I think this conviction's gonna come from the lab," Running Deer said.

"Or he just keeps his mouth running and slips up," Monroe added.

Running Deer checked a message on her phone. "We found an old-school camcorder in his car. Forensics is running it now, getting a transcript."

"Did they look at the tape?" asked Sloan.

"Just a few minutes. They only just found it. Apparently, he was running through lines or something . . . talking to the camera."

"He was practicing for his big moment," Jessica observed.

Jessica tuned out the words coming from Kaufman's mouth and focused on his body language. Initially, she had thought he was performing to the other agent in the room, but now she realized he had shifted his position as much as he could with his hands cuffed to the table to make sure the camera saw him. He knew he was being watched and recorded. She wondered if his presentation was for now or posterity.

"There's gotta be other people involved, right?" Sloan asked.

"I'm happy to go dig through the records in the other room, because I think I've had enough of him," Jessica said.

They excused themselves and went into an adjoining conference room filled with cardboard boxes containing binders of printouts, thumb drives, and all the other evidence the FBI had been collecting during the investigation.

Sloan frowned. "I hate this part of the job."

"Could I make it better for you by tossing some of this evidence into a swimming pool and letting you dive for it?"

"You might . . ." Sloan began thumbing through a binder filled with witness testimony.

Suddenly, Jessica looked up and over to the conference room. "That fucker's stalling."

"Stalling for what? Danny Ocean to pull a heist? A rescue team to save his ass?"

"I don't think he wants to be rescued. I think he is electrified about the idea of some kind of televised trial," Jessica said.

"Seems like a dumb way to achieve stardom."

"From our point of view, sure, but you click on your television and it's nothing but documentaries and reenactments of famous criminals. Jeffrey Dahmer's a goddamn franchise." She shook her head.

"I didn't think about it like that," Sloan admitted.

"The Tiger King got to star in his own documentary via a video call from jail. We talk about the lines between real life and fiction being blurred; the lines between celebrity and infamy don't exist anymore. If this guy doesn't go to the electric chair—which he probably won't—he's going to be around forever." The anger in her voice ramped up. "You don't think he'll shut up now? It's never gonna end. Even guys like Ted Bundy, who were electrocuted long before this current fascination with criminals, don't go away. Oh, look, we found some audiotapes of him talking about stuff. Oh, here's something new to report on. I mean, people like the Menendez brothers get treated like political prisoners. And they point-blank murdered their parents," she said, fuming. She glanced at the other conference room. "We hear a bullshitter, but other people, they're going to hear truth."

Slumped forward, her arms resting on the back of a chair, Sloan said, "I hear you. How can we stop this guy from getting his pulpit?"

Jessica dropped a file back into the box. "Is this really his whole plan? Is this how he planned to go out? Some revenge killings? No, no! There's more; he's got to have accomplices," she concluded.

"The FBI couldn't care less about that," Sloan said.

"Hold on a second . . . Elder Schilling sent me that list of names."

"People Kaufman knew when he was in Brotherhood?"

"Yeah, there are ten of them."

"They all left too?"

"Or were kicked out," Jessica said.

"Do we want to look through these files and see if any of them pop up here? I could ask if they have an electronic index," Sloan suggested.

"No, we can do it this way. I wish I'd thought of it earlier," Jessica said as she held up her phone and showed Sloan the Nia Stratos avatar app.

"Nia, tell me about Hiram Taylor," Jessica said.

"I'm sorry, I can't talk about REDACTED," Nia's avatar said.

Sloan's eyes lit up. "Redacted" didn't mean that the AI avatar didn't know. It meant that specific name had been excluded.

"How about Joseph Tanner?" Jessica asked.

"I apologize, but I can't talk about REDACTED," the avatar said.

Sloan ran into the other room and grabbed Monroe and dragged her into the evidence room.

Of the names on Schilling's list, Nia's avatar refused to talk about three of them: Hiram Taylor, Joseph Tanner, and Nephi Jensen.

Two of the men lived in Las Vegas. One lived outside of Reno, Nevada.

"What does this mean?" asked Monroe.

"While that asshole's bloviating for time," Sloan told her, "his three buddies are running around doing God-knows-what."

CON

Jessica, Sloan, and Monroe returned to the conference room where the rest of the investigators were watching Kaufman's interrogation. Monroe had texted Nowitz some questions to ask.

"How would you describe your relationship to Nephi Jensen?" Nowitz asked.

Jessica and Monroe had carefully crafted the question to not include any information about how they knew the name. They wanted Kaufman to think it was entirely possible that Jensen had been apprehended and was in a nearby room like this one.

In some situations, this could create a prisoner's dilemma, where two suspects who work together fear that the other one might try to implicate them. This often leads to admissions of guilt but phrased in such a way that the other person is largely responsible.

But Jessica and Sloan knew that Kaufman wouldn't fall for a simple ruse. What they wanted to see was his reaction.

Did it catch him off guard? Did he change the topic? Did he hesitate? These would all be signs that he wasn't anticipating where the questioning had gone. He had the disadvantage of not knowing how much they knew. Regardless of whether he thought they were questioning Nephi Jensen, denying knowing who he was could reveal him as a liar.

"Well, man, that's a name from a long time ago. I grew up with a guy named Nephi Jensen," Kaufman said after a moment.

"Took too long; that's a tell," Sloan noted.

"Yeah, but he knows I spoke to his father. He thinks he's safe right now," Jessica said.

"Let's see how he reacts to the next question," Monroe said.

"How about Hiram Taylor and Joseph Tanner? Do you recall them?" Nowitz asked.

Kaufman's face froze for half a moment. His eyes darted from Nowitz to the camera, then quickly back to his interrogator.

"Rabbit. That's a trapped rabbit if I've ever seen one," Sloan said.

"Who are those people?" asked Agent Running Deer from the other end of the table.

"We pulled those names from a confidential informant. We think they're accomplices," Jessica told her.

"Accomplices to the murders?" asked Running Deer.

"We don't know."

"Are you going to keep naming everybody I went to middle school with? Do you want to just get out a yearbook and have me circle names?" Kaufman asked.

"I'm pretty sure he did not go to middle school, and he did not have a yearbook," Jessica said.

"I imagine he spent a lot of time trying to figure out how to act like a normal guy and not some dude raised on a commune," Sloan added.

"Tell me something, Agent Nowitz: Does God ever speak to you?" Kaufman asked.

"All right, he's decided to flip the whole conversation away from himself because he's not comfortable. We need to figure out where his friends are and what they're up to," said Jessica.

"I just sent a text message; we're gonna have them picked up," Monroe replied.

"That's assuming they're at home or work and not out doing God's work for Kaufman," Sloan said.

"Yeah . . . Come with me," Jessica told her.

They followed her back to the records room. Jessica started riffling through boxes.

"Where are the drives with the surveillance videos?" Jessica asked.

"Over here," Monroe said, pointing to two boxes containing hard drives and DVDs.

Sloan pulled a laptop from her bag and pushed aside a stack of folders to make room. "Where do you want to begin?"

Jessica crossed her arms and backed into a corner of the room. "What has he told us?" she pondered. "What is he capable of?"

"Isaiah said he had visions of fire," Monroe offered.

"He blew up his storage unit and torched the ranch. Clearly, he has access to explosives and incendiary devices," Sloan added.

"We need to make a list of anybody we think he's been in contact with and warn them," Jessica stated.

"Places of work, companies he's dealt with?" Sloan asked.

"All of it. Not just here. California, Idaho; we need to tell the folks in Brotherhood too. They should be on the lookout."

"I'm on it. Let me reach out to Vera Pinellas. She's been coordinating with local agencies," Monroe said.

"This is a big town for conventions, and I've got a list here. There're at least two dozen going on right now," Sloan said, looking up from her laptop.

"Do any stand out?" Jessica asked.

"Let me take a look. We've got a convention for journalists. There's something called You Con, which is a convention for live streamers. Shit. That might be of interest. Ditto Nevada Ministries. I don't think the American Dental Technology Group is going to be a target, but

God, I don't know. And that's even assuming he wants specific targets. It could just be a body-count thing."

"Lord, telling the police in Vegas to be on the lookout for anybody suspicious is like trying to spot a drunk at Mardi Gras," Monroe remarked.

Jessica looked at the pile of hard drives. "Hold on. Let's just focus on any security camera footage from near the ranch." She pulled a black box from under a pile and handed it to Sloan. "Plug this in," she instructed.

Agent Running Deer poked her head into the room. "You guys should know, he's asked what time it was twice now."

"Damn it," Jessica said. "How's that coming?" she asked Sloan.

"It's hooked up. There's like twelve different folders in here. What are we looking for?"

"What time did we show up at the warehouse where the salt delivery was made?" Jessica asked.

"That was around 2:40 p.m.," Monroe replied.

"What footage do we have of the highway leading from the ranch back toward Las Vegas?" Jessica asked.

"We've got a gas station camera. It can't pick up license plates, but it can spot the make and model of cars," Sloan said.

Jessica walked over to where Sloan was sitting and leaned in to stare at the screen.

The gas station camera's point of view showed the pumps in the lower half of the screen and the highway at the top. Cars drove by but were cut off approximately two meters from the ground.

"I'm going to run this at 5x speed so it's slow enough," Sloan said.

It wasn't a well-trafficked route, but there was a steady cadence when Sloan sped it up. They saw a tractor trailer, a minivan, and two pickup trucks speed by to the east for Las Vegas and an empty car hauler heading west.

A fire truck flew by the camera, heading west toward the ranch.

"That would have been when the neighbors called to report the fire," Sloan remarked.

"All we got is a bunch of random cars," Monroe said.

"Play it again," Jessica urged.

Sloan scrolled back to the time stamp and let the video play, this time at only 2x speed. She paused on each vehicle.

They studied each frame, but there wasn't enough to see anything other than the general types of cars and trucks.

Monroe pointed to another box. "Do we want to look somewhere else?"

"You've been all over the footage that you gathered from the storage unit explosion, right?" Jessica asked.

"We tracked everything down," Monroe replied. "I don't know if that's going to be much help. That explosive charge could have been set up a long time ago, and we still haven't done a real sweep of the area for any of his hidden cameras. I think the ranch caught him by surprise."

"Are we making an assumption here?" Jessica asked.

"Let's go back to before we showed up at the warehouse and watch from that time on," Sloan suggested.

"Do you think something else spooked him?" Monroe asked.

"Maybe," Jessica said.

Sloan started the video two hours earlier and let it play.

A new collection of random vehicles passed by the camera: tractor trailers, personal vehicles, a cable van.

"I don't even know what we would do if—" Monroe began.

"Shut up. I'm sorry . . . but hold on," Sloan said as she navigated back to a certain frame.

A white utility van was heading east. It was nondescript, other than a partial red logo barely visible in the frame.

"It's a van, but . . ." Monroe began.

"Hold on," Sloan said impatiently.

Her fingers tapped on the keyboard. A new frame showed up. This time, the van was at the right edge of the screen.

"We can't see the logo, but we can do a search," Monroe suggested.

"No, you don't understand," Sloan said, tapping her keyboard again. The van was back to the left edge of the screen.

"What am I not seeing?" Monroe asked. "We still can't make out the logo, and I don't know why that van is any more suspicious than any of the other vehicles that we saw driving past."

"It's not the same van," Jessica said in a low voice. "Check the time stamps."

"Look," said Sloan as she slowly went through the timeline at each point one of the vans drove by.

"Oh," said Monroe. "When was this?"

"Twenty-five minutes before we showed up at the warehouse," Sloan said.

"All right, we can start looking through logos and see if we can find who owns those vans," Monroe suggested.

Jessica snapped her fingers as she thought of something. "Sloan, the guy that got burned alive in the sauna—they said he sold off his contracting company, right? What was his name? Alexis Weissnott, was it? What was the name of the company?"

"Mesa Surveillance. Oh damn! All the resort properties use a security system where only authorized vehicles are allowed in," Sloan said.

"The convention centers use that system too!" Monroe exclaimed.

Jessica bolted out the door and ran to the other conference room. "Everybody, get out your phones now!"

EXIT ROUTE

Sloan and Jessica were sitting on desks, along with the rest of the investigators in the FBI bullpen, watching the television monitors that had been dragged in to show the situation.

The only sounds were the ongoing narration from a reporter aboard a television news helicopter hovering over the Las Vegas Strip and the radio chatter of the bomb-disposal technicians working across the city as they tried to defuse the bombs.

Jessica was both sad and grateful that Las Vegas had been designated a high terrorism threat locale. Law enforcement here had extensive training and multiple teams in place to handle situations like this.

It had not been difficult to find three matching vans using Vegas's many live-traffic cameras. The only problem was, one of the vans was already three stories underground: at the Avenue, Las Vegas's tallest hotel.

The second van was found inside a parking garage adjacent to the Cube, a massive concert venue covered in the world's largest electronic sign.

The third was spotted driving down Las Vegas Boulevard toward the densest part of the Strip.

The quick-thinking response team managed to distract the driver of the third van by staging a collision of an ambulance with an unmarked police car in the middle of the intersection.

This gave plainclothes policemen enough time to start pulling people out of vehicles behind the van while two uniformed officers at the front of the intersection waved the cars through and around the accident, making it appear as if they were trying to ease the traffic jam.

When it was the van's turn to move, the police officer held his hand up. The other officer said something to him, engaging the first cop in an argument. The two men got quite animated—a little too Improv 101 for Jessica's taste—but the act did its job. All eyes were on the uniformed officers, including those of the van driver.

"Remarkable," Sloan whispered.

"That's their undercover SWAT team," Monroe pointed out. "They've been training with federal agencies for several years now on these kinds of situations."

"Things have changed a bit since I was a cop," Jessica remarked.

"The crazy ironic thing is, one of the training facilities is that old Mormon cult ranch in Texas that the government seized," Monroe said. "It's a whole town they use for practicing these situations."

"Speaking of which, any word from Brotherhood?" Jessica asked.

"They got the notice; they've set up a perimeter," Monroe told her.

"I just hope it's only these three vans."

"I hope they get everybody out," Monroe said.

The camera operator aboard the news helicopter panned toward the throngs of people being evacuated from the hotels and into the side streets of the Las Vegas Strip. The plan was to clear all the large buildings and disperse the public as widely as possible. Internationally, there had been an alarming increase in situations where terrorists planted backup explosives at evacuation locations, in some cases creating even more casualties than if people had remained inside the targeted venue. One kilogram of explosives can do more damage in a tightly packed tunnel of people than in a wide-open space.

The helicopter camera operator panned back to the staged drama at the intersection. The van was still being held up by the SWAT team member disguised as a traffic cop.

"The driver has to know what's going on, doesn't he?" Sloan asked.

"I think he's waiting to see what they're going to do next," Monroe said. "What else can he do?"

"The radius is cleared," called out somebody from the back of the room listening in on a scrambled police frequency.

The SWAT officer suddenly drew his gun and aimed it at the driver's side of the windshield, his mouth opening in a yell.

The driver floored the vehicle, heading straight at him.

The police officer started firing rounds into the window. Bullets pelted the van from other angles from hidden SWAT snipers.

As the van roared into the intersection, a fire truck flew out of nowhere from a side street, slammed into the van, and pushed it through a chain-link fence and into a construction area.

The reporter aboard the helicopter lost all professional composure and started screaming, "Run, run, run!" to the firefighter who'd rammed the fire truck into the van.

A figure leaped from the fire truck, landed on the dirt, sprinted away, and jumped into the back of an armored van that was already in the lot.

Jessica noticed that vehicle for the first time. "They really planned this out."

"They do now. Terrorism's bad for business," Monroe told her.

The camera focused on the bullet-ridden van, which was wedged between the fire truck and a pile of concrete blocks.

An instant later, it was a black cloud. A low roar could be heard over the reporter's microphone, and the camera shuddered as the sonic wave hit.

"The other two just blew," somebody said from the back. The open radio channel was filled with shouting.

The camera operator swung the lens to a large brown cloud of dust and smoke in the street behind the Avenue Hotel.

"It looks like they were able to tow it out of the garage, thank God," Monroe said.

"What about the Cube?" Sloan asked.

Somebody called out from the back. "They pulled it to the other end of the garage. There's going to be structural damage, but we probably avoided the worst of it."

"I don't know if we avoided it," Jessica said quietly.

The helicopter pulled back to reveal three clouds of smoke billowing from the targeted locations around Las Vegas.

"How far apart was the timing?" Sloan asked.

"Close," Monroe said. "I'm guessing they were manually triggered, and when our guy on Las Vegas Boulevard blew his, so did the other two."

"Kaufman checking that clock . . ." Jessica sighed. "So, we found the names of three people; we found three vans."

"Are you saying there are more?" Monroe asked.

"Weissnott's company had five vans. If you're using timers, you don't have to have a driver for each one; you can just park it," Jessica pointed out.

Nowitz, who had returned from interrogating Kaufman, called out, "What are you saying?"

"I'm saying we might have two more vans out there," Jessica told him.

"Fuck. And once they know these blew, those are gonna go too." Nowitz shook his head.

"We told a ton of other agencies to be on the lookout," Sloan said.

"Did we?" Jessica asked the room.

"Yeah, Pinellas was doing that," Monroe concurred.

"Where is Pinellas? I'd like to double-check," Jessica asked.

Monroe looked around the room, then pointed toward a desk at the corner. "She was working there. Maybe she stepped away."

Jessica walked over to Vera Pinellas's desk.

There was an emergency response binder filled with telephone numbers for all the different law enforcement agencies across the Southwest. Multiple file folders and a notepad with addresses and names of witnesses.

Sloan walked over and stared at the desk, then at Jessica, and called out, "When was the last time somebody saw Vera Pinellas?"

"She headed back to the Reno office last night," said Agent Running Deer.

Sloan slid the notepad aside. Underneath was a car key.

Jessica's eyes widened. "Soraya," she breathed.

"Everybody get out now!" Sloan screamed as she pulled Jessica by the arm.

HOMECOMING

Brotherhood Police Sergeant Jefferson was standing in front of the barricade at the entrance to town when the van with the Idaho State Police decal on the side pulled up.

The church leaders had parked pickup trucks bumper to bumper to prevent anyone from going through without permission. The eight other men on the Brotherhood police force were standing in different locations around the town, forming a perimeter. Another two dozen men holding rifles were located near the general store and surrounding the prophet's temple.

The driver rolled down the window and greeted him. "I'm Officer Lawson. I was told to bring some backup radios."

Jefferson studied the woman's face for a moment; she looked familiar. He wondered if he'd met her at a law enforcement conference.

"Make room!" he shouted to a man in a truck blocking the entrance.

"Where should I park it?" she asked.

"The municipal station, first building on your left," Jefferson replied, waving her through the gap.

She gave him a nod and then rolled up the window.

Once she was clear of the vehicles, Soraya, a.k.a. Vera Pinellas, stomped on the accelerator.

Police Chief Matthews was standing on the roof of the munic-ipal building with a pair of binoculars when he saw the van race down the main street, jump the curb, and head straight into the Prophet's Tower.

The explosion was so loud he couldn't hear himself scream.

LAST MAN STANDING

Sloan McPherson hung up her call, slid her phone back into her pocket, and sat down on the curb next to Jessica Blackwood.

Firefighters were still spraying water on the side of the FBI building where the bomb had blown it wide open.

So far, they'd been able to piece together that Vera Pinellas had one of the vans from Kaufman's fleet detailed to look exactly like a Nevada Department of Public Safety vehicle and another marked as Idaho State Police. Sloan and Jessica had laid eyes on the Nevada van several times. All it took was two sets of decals and the vans looked official.

She'd parked the Nevada van next to the FBI building, mere meters from where the bullpen was located.

Monroe was pacing back and forth, occasionally checking her phone and sending furious text messages. "How the fuck did we miss this?"

Jessica was calm, having accepted fate.

"We were always looking in the wrong direction. That was their plan."

"She tries to blow us up, blows up the temple, he tries to take out a few city blocks in Las Vegas yet is around to talk about it. I don't get it. What was the plan?" Running Deer asked.

"It wasn't a plan; it was two plans—two very angry people working together, but they wanted different things," Sloan explained.

"What did Vera, or Soraya, or whatever the fuck her name is, get out of this?" Running Deer asked.

"She hated that place, and she hated the FBI for never putting a stop to it. I don't know how much she believed in Lehi's apocalyptic vision, but certainly, making it come true was the ultimate fuck-you to the men who made her life terrible," Jessica said.

Monroe looked up from her phone and asked, "Well, who sent us the photo of Nia?"

"My bet? That would have been Vera," Sloan replied. "Isn't that how she got on this case in the first place?"

"Damn," Monroe replied. "Once we knew this was statewide, it made it easy for her to insert herself. She had a reason to be working out of the Las Vegas office." Monroe looked back toward the pillar of smoke over the FBI building. "And park that goddamn van ten feet away from us."

"She was also coordinating contact with other law enforcement agencies. God knows what she was passing on and what she wasn't," Sloan said.

"So Lehi just used her," Running Deer said.

"I'm inclined to think it was the other way around," Jessica said. "She probably had a death wish for a long time. Lehi, on the other hand, fancies himself as some new dark messiah."

"Why blow up the warehouse and torch the ranch?" Monroe asked.

"Vera was never more than ten feet away from me when we went to go look at the ranch," Sloan said. "She was probably afraid we'd find something—clothes, a SIM card, I don't know. But, goddamn it, she was there every time something happened. She probably triggered the warehouse explosion; there could have been something there connected to her as well. I think it might have been covering her tracks, not his."

"She might have recruited the other drivers, not Lehi. Given the fact that he killed two of his followers and almost succeeded with another, he might not have been the charismatic leader he thought he was—or we suspected," Jessica said.

Monroe rubbed her temple. "What a fuckup . . . what a fuckup," she muttered.

"Bullshit," Sloan snapped. "Not from how I look at it. The only person killed in the Las Vegas bombings was the dumbass driving the van. Now, I can't speak for who was in that temple, and maybe it's unprofessional of me to say this, but I'm not going to lose any sleep over that. The kids that Lehi took out, they were dead before we even knew something was up. So yeah, this sucks, but there are fuckups and then there are fuckups, and I'll take this one over a real fuckup."

"Yeah, maybe. I just feel stupid," Monroe admitted.

"I'm just glad we're able to feel anything right now," Sloan said.

"Thanks to you," Monroe said.

"It was Jessica who noticed that Vera was missing, but I'll take her compliment because she'll probably reject it. But wouldn't you say we got lucky?" Sloan asked Jessica.

Jessica was deep in thought. "I'm glad we're alive."

"I feel like there's a 'but' there," Sloan said.

"I agree, this could have been way worse. And I don't think we should be tearing ourselves up over it. We inherited a dysfunctional situation. We had a one-in-a-million monkey wrench thrown into the case by one of our own betraying us. And had things gone the way Lehi wanted, way more people would be dead—that's for sure."

"Are you worried about Lehi running his mouth and getting a following?" Sloan asked.

"I used to think people had a pretty clear idea of what was right and what was wrong, but then I watch social media cheer on murderers killing CEOs in cold blood. Or gleeful that some part of the country they don't agree with gets beset by a hurricane or a wildfire," Jessica said. "Vera, as horrible as the things she did were, was acting out of pain. Lehi, on the other hand, was driven by ego, and even worse, people are going to be all too willing to feed it."

ABOUT THE AUTHOR

Andrew Mayne is the Amazon Charts and *Wall Street Journal* bestselling author of *The Girl Beneath the Sea, Black Coral, Sea Storm, Sea Castle,* and *Dark Dive* in his Underwater Investigation Unit series; *The Final Equinox* and *Mastermind* in the Theo Cray and Jessica Blackwood series; *The Naturalist, Looking Glass, Murder Theory,* and *Dark Pattern* in the Theo Cray series; *Angel Killer, Name of the Devil,* and the Edgar Award–nominated *Black Fall* in his Jessica Blackwood series; and *Mr. Whisper* in the Specialists series. He was the star of A&E's *Don't Trust Andrew Mayne* and swam with great white sharks using an underwater stealth suit he designed for the Shark Week special

Andrew Mayne: Ghost Diver. He worked on creative applications for artificial intelligence and served as the science communicator for OpenAI, the creators of ChatGPT. He now serves as CEO of Interdimensional.ai. For more information, visit www.andrewmayne.com or find him @AndrewMayne.